W9-CBD-263

RED BAKER

Books by Robert Ward

Four Kinds of Rain

Grace: A Fictional Memoir

The Cactus Garden

The King of Cards

Red Baker

The Sandman

Shedding Skin

Cattle Annie and Little Britches

RED BAKER

Robert Ward

With a Foreword by Michael Connelly

St. Martin's Minotaur

New York

SWAMPSCOTT PUBLIC LIBRARY

RED BAKER. Copyright © 1985 by Robert Ward. Foreword copyright ©
2006 by Michael Connelly. All rights reserved. Printed in the United
States of America. No part of this book may be used or reproduced in any
manner whatsoever without written permission except in the case of brief
quotations embodied in critical articles or reviews. For information,
address St. Martin's Press, 175 Fifth Avenue, New York, N.Y. 10010.

www.minotaurbooks.com

Library of Congress Cataloging-in-Publication Data

Ward, Robert, 1943–
    Red Baker / Robert Ward ; with a foreword by Michael Connelly.–
1st St. Martin's Minotaur pbk. ed.
        p. cm.
    ISBN-13: 978-0-312-36274-4
    ISBN-10: 0-312-36274-9
    1. Iron and steel workers—Fiction. 2. Layoff systems—Fiction. 3.
Unemployment—Fiction. 4. Psychological fiction. I. Title.

PS3573.A735R4 2006
813'.54—dc22

First published in the United States by The Dial Press

First St. Martin's Minotaur Paperback Edition: September 2006

10 9 8 7 6 5 4 3 2 1

This book is dedicated to
Celeste Wesson and Shannon and Kevin,
with all my love.

Special thanks to friends and family who hung in with me down the line. In Baltimore, my deepest gratitude to William Kelch, who drove me around to union halls, unemployment lines, bars, and other hangouts and who was the finest guide and friend a writer could have; to Vic Covey, and his wife Ginny, who taught me about the steel industry and answered endless questions; and to Dr. Ted Trimble, who got me started and gave me support all the way through. And to Ned Myers, friend and brother.

In New York, special thanks to my editor Joyce Johnson for her courage and brilliant editing; to my agent and friend Jay Acton, who believes in my talent and kept coming up with money-making projects for me so I could finish the book; to my friends Morgan Entrekin, Bob Asahina, Paul Bresnick, and Gary Fisketjon, who all read early drafts of the book and made valuable suggestions; and to David Black, who is always there at 2 A.M.

And very special thanks to Larry Sullivan, for his warmth, wit, and brains.

I, RED BAKER

"It was supposed to be a walk." That's what Red Baker says near the end of this wonderful and heart-searing story. When everything has gone wrong, when the plan has gone awry, when it is the end of the line and the chips are down, Red laments about how it was supposed to be. And while with that one line he speaks directly of one disappointment, he might as well be summing up a lifetime's pain. With that one line we know all the frustration of the man who is Red Baker. And we know it about our own lives as well. Very simply, *it was supposed to be a walk.*

In this novel, and perhaps all of his novels, Robert Ward writes about the betrayal of ideals. He writes about the corruption of meritocracy. Red Baker, steel worker, husband and father, has pushed himself through countless days with the simple idea that if he was a good man and did the right thing then there would be a payoff, something waiting for him at the end. Yes, he is flawed. He is by no means a saint. He is a man who rails against the limitations of his life. But he still operates with the hardwiring of a basic belief; that if you walk the line, then it takes you to the place you want and deserve to go. This is the story of Red's betrayal, of his learning to leave such notions behind, of his realizing that life is never a walk.

With this novel Ward clearly and deftly makes the jump. By that I mean he achieves the elusive transcendence that every writer works and prays for. In *Red Baker* one man's story becomes our story, his conscious becomes our collective conscious. His journey is our own. I am Red Baker and so are you. It is why this book is important. It is why it should always be celebrated and always in print.

It is a story that in many ways defies classification. It is a literary novel, a crime novel, and a novel of social reflection. And on some levels it is even a love story. I believe Ward achieves all of this by bringing a reporter's eye to the story. A veteran journalist by the time he wrote this story, the author dispassionately uses his skills as an observer to build the world in which we travel. We know it to be real. We know it to be true. Never didactic and always riding with the idea of less being more, Ward writes of the places he knows, the Baltimore where he grew up. He does this sparely but brilliantly, offering us a story for the ages. A story as important now as it was then.

I think it is appropriate to note that Ward was inspired to write this story about a laid-off steelworker without hope, pride, or prospect ("transferable skills," as it is termed in the book) at a time when the book business was publishing and celebrating stories about self-indulgent users with money to spare and opportunities to ignore. At the time, stories about upwardly mobile professionals were upwardly mobile on the bestseller lists. But Ward didn't put his finger up into the wind to check the current. He went against the trend and pulled this story from his heart. It was about his place, his town, and his people. He told me once that he had spent four years laboring over a book that was the wrong book, that was going nowhere and taking a long time to get there. Lying awake in bed one night, the inspiration for *Red Baker* suddenly came to him, along with the first line of the story in which he introduces himself. "I, Red Baker...."

Ward rose from the bed (and the dead with that wrong book) and gave us Red Baker in only six months. The story burned to come out, and it did so to across-the-board acclaim.

But to be sure, the treachery of idealism and meritocracy does not exist only in literature. The publishing story of *Red Baker* is a case of life imitating art. Deeply moved after reading the manuscript, Ward's agent predicted great things and immediately set the novel for auction. Copies of the manuscript were made and sent to thirty publishers. An auction day was announced.

It was supposed to be a walk. But on the day of the auction the agent's phone never rang. Robert Ward had gone against the trend and thirty publishers said no thanks.

Eventually, one editor and one publisher stepped forward and agreed to publish the book. There were no riches for Ward but the glorious critical response to the novel validated his work and the publisher's gamble. We now have this fine novel at which to marvel and learn from.

Life may not be a walk but it is not without its redemptions. Red Baker learns that in this book and over the years since its publication Robert Ward has learned it again and again. On many occasions he has opened his mail to read letters from the people who have found this book and taken it to heart. Many of those letters simply begin with the words, "I am Red Baker...."

Read on and you will be Red Baker, too.

—Michael Connelly

RED BAKER

The story I am about to tell you is how I, Red Baker, lost my job, my pride, my family and came damned close to losing my home and life, but through an act of ingenuity got them all (for the time being) back again.

There never was a story with a happy ending in Baltimore, but this comes as close to cutting it as any I have heard.

What happened was this:

In the winter of '83, the year the President and his band of television writers were telling us how the economy was on the big climb, 60 percent of the work force at Larmel Steel were told they could grab their lunch boxes, clean out their lockers, and make tracks for home. We weren't supposed to be bitter because we had a whole week's notice.

Not that it was any huge surprise. They don't ship steel because they got a soft spot for erecting buildings, and the truth is we weren't exactly creating a whirlpool of business. But it came as one hell of a blow anyway.

I remember the way the mill looked that last night. Like one of those ghost towns you see in John Wayne movies. I walked past the slag heap, gone cold now that the furnaces were shut down. All the machinery sitting there with the fine steel dust settling over it, the guys walking around slowly in the unnatural quiet, staring at one another blank-faced and blinking in the lead-dull light. I waited there for my friend Dog Donahue to get his jacket and stared at the tilting tables on the blooming mill, where I had spent the last twelve years of my life turning the huge bars of steel over with my tongs. So many days dreaming of getting the hell out of here. But now that they were shutting the place down—rumor had it that it might be for good—I would have given about anything to climb back up there, put on protective goggles, and get back to work. Already I missed the clack of the tongs as Dog and I guided the molten steel through the pass to shape it down. I could see old Billy Bramdowski working up in the pulpit, waving down to us, smiling and yelling encouragement. It was like something was cut out of me, which came as a shock because I never figured to miss all that smoke and belching noise.

All over the place—in the rod mill, in the chem plant, out in the yard—it was dead and dark, and I felt a fear overtake me, sending electric sparks through my chest and arms. A fear which pissed me off, made me want to smash something down, break it off. But what? Who?

Before the silence got too much, I walked outside to the parking lot, pulled the collar up on my parka, and looked up at the black sky and the white snow flakes, which drifted down through the high-tension wires. The moon was white, perfectly round, and all around me guys walked slowly to their cars and trucks, some of them with their heads down, others huddled together for a last few words before they made it home. I didn't have to join them to know what they were talking about. There was only one thing on anybody's mind. Was this the last time we all walked out of Larmel? And if so, what the hell was going to happen to us?

Finally Dog came out, carrying his lunch pail and wearing the red-and-white-checked hunting jacket me and Wanda gave him last Christmas. He looked at me, smiled with his big-gapped teeth, and punched me in the arm with his huge fist.

"Let's get outta here, Red," he said.

"You said it, Doggie."

He turned around and looked at the silent, dark machinery and then turned back to me.

"You know what it is?" he asked.

"No, what's that?"

"It's the fucking Nips. Fucking Nips sending that steel over here, kicking our ass. You know why? They got fucking slave labor over there. Between the Nips and the government we got a snowball's chance in hell. They stop those imports, we're back in business. But there's no way they're gonna do that. Big shots in Washington could care less, you know that."

"Come on, Dog," I said. "Let's get on down to the Paradise, get us a couple of drinks. It's cold as hell out here."

He nodded his big head, and we walked across the lot, our boots making crunching noises on the tar.

"Nips'll be running this country soon. You hear what they did to Blackwell's?"

"No. Why don't you tell me, Doggie?"

He looked at me and gave a little half smile.

"Wise ass," he said. "You know all right. They bought the whole fucking place and turned it into a warehouse. Think the city gives a shit? No way, jack."

I nodded but didn't say anything. Dog was on a roll, letting it all out.

If the Nips had to take the heat for it, that's the way it fell for now.

We climbed into his pickup, and the seats were frozen, the plastic smooth as glass. I reached into the glove compartment, pulled out a pint of Wild Turkey, took a long belt, and handed it to Dog, who chugged about half the bottle.

"Hey, gimme a break," I said.

"Shit," he said, handing it back to me, "what the hell we gonna do now?"

"How about starting the truck?"

He looked at me with his big head tilted sideways and that strange glint in his eye as though suddenly he didn't know me at all.

Then he laughed and took the bottle back.

"I don't need this, Red . . . I mean it."

"Yeah, yeah, now how about starting the engine?"

He turned the key and mashed his foot on the accelerator, and the old Ford sputtered and died out.

"Don't flood the son of a bitch, Dog!"

"Hey what's this, driving school?"

I said nothing more but took another hit of the Wild Turkey and stared out at the snow, which fell gently on the window.

He hit the gas again, and this time it turned over and we started

out of the lot. I tried not to think what I was going to tell Wanda and
Ace, tried keeping my mind on the Paradise and Crystal, and then I
shut my eyes a second, and the whiskey flooded my mind with pictures of me and Crystal on the highway down in Florida, weeping
willows hanging over the car and orange juice stands everywhere you
looked, and then a long white beach, the sun burning down on us,
the brightest, whitest sunlight you ever saw, and she and I standing
at the ocean's edge.

For about thirty seconds I was right there, with my pants legs
rolled up and Crystal in her new bikini showing off that fine, tight
little ass of hers, and then Dog's gruff, low voice wiped the whole
thing out and we were out on the North Point Boulevard, passing
Bud's Bait and Tackle Shop and Mickey's Package Goods with his
pink blinking neon sign.

"Hey, Red, what was that thing that guy wrote inna paper?"

"What thing was that?"

"You know. The one that guy wrote the other day."

"About the Colts?" I said. There never was a time so bleak I
didn't enjoy putting on the Dog.

"No," he said. "For Chrissakes, I'm not talking about the fucking
Colts, the thing that guy wrote who interviewed us downa plant?"

"Hey, who gives a shit? Let's get that heater going. I'm freezing
my balls off."

Dog took a long, furious breath and stared at me.

He had his teeth clenched together, and his eyes knitted up so he
looked like he had one long brow.

"You look real good when you get pissed like that, Dog. Kind of
like one of them Neanderthal men."

"Hey, I'm going to start acting like one if you don't tell me what
that guy wrote, Red."

"Which guy was that?" I said, barely able to keep from smiling.

But I guess I pushed it too far. Because Dog jerked the steering
wheel to the right and slammed down hard on the brakes. My shoulder bounced off the door, and my head snapped forward, bashing
into the windshield. He reached his huge hand over and grabbed my
jacket collar.

"Goddamn it, Red. Don't treat me like no dumbass. You know
what that guy wrote. Now tell me . . ."

Sweat beads broke out on his forehead, and he had that big-eyed look which I'd seen all too many times over the years. I can handle myself okay, but nobody wants to mess with the Dog.

"I'm starting to remember a little," I said. "The asshole wrote that what we had were 'nontransferrable skills.' "

As soon as I said it, Dog began to nod. He took his hands away from my throat and slumped back in his seat.

"Nontransferrable skills. It was right there, but I couldn't remember it. Stayed up all night trying to get it."

"Yeah, I know what you mean. Old songs get me that way sometimes."

"This ain't no song, Red. He's telling us we're through."

"Hey, fuck him and the horse he rode in on. We'll be back in there in two weeks. Meanwhile, we'll get a line on some new jobs. Collect a little of the old unemployment. Lay back some. I been working too damned hard anyway."

The Dog wiped his head and bit his lower lip.

"Nontransferrable skills," he mumbled under his breath. "What's he think we are, just a bunch of assholes? You hear what they're saying, Red? That the mill ain't ever gonna open again. Between the Nips and Walsh Brothers up in York, Pennsylvania, we can't compete. Those guys got automation."

"Hey, don't worry so much, Doggie. Come on, let's get down to the bar. We can't settle this all tonight. Take it one day at a time, partner."

I reached over and gave him a pat on the back of his neck and felt the muscles all bunched up tight. I didn't blame him, really, and there was nothing more I could say because the truth was that Walsh Steel could go from ingot to bloom to billet to a roll of wire in about half the time we could. If you were building a shopping mall, you sure as hell wouldn't come to us.

But I told myself not to dwell on it. Something would turn up; it always had before. Red Baker's Philosophy: You're usually up to your head in mud, but as long as you can keep breathing you're ahead of the game.

Dog started the truck up, and as we rode through the blowing white snowflakes I felt the whiskey cutting through me. For a while there, as we passed Gino's and Graybar Electronics and Luby Chevrolet with its new PAC MAN LOVES LUBY sign, I felt all warmed up and loosey goosey, and I was almost able to pretend it was just a regular night, stopping in for a few whiskeys at the Paradise, trading lies and bullshit with the boys, and flirting with Crystal before I headed on home to my wife and kid.

When I entered that dark gin mill, the first thing I heard was Mick Jagger singing "Satisfaction." Up on the red velvet platform in the middle of the bar Crystal danced in her white spangled body stocking. She was bumping and grinding her sweet tight ass, and she gave me a little wave and a big smile. There were quite a few of the boys in there—but they weren't yelling encouragement like they usually do or bringing out the dollar bills so she'd drop one of her straps and show them her perfect pink nipples. Instead this was a bar of hard-hatted, grim drinkers, staring down into their whiskey glasses and talking low to one another like there had been a death in the neighborhood.

The one thing Dog and I did not need was grim, so I waved back to her and did a little dance shuffle with my feet, like I was getting ready to raise some serious hell. Crystal laughed at me, and just seeing her smile sent a shot of adrenaline through me.

Dog and I sat down at the horseshoe bar and ordered our Wild Turkey from bleary, blond, hound-faced Deena.

"Fucking morgue in here," Dog said, gulping his whiskey and beer and ordering another before I could even get started on my first.

"Need some fun!" he shouted, banging the bar with his glass.

"Go baby!" I called up to Crystal, and she tried her damndest, shaking and shimmying as the old, scratched Rolling Stones record burned into my ears.

Already I could feel a dull ache slipping away from me.

"God, she is one fine-looking woman," I said to Dog, who was smiling at her himself now. Crystal has that magic you can't explain. Just seeing her with her short haircut and this little-kid enthusiasm makes a man feel close to joy.

"I thought she was going to be singing down at the Starlight Lounge," Dog said, drinking another Wild Turkey.

"Yeah, but they say they're broke. Laid her off. Just when she was getting good playing the piano too. She did a rendition of 'Misty' a couple weeks ago near broke my heart."

"Shit," Dog said. "There's only one thing she gonna break for you, and that's your head when Wanda finds out."

"Hey," I said. "You're moving into a sensitive area, son. I'm half in love with that woman."

"In love with her tight little bod," Dog said. "You got to admit she's got a better ass than she does a voice."

This actually offended me, so I attempted to burn Dog with my cigarette, our old high school trick. He jumped back and laughed.

"Fucking broke Romeo," he said. "Shit."

He pounded me on the back while I sulked some. I don't know why it is, but friends do love to see one another suffer.

Crystal kept right on prancing about, shimmying and shaking and then coming real close to me and reaching down and kissing me on the forehead while whispering, "Hey, Red Baker," and I reached up for her, but she stepped back and danced down the other end of the bar, trying to cheer up the grim guys down there. Looking at her I thought of those USO girls. It occurred to me that she was kind of a welfare worker of the body, using her natural delights to keep the whole, burned-down, wasted town afloat.

And thinking that made me love her all the more.

"Buy you a drink, Red?"

I turned and saw Billy Bramdowski, who worked up above me in his glassed-in pulpit. It was up to Billy to move the big tables I worked on from side to side, guiding the molten steel into the right pass while I turned it with my tongs. Just like Dog, he was part of our team, and I trusted him completely. He was a real pro up there, something like an artist the gentle way he moved all that red-hot steel, and he better be too, because if he jerks the table too hard I got a hot bar of steel flying off the table onto my legs. Just last year Tom Chenowith lost his right leg when one of the other pulpit operators showed up with the shakes from too much booze. But Dog and me didn't have to worry about that with Bill, because usually he was a sober, mild-mannered guy. Only tonight he looked about as down as the rest of us, his face red from drinking and his blond hair matted to his head.

I put my arm around his shoulder and gave him a hug.

"Look like you been doing a little drinking tonight, Bill."

"Well why not?" he said. "Celebrating some."

"Celebrating what?" I asked.

"New baby, Red."

"You had another kid. Nobody said anything to me . . ."

"No, not yet. Just found out. Jennie's expecting. Number four."

"Hey, that's great Bill," I said, thanking God it wasn't me.

"Yeah, real timely, huh?" he said, laughing and calling Deena over.

"Hey, you hear that, Dog? Billy's wife is having another kid."

Dog gave me a look like this guy should be packed out to the farm but managed a couple tinny congratulations.

"Four kids," Billy said, staring into his beer. "Right on time."

"Hey, we'll be back in there soon," I said.

"Hey, I know it," Billy smiled. He winked at me and started to push his money at Deena, but I grabbed his hand and reached for my wallet.

"Tonight, I buy you a drink."

But Billy pulled away from me and waved his arms.

"No way. We're having the kids, and I'm buying the booze. What the hell, Red, this is the last night I'll get out in a while. Two o'clock feedings, you know?"

"If you say so, Bill."

"I say so," he said in a voice that was too loud and hearty for him.

"Hey," he said, pointing to the stage. "Look at that woman dance!"

Billy started waving to Crystal, who saw him, waved back, and began to get all inspired, touching the inside of her hard thighs and darting her sexy tongue in and out of her mouth like a snake.

"Alll riiight!" Dog yelled, pounding the bar.

"Do it Crystal," Billy said, taking ten dollars out of his wallet and throwing it up on the stage. Crystal winked at him and ever so sexily picked it up without missing a beat. She stuffed it into her bikini bottom and pranced on down the bar and began slithering around the fire pole that was in the center of the stage.

This sent Billy and Dog and some of the other boys over the edge. They were screaming and yelling, and though I joined them, I was miserable as hell.

"Good times," Billy yelled. "Good times . . . Have 'em while you can!"

He pounded me on the back and walked down the bar toward the men's room.

"When did he become such an ass kicker?" Dog said. "He's always been on the quiet side."

"World's full of surprises," I said, looking glumly up at Crystal. I know it's wrong and outdated, but I was thinking of her as my girl and wished to hell she was crooning her tunes down the Starlight Lounge instead of shaking her ass for all of Baltimore.

Finally her set ended, and she tossed a gold lamé shawl over her shoulders and hopped down off the stage.

"Hi ya, hon," she said, coming around the bar and standing behind me. I couldn't resist it any longer and didn't even give two shits who saw. I put my arms around her and held her tight. Just seconds ago she'd seemed like the Queen o' Sex up on the stage, but now she had changed into this innocent little girl, and I wanted to protect her, hold her safe from all the trouble the world loves to lay down on you. That's the glory of women for me. They are all at least five different people, every time, and I'll never understand how they do it. I mean, keep all those separate personalities straight. What amazes me is that they don't even seem to know it. It comes natural to them, and if you ask them about it, nine out of ten will tell you a logical explanation for each of their different parts, which sounds good while it's being told but, when you think back on it, never adds up to anything like the whole story.

Even Dog cheered up just standing next to her.

"I heard you boys got the pink slips today. Well, join the club. The Starlight just told me they're going to go with a jukebox. I won't be singing there anymore. Got to be the slut queen here instead."

She smiled so sweetly when she said it that I gave her a squeeze.

"Hey, don't run yourself down, hon," I said. "You are the queen of every steel man's heart."

Crystal gave me a little peck on the cheek and winked. "A girl has got to try to find her fun where she can, hon, but you know my heart belongs to song."

"And you can sing with the best of 'em," Dog said. "They ought to let you put your piano up there on the stage and do your numbers right here."

"Vinnie isn't interested in my *voice*," Crystal hummed.

Billy Bramdowski came back from the men's room. I noticed he had put on some weight around the middle. He smiled and gave Crystal a hug.

"You're wonderful," he said. "Isn't she terrific, Red. Hey, Crystal, you hear about Jennie? She's having a baby."

"She is?" Crystal said. "That's wonderful, Billy."

She shot me a look then, and I looked away. There had been times when we were together late at night dreaming about Florida, when having kids together seemed like the most natural and logical thing in the world.

"Yeah," Billy said. "Four babies and no job. But we're going to hang in there. Count on that!"

"That's right," Crystal said. "I'll tell you what, I think the bar ought to buy us all a drink to celebrate Billy's kid. What do you say, Deena?"

Deena broke into her horsey laugh and started taking the orders, when behind us I suddenly heard a voice that sounded like a file being rubbed across steel.

"Hey, what's this, charity day? Since when do you buy my customers drinks?"

Without even turning around I knew who it was. None other than Vinnie Toriano, the owner of the Paradise Lounge.

"No, Vinnie," Crystal said. "I just thought since Billy's wife Jennie is having a baby, you wouldn't mind springing for a round of drinks."

I turned and looked at Vinnie. He was fatter than ever, wearing his light green leisure suit and a silk shirt with this paisley print that looked like the bugs we looked at in night school class down Essex Community College. Parameciums. Though I would guess a paramecium had more soul than Vinnie Toriano. I'd known this moustachioed grease ball since we were kids, about as long as I'd known Dog, and you'd think by now with all of us pushing forty he'd mellow out some. But he still talked in his Godfather voice, still had to be the hard guy who gave people shit. Still hung around with his two goons, Frankie Delvecchio and Joey Capezi, both of whom had faces like hatchets and mean ferret eyes, though Joey wore a toupee these days. They were with Vinnie now, standing a few feet away, just staring at Dog and me. Old wars from childhood, which they would never forget.

Vinnie looked at Billy Bramdowski and slapped him on the back.

"You having a kid, Bill. That's fine. I'll be happy to buy you a

drink. Have whatever you want. These other jerkoffs want to drink
with you, they got to pay cash."

"Christ, Vinnie," Crystal said. "Don't be such a douchebag."

"Hey," Vinnie said. "I heard what happened to you down the
Starlight. You want to be out in the snow like Baker and Donahue
here, that can be arranged."

"Hey, Vinnie, leave Crystal out of it," I said. "She was just happy
for Billy here, that's all."

I wanted to say a hell of a lot more than that and could feel the
anger rising in me, but I knew starting trouble wouldn't do Crystal
any good. Next to me, Dog was half off the barstool. Behind Vinnie,
Joey Capezi and Frankie Delvecchio inched forward a little, moving
together like they were attached at the waist.

"Hey, it's like I say, Bill," Vinnie said. "You want a drink, you got
it. You're having a baby, that's just fine. But what are *you* celebrating, Baker, getting laid off down the plant? Or maybe you got some
new plans. Like running for mayor!"

Joey and Frankie laughed in unison, only Frankie didn't make any
noise. He just opened his mouth and moved his head up and down
like a spring doll of Gino Marchetti I once had in the back of my first
car.

"That's all right," Billy Bramdowski said. "If my friends can't
drink with me, then I'll pay for everybody."

"Suit yourself, sucker," Vinnie said, curling his fat lower lip into a
snarl aimed at me and Dog. "As for you, Crystal, how many times I
gotta tell you, when you're working I want you behind the bar or
mixing with the customers. Baker here ought to be home with his
family anyway."

"Leave my family out of it, lardass," I said, stepping down from
the bar.

"You telling me what to do in my place, Baker?" He turned and
looked at his two boys, who took another step up.

Dog slid off the bar and picked up a bottle of National Bohemian,
and I saw doubt in Vinnie's eyes.

"You know?" Frankie said, "I don't know why you don't throw all
three of 'em out of here, Vinnie. Broad ain't got any tits anyhow."

I was about to move forward when Crystal suddenly turned and
slapped Frankie right in the face. He fell backward, and somebody

sitting at one of the tables managed to stick his foot out, sending him ass over heels on the floor.

"Don't you ever talk to me like that again, you sleazebag. You want to fire me, Vinnie, I'll walk right out of here now. You want that? Tell me. Just say so."

Now Vinnie stared hard-faced at Dog and myself. I caught a shot of Billy from the corner of my eye. He was picking up a bottle.

"Hey, let's take it easy," Vinnie said. "Everybody's getting too damned upset. Let's all cool down, what you say?"

He wasn't about to fire Crystal just yet. She was the bar favorite, and the fat boy would have lost half the regulars.

Besides, it wasn't any secret that Vinnie had about as big a crush on her as I did, which was half what all this was about anyway. He had recently opened another place down in Curtis Bay called Mona Lisa Pizza, which was modeled after some Wop museum he'd seen on one of his Mafia charters to Italy. This place was his pride and joy, made from Formstone, with stained-glass windows and a moat full of plastic goldfish. Inside there were two rooms—the Da Vinci and the Michelangelo—and girls dressed like peasants with pretorn dresses, which Vinnie had gotten from seeing the movie *Spartacus* (there were also a lot of crucified Christians in the movie, but he couldn't figure any way to work that into the general theme). In the midst of all this splendor, you might expect Roman slave girls to bring in suckling pigs and all. But the best that simple-assed creep could come up with was pizza with names like El Greco's Supremo and Attila's Revenge. The point being that just last week Vinnie had suggested to Crystal that the Paradise and Mona Lisa and all the rest of his greasy kingdom could be hers and his if only she would put out for him from time to time. She had told him that there was as much chance of this happening as the Colts staying in Baltimore, and now, in his stupid, savage way, he had to break her chops and mine whenever he had the chance.

But tonight he had pushed it too far, and he knew it. His fat belly was quivering with fear and hatred, and he was breathing in short, deep bursts. Behind him Frankie picked himself off the floor and looked at Crystal with those little eyes, narrow slits like the edge of a knife.

"You're gonna be sorry for that," he said.

"Shut up, Frankie," Vinnie said. "Go out and get the car started. Joey, you go with him."

"No broad's going to push me around and get away with it," Frankie said.

"You bother her and it'll be carnival time for you, shithead," I said.

"You think so, Baker? You think so?"

"Come on—right now."

I stepped forward, but Dog grabbed me from behind and Vinnie and Crystal both jumped in the way.

"Frankie," Vinnie said, "go out and warm up the car. Crystal, get back up on that stage. What the hell am I paying you for?"

"Sure Vinnie," Crystal said. She gave him a sexy, mocking little pout and then ran the back of her hand across his cheek. Vinnie turned red-faced and backed away from her, stunned.

"Am I gonna see you tonight, honey?" she asked me.

Vinnie heard this as he followed his cretins out the door. But when he got there, he turned back and looked at me. His gold chains were shining in the hot red lights from the stage.

"You gonna push it too far one time, Baker."

"Blow it out your ass, fat boy," Dog said. "You scare nobody!"

"You'll see. One of these days. You'll both see!" Vinnie waved his fat finger up and down and twisted his lips so he looked like a blowfish. Then he turned and made a movie exit out the door.

"You're breaking his heart, honey," I said to Crystal, putting my arm around her shoulder and feeling her perfect, smooth skin.

"Just like you're breaking mine, Red."

"Hey, hold on."

"*Am* I going to see you tonight?"

I stared down at my drink, ran my hand through my hair.

"I can't tonight, hon. I gotta go home and break the news to Wanda and Ace."

Crystal fluttered her long lashes and shook her head.

"Well then, I guess I'll just have to find someone else to listen to my records with me."

She looked at me and then over at Dog, who was having a drink with Billy.

"Count me out of this one," Dog said. "Life is trouble enough without humping you, Crystal."

"Well, you'll never know what sweetness you missed, hon," she laughed.

I felt a pain go right through me to the bone, and I wanted her so badly I almost grabbed her and hustled her out to Dog's truck.

"Tomorrow night," I said. "Can you make it then?"

"Maybe, Red," she said. I guess I got so long-faced that she kissed me, and she whispered, "You know I can. I love you, honey." That cheered me up, and I ordered another round.

"Gotta dance, hon," she said. She went back behind the bar and blew me a kiss on the way up to the stage.

"Son of a bitch," Billy Bramdowski said. "That is one beautiful woman."

"Kicked old Frankie's ass too."

"Yeah," I said, "some woman."

Dog looked over at me and shook his head.

"We're out of fucking work and you're in love. Ain't life wonderful!"

But I didn't hear him. I was busy staring at her dancing and moving to Aretha Franklin, shaking her ass, and running her hands up and down her smooth, flat belly, and I thought of the snow outside, and of Vinnie and his crooked moustache that looked like a caterpillar trying to crawl off his face, and of the plant closed down, dark and silent, and then Crystal and I were in that big white convertible moving across the endless sun-baked road, heading down through the palm trees to the land where dreams didn't die.

When Dog left me off in front of our row house on Aliceanna Street, I suddenly had an attack of the Red Baker Special Express Guilts. Began feeling all clammy and wet, like old cardboard left out in the sleet and snow. I mean, what was I doing hanging out there at the bar, seeing Crystal, when I should have been home taking care of my family, figuring out our next move?

Like a high school jerk I stuck a piece of gum in my mouth so Wanda wouldn't smell the booze and then spat it out on the street, remembering that Wanda knew the only time I chewed gum was when I was drinking hard whiskey. Maybe that was the whole problem, I thought, as I looked in the window and saw her arranging some daisies she'd just bought. You want someone to know you, to share your every secret, someone who you can fill up the lonely mortal space with, and then after they do, you feel all empty and hollowed out. They steal your secrets, they know the fear under your charms. You're whittled right down to the bone.

So you go out in the street, where you can kid yourself that you're a different man, acting out a new part with a stranger.

The thought of all that, plus losing the job, made me want to head down the street to Slap's Tavern, but I made it into the house and tried for an optimistic smile.

"Hi," she said in that flat tone of voice she used when she had been hurt or disappointed. "Where have *you* been?"

"Well," I said, taking off my wet coat and hanging it on the wood peg by the stairs, "I could lie and tell you I was visiting sick orphans down at the Children's Hospital or reading to the blind over at Church Home Hospital, but the truth is I just came from the Paradise, where Dog and I celebrated the losing of our jobs with a few beers."

"I see," she said, turning her back to me and going on with the flower arranging.

"Where's Ace?" I said.

"He's down in the basement talking on the telephone. We've been waiting to have dinner."

"Hell, I'm sorry."

"I know," she said, and she sounded goddamned exhausted. I wanted to come over and hug her and tell her that I really meant it, I *was* sorry, but there didn't seem to be any way of pulling that off just now.

"I already know about the layoff, Red. We knew it was coming, and I guess I half expected you to be late, but you could have called."

"I'm sorry, Wanda. Look, it's been a tough day."

"Yeah," she said, "I know it has, but you still should have called."

I shrugged and rubbed my jaw, trying to figure out how to move past this, to tell her what I wanted to say, when Ace came into the room, spinning his basketball on his index finger.

"Hey, Dad, look at this."

He spun it hard and then let it slide from finger to finger, still keeping it going. Wanda and I stood there looking at him, and she couldn't help but smile.

"I could never do this until today," he said. "I mean, I couldn't even do it on one finger, and now it's easy to do it on all five."

"Hell, kid, I played ball for twenty years and still can't do it at all."

"That's okay," he laughed. "You can't stop my drive shot anymore either."

He began to dribble the ball toward me, and Wanda jumped out of the way, sitting down on the blue couch as Ace faked to his left, then his right.

"You'll never make it to the door, kid."

"The only way you can stop me is to foul. Old guy!"

He gave me a little shoulder fake and a stutter step, while Wanda yelled, "Watch out for the lamp, Red. No dribbling in the house," and then I dodged for the ball, missed, and he would have been by me for sure except for the last-ditch Red Baker defense, the Fatherly Hug. I grabbed him, and the ball squirted free, bouncing onto the shag rug and knocking over the picture of Wanda's mother, Ruth, which sat on the end table next to the couch.

"You lunatics," Wanda cried, but she was laughing with us. "Look what you've done to Ruth."

"Nothing time ain't done worse," I said, quoting the words of Buck, my old man five years' dead.

"Red!" Wanda said. "That's no way to talk in front of Ace."

"Yeah," Ace said, "you're going to screw up all my values, Dad."

"Yeah," I said. "Next thing you know the kid will be a teenaged alcoholic."

"No, glue sniffer," Ace said. "Or ludes. I'll get into ludes and hang out on the waterfront, bumming dimes."

"No way," Wanda said, smiling at both of us and looking about ten years younger. "You'll do nothing of the kind."

"What the hell?" I said. "This boy's talking like a regular loon-a-tick."

I grabbed him again and wrestled him down to the floor. He was bigger than me, but I still had the upper-body strength on him.

"Now you two cut that out this second. Red, you get upstairs and get yourself cleaned off, and Ace, you come out here and help me set the table."

"Okay, Mom," Ace said. He picked up the ashtray with "Yellowstone National Park" on it, passed his hand over it, and made it disappear.

"Ace?" Wanda said. "Don't do that. You'll break the ashtray."

"I don't see any ashtray," Ace said. "You see it, Dad?"

"What ashtray?"

"You two are going to drive me crazy."

"You mean that ashtray sitting over here?" Ace said, picking up the ashtray from the end table.

"I don't believe he did that," Wanda said. "You ought to get into the movies, Ace. You're getting real good with that magic."

"I just hope he's that good with his studies," I said.

"Don't worry, Dad, I'm tearing up the books. Got a fifty in a math test today."

"Ace," Wanda said, "you didn't."

Ace smiled and shook his head. "I forgot a few points. Got an eighty-five. I'm doing okay."

Wanda shook her head, and I took the opportunity and reached over and squeezed her hand. I thought she might jerk it away, but she held on to me tight and smiled again.

"Now go get cleaned up, Red. I got a roast in the oven."

"Okay, okay . . ."

I started up the steps and looked down on them standing there in the living room, smiling at one another, and suddenly I felt this thrill pass through me. Not like the one I had with Crystal. Something deeper that brought tears to my eyes.

They were mine, my wife and child. The thought amazed me, like I'd been given a bright gift. There was no way I could let them down.

I sat in the bath, letting the hot water soak into me, trying not to think of what lay ahead—the unemployment lines, the agonies of looking for work. Just be cool, lay back, take it one step at a time.

I was half asleep in a blue daze, staring at the white tiles and dreaming of that sunshine highway with me and Crystal on it again, when Wanda came into the room.

"I need to talk to you, Red," she said, sitting down on the toilet seat with the pink, fuzzy cover on it.

"I kind of figured this was coming," I said, shutting my eyes.

"Red, I'm not here to attack you. I don't really care about tonight. I know how bad you feel, but there's just something I've been thinking about. Stuff I've got to say to you."

I looked up at the mirror and the blue plastic shower curtain with white whales on it, and suddenly it seemed like I was in a hospital somewhere, being talked to by a doctor who was about to tell me how long I had left.

"All right," I said. "Shoot."

"Well, it's just this. We've been through hard times before, and I've always stuck by you, but I don't plan on going through any more craziness. I don't want this to sound like a threat, Red. I'm just trying to state some facts, because I've been thinking a lot about all this since that time you ended up in jail for driving down the Pulaski Highway the wrong way."

"Hey," I said, looking down at the water, which was red-gray from the dust on my skin. "That wasn't my fault. I was with Dog and Henry, and they were in the car ahead of me, and they got lost in the rain and fog and headed down there on the wrong side of the divider. I was only following them, you know what I mean?"

"Red," Wanda said in this calm way she has, which scares the shit out of me because I know she means business. "Red, we went all through that, and you don't have to explain it, any of it. All I'm saying is this. I've worked hard for this family, and I'll work for the rest of our lives, but if you go off half-cocked this time, drinking with Dog, and going on the dope, and turning down jobs, and running around, well, then I am going to take Ace and I am going to move to Ruth's. Do you understand?"

"Come on," I said. "It's been a hard enough day, you know? I don't need to hear about my family walking out on me too."

"I didn't say I'd walk out on you, Red. You know that. You could be down to selling apples on the street and I would never leave you if you showed some pride in it, but I won't be here to see you destroy yourself, and Ace."

"Who said anything about me destroying myself?" I said. "Is that all the faith you've got in me? You think I'm a crazy man?"

"No, I don't, Red. I think you're the best man I've ever met. But I'm thirty-seven years old. I can't go through all the dramas anymore. Coming down to the hospital to see you in the emergency room? That's over with for me."

"Okay," I said, taking her arm and pulling her up next to the tub. "Don't you worry. I'm going to get over to the unemployment tomorrow, and I'm going to take the first job they can find me, and I'll stick with it until this thing blows over. No sweat."

"All right, Red . . . You know what, you ole sweetheart . . . you know what kills me? Every time you tell me this stuff, I believe it. Even now. But don't disappoint me again, hon. 'Cause if you screw it up this time, I don't think I can go round anymore."

She spoke so softly, so sadly that I knew she was dead serious. And suddenly all thoughts of Crystal and being a footloose kid just vanished from my head. I held her close to me and kissed her on the cheek and then on the lips.

"There's something I want to say," I said. "I've screwed up a lot, Wanda, and I know it. But don't think I take you and Ace lightly.

You're the most important thing in my life. That kid has got talents
. . . I want him to keep taking his music lessons, I want him to go
to basketball camp out at College Park this summer. And I want you
to be able to do what you want. I'm going to get us money, babe, you
can count on it."

She smiled, and I kissed her cheek. "God, you smell good," I said,
meaning it too.

But she splashed me and pulled away. "Red, there's something
else I have to tell you. I got my old job back down at Weaver's Crab
House. I start Monday waiting tables."

"Honey, you don't have to do that. You should get to stay home."

"I don't mind, Red. I been home too much lately."

I knew this was a flat-out lie. Wanda had lately learned how to do
screen painting, which is a Baltimore art form, painting cows and
waterfalls on screens. People put them in the windows, breaks up the
brick in the neighborhood. She'd gotten real good at it too, even had
a write-up in the Sun papers. All her life she had wanted to be good,
really good at something, and this was it. I knew how much she
hated to give up her time to wait on lawyers who wanted to drink
beer and eat crabs. But I also knew we wouldn't make it for long
without the money.

"Goddamn, Wanda," I said, holding her close to me. "You know I
love you, honey. Nothing's going to change that. I won't let it."

I smelled her sweet, lovely skin and lifted a silent prayer to the
heavens.

"Please, God, if you're up there at all, don't let me fuck up again."

The next morning was cold and gray, and the snow had turned into a mush which fell from the sky like old grits. Dog came by in his pickup so we could head on down to the pissant humiliations of the unemployment line. I was already feeling the grimness overtaking me as I stared out of the window. The right windshield wiper wasn't working smoothly, and every time that sucker swept back and forth it made a squeaking sound that cut through my eardrums and made my temples ache. But if I wasn't looking like Mr. Snappy, Dog had gone me five degrees better. He hadn't bothered to comb his hair, which stood out in clumps on his head and made him look like one of those punk rockers. His breath was so bad it could have melted the dashboard, and he wore the exact same work shirt he had had on the day before, which had given yesterday's mill odors a chance to really bark right out at you. Though it was only eight-thirty in the morning, he already had the Jack Daniel's in his hand, and when we hit the potholes and mush humps in the road, the booze would dribble down his chin as if he were one of those old-bag booze rummies you see down on the Block.

I wanted to say something, maybe suggest he head on home and take a shower and shave, put a little Brylcreem in his hair, but I was too damned low myself to have to play cheerleader to him. Besides, he wouldn't have done it anyway. You could tell the way he was going about the whole thing that the entire purpose of this getup was to make it impossible for him to get a new job. In his heart he was still counting on the mill to reopen. And I couldn't blame him much. It's a hard, cold thing to have to change jobs at forty. No matter what you say the night before, you keep hoping some miracle will fall from the sky like a streaking yellow comet and that when you awaken things will be all right, the plant open again and your sweaty, clammy fear and fury will be just a cheap bad dream.

You might as well dream of being sixteen again, heading down to Ocean City in your '49 Ford, a case of National Boh and all the hard crabs you can eat sitting in the backseat.

So I could understand how the Dog was feeling that morning. But damn it all, I wanted the boy to at least act like we had a shot at pulling this thing off. Instead he said next to nothing as he stared straight ahead at the gray, ratty streets, and finally I broke the silence myself.

"Listen, son, hang in there. We're going to get us jobs soon enough. The way I hear it, they got some real big-shot positions down there for us. I mean, we're talking serious stuff. Movie stars and talk-show hosts and president of Spam . . . the thing is they got so many good jobs it can confuse a man just hearing about 'em all."

I figured this would lighten the Dog up, but it was no go. He hadn't even heard me.

"What it is, is I can't stand this shit," Dog said, slamming the heel of his hand on the steering wheel.

He took a long pull on the Jack Daniel's bottle and sighed deeply. I watched him from the corner of my eye and could see him sliding down, way down into the blue hole where friendly voices could never reach him.

And when we finally turned the corner to Madison and saw the line waiting in the slate sleet, I almost fell right through the world with Dog.

There were at least a hundred guys standing there with their collars pulled up, some with baseball hats on, some wearing parkas or yellow rubber rain hoods. Most of them were standing stock-still, not even talking, and for a brief second I got the feeling that I was looking at a photograph I'd seen in night school of the Great Depression. It was just like a soup line. And then somebody would sort of bounce around a little, a kind of halfhearted warm-up jog, like they were waiting to run back a kickoff. But there sure as hell wasn't any ball on this field of concrete.

"Do you believe this shit?" Dog said softly under his breath. "Can you fucking believe it?"

We stood out in the line, getting gray sleet down our collars, blowing steam on one another, and cursing for two hours, rats waiting for cheese. But for all of that it was nothing compared to the unemployment office itself. They tell me the steel mill is depressing, what with the big machines booming, the smell of burning steel, and the heat that cuts through your skin and leaves iron filings in your pores. But I'll take a life sentence there anytime compared to the green-walled, gray-metal–desked room, with brown-suited little Negroes and blue-haired, age-spotted ladies who sit behind those desks and stare up at you as if you were a lifer down Jessups Prison coming up for parole.

We stood just inside the door, waiting to get up to the first plateau, a gray metal desk behind which was a skinny black lady with her hair waxed to her head by maybe forty cans of Spray Net. She had dips and whirls and bobs going, kind of looked like one of the Supremes. I got to thinking of her as Miss Motown and told Dog that, but once again he was lost on me, his eyes bulging out of his head, his body tense, coiled.

"Man, I gotta get out of this place," he said. He looked around the room, his eyes never landing on anything but darting like dots in video games.

"Place reminds me of a troopship in Nam. Same fucking green walls. I still remember the day we was overrun, got the shit blown out of my leg, fell down in one of those ditches with water in it and these blue flowers. They say you can't drown in a bathtub, but I could hardly get myself out of there in time. Head down, this hole in my leg, and those floating blue flowers that stuck to my body. Finally I made it to the pool's edge, and I musta fallen asleep. Next thing I know I wake up and I'm staring at these puke-green walls. Peeling paint, and they told me the choppers got me out, but I couldn't stand looking at them walls. You could see the bumps of the concrete in it . . . Fucking crazy, right, Red?"

"No, you were shot."

"But they told me, this doc, that the green was there because it was restful. Made me want to puke, nothing restful about it. Then I remembered the night we got busted, Red, they took us down to the lockup, same fucking walls. You hang around long enough, green walls going to get your ass!"

"Hey, take it easy, Dog. No use harping on it. We got a few more hours to go yet."

But what he had said had gotten to me some now. All that metal, all these slumped-over guys, some of them trying to talk and act casual like this wasn't a big deal. They weren't the worst, though. The worst were the guys in the lines to the left. These were the unskilled workers' lines. The Motown lady's whole job was to process you through and then to decide which line you belonged in, skilled or unskilled. If you got put in the unskilled, it looked like the shock of it made you age twenty years in a minute. There were guys there so droopy, so wasted that they looked like they were going to ship them out back behind Big Burger, grind them up, and use them in the special sauce.

Dead-eyed guys. Bent-backed guys.

Guys with the shirts hanging off of them, so they looked like store manikins you see down at Ralph's Menswear on Broadway. You know the kind, a dummy with an arm fallen off, and a two-tone acetone shirt, and pants made out of polyester, look like they're made to start fires, and under this sad-assed display dope words are scratched in by Mr. Ralph, the fashion expert, which say MISTER SHARP DRESSER. Or HIGH SPIRITS. Or OUT ON THE TOWN.

I told myself no matter what, I wasn't going to let Miss Motown send me over to the unskilled department. I'd goofed on that before and got offered a new career stuffing newspapers with the Sunday supplements along with junkies and Thunderbird winos from down on Pratt Street.

Not today. No way.

"Hey, you guys," a voice suddenly called out. Dog and I looked up in front of the dead line, and there was fat Henry Hollister. We hadn't seen him before because he had had his three-hundred-pound carcass spread out on the floor.

"How's it going, fat man," Dog said, laughing a little and poking me in the ribs. Just seeing Henry always cheered Dog up.

He looked a hell of a lot like Curly in the Three Stooges, and he had the same sweet stupidity. As a kid he was often the gang's mascot, making dumb jokes about how fat he was, like pretending he was a dirigible and running around with his arms outstretched, yelling whoom, whoom! And pulling stunts like mooning the couples who were parked out at the reservoir. He had guts though, got to be one hell of a football tackle in high school, and both Doggie and I have always had a soft spot for the old boy.

"Doing real good, boys," Henry yelled. "Might get me a job selling donuts at Harborplace. Boy, will that be temptation."

He rubbed his round, soft stomach with a circular motion like he was helping all those little round donuts to roll on through there, and Dog and I cracked up.

"How's the Babe?" I yelled. The Babe was Henry's girlfriend, a two-hundred-plus former stripper at the Club Peacock. Everybody we knew thought Henry had lost his pea brain when he hooked up with her, but she had turned out to be good for him, or as good as any woman could expect to be, given Henry's proclivities for long drinking binges and getting fired off jobs. The latter was his specialty. Like most fat people he was sensitive—92 percent of them are sensitive about being fat (and nothing else)—and when some guy would mention his monstrous size in an unfavorable light, he would take to pulling his famous *National Geographic* bull rhino act, trampling the perpetrator of the unkind remark and everything in his stout path. Naturally this gave him a certain reputation at the bars. "You hear who Henry run up on today, crumpled up Leroy Selkirk, put a heel mark on his cheek." But it didn't go over extremely well with his employers, who one after the other reluctantly let Henry go. As a result of his deep sensitivities, Henry was just about unemployable, but to look at him standing there waving to Dog and me you would have thought he was John Beresford Tipton getting ready to give away another million bucks to some poor war orphan with big round eyes.

"Me and the Babe doing fine," he said. "She's working down Mc-Cormick. Come home smelling like spice cake every night. Whewooooooooie!"

Doggie laughed hard and put his arm around me.

"Shit," he said. "Henry in a donut shop, ain't that fine?"

"He is a handful," I said, still laughing.

Dog laughed with me for a minute or two more, then turned away and began itching his scalp so hard I thought he'd rip out his remaining hair.

"Red, this place is really getting to me. I need some air. There's a coffee truck outside. How about saving my place in line, okay?"

"Sure," I said. "But we're getting a little close up for you to be leaving. Once I get there I got to go on through."

"Don't worry. I'll be back in plenty of time. You want some coffee?"

"As long as you're going."

"Thanks, pardner."

Dog smiled as if he had been let off a life sentence and headed for the door. When he opened it, I could see the wall outside of twisting, roaring snow.

About forty seconds after he was out of the green-walled room, the line started moving along like there was cancer eating the other end of it. I got down and started fumbling with my drenched, stubbly work boots, pretending that my lace was untied, but a big greasy-haired guy named Al Rourke, with a head like a medicine ball and eyes like they were cut out of a pumpkin, began bitching at me.

"Come on, Baker. Quit the stalling. Dog's out of line, it's his problem."

"Take it easy, Rourke. I'm moving as fast as I can."

"Well, get on with it. I want to get out of this place."

Finally there was no holding it back any longer, and I found myself up to the information desk, face-to-face with Miss Motown. Close up her hair looked like sea kelp and smelled like the dissected frog down at Patterson High.

She asked me the essentials—name age address—and then got around to my work.

"Rougher down at Larmel Steel." I smiled at her. "That's a skilled position."

She tilted the maroon, heart-shaped glasses, with the gold-link chains which hung around her neck, and looked at me as if she was checking out a leprosy victim.

"Rougher? I'm sorry, Mr. Baker. That falls under the category of unskilled laborer. You go to the line on the left please."

"Now wait a minute, Miss . . ." I looked at her nameplate, which sat on her desk like a big black razor blade. "Maybe you don't understand just what it is a rougher does. I turn bars of steel that are hotter than hell. I don't do it right, the steel jumps the track and somebody ends up walking on stumps for the rest of their life. There's plenty of skill in that, you better believe it."

She looked at me and touched her hair, which bounced up and down, all one big spring.

"I'm sorry, Mr. Baker. Under our present laws your job is categorized as unskilled work. The line on the left, please!"

"I don't give a damn about your categories, lady," I said. "It's got more goddamn skill than what people do in here, and I'm going to the line on the right."

"Mr. Baker," she said in the even, strained tones of a woman who had seen the light when she read the rules, "you're unskilled or I call the guard. The choice is yours."

"Yeah, come on, Baker," Rourke said behind me. "You gonna shit or get offa the pot? There's other people wanta get home too."

I turned and looked him in the eye and then past him, searching for the Dog.

"Listen, Rourke, I've had a long day. Don't push your luck, okay?"

"If I was you I'd shut up, Red," he said, making a fist.

"Why don't you open your hand, Al, before I stick it up your ass."

Rourke's head jerked back as if I'd slapped him, and he narrowed his slitty eyes as thin as paper cuts.

"Mr. Baker, will you please take your card, sign it, and go to the left line?" Miss Motown said.

"You ever sing with Diana Ross?" I said. "You look a lot like the Supremes."

"Listen, Mr. Baker, either you move or I call the guards. Take your pick."

I turned back around to Rourke, and there, three feet away, was Dog, his big brown head covered with snow and his mouth hanging open in a surly way as he stared at the space he was supposed to occupy.

"Excuse me, Rourke. I'm getting back in line," Dog said politely.

Rourke's head swiveled around like a periscope. "Your place in line is back there, Donahue," Rourke said, pointing to the unseeable rear.

Dog looked at me and smiled, nodding his head back and forth, holding the coffee and donuts tray in his two flame-red hands.

"Hey, Rourke," Dog said, smiling politely and putting the cardboard tray down on the corner of the desk, which made Miss Motown's deep-penciled eyebrows raise almost up to her lacquered hair.

"You know what, I think I saw your ass in the back of the line. Maybe you oughta go back there and screw it back on your neck."

Rourke waited a second, as if to sort all of that out, and then nodded slowly, as if he'd almost caught up with it.

"You want some trouble, Donahue? Is that it?"

"I'm sorry, Rourke," Dog said. "I had it all wrong. I thought your ass was back there when it's right here on your shoulders."

"Dog," I said, trying to play peacemaker.

But I was a lifetime late.

Rourke reached forward, grabbed Dog by the lapels, and picked him straight off the ground. Dog looked shocked, like he'd seen a miracle. He goes two twenty in the winter, and nobody I ever recall had budged him. When he went up his hands flew out, upsetting the snack tray, which flew up in the air, the brown, steaming coffee flying all over Miss Motown, who gave out with a bloody scream. Her little opera was short-lived, however, because when she saw Dog kick Rourke squarely in the nuts with his dangling knee, she threw her hand over her mouth in horror. Rourke doubled over like a manikin, and Dog gave him a good chop on the back of the neck, which put him flat out on the wet green tile.

Rourke didn't move, so I bent down to see how he was breathing. I turned him over and saw a mean red bump rising on his forehead.

"Hey, Al," I said. "Al, you all right?"

He moaned a little and opened his eyes.

I looked up at Dog, who was still pumped up, his eyes wide open, his teeth clenched tight.

"Hell," Dog said, shaking his head. "Hell . . ."

But now Miss Motown had come to her senses. She slid out from behind her desk, coffee dripping down her face, and she started flinging her arms out in an umpire's "safe" sign.

"No way," she yelled. "No way! You are out of here, mister. There's no way this kind of violence is allowable."

"Hey," Dog said, really sounding sorry. "I didn't start it, I just—"

But she shook her head, put one hand on her hip, and pointed the other at the door.

"Out, out, out," she yelled.

"Okay, okay," Dog said.

"Hell, I'll go with you, Doggie."

But the Dog smiled and shook his head, putting his hands on my shoulders.

"No, Red. You're almost through. I'll meet you over in the mall bar."

"Hey, I don't need this shit," I said.

"Nah, you got to go through. It's all right. You stay around and tell Al I'm sorry. I shouldn'ta kicked him so hard. Just lost my mind."

I looked down at Rourke, who was groaning and picking himself off the tile. He looked younger and sweeter waking up.

"Hang in there," Dog said. "You hear something for me, let me know later."

"Okay," I said. "Take it easy, Dog."

I watched as Dog left, some of the men slamming him on the back and pointing down at Rourke, who was not one of your most popular people at the mill.

It was two more hours in the left line before a man with a face like an Indian wood carving gave me restful green-colored cards on which I had to print the names and addresses of two places I'd applied every week. This same helpful jerkoff then came up with his "listings" (as he called them), all the exciting new career moves an out-of-work rougher could hope for. Wonderful jobs like Deliverer of Telephone Books and Car Wash Technician, both of which paid one hundred dollars a month less than unemployment benefits.

Technically he could have turned me down for any benefits for refusing to go out on those jobs, but he looked about as whipped as I felt.

His eyelids hung down over his face like two broken blinds in a Baltimore Street flophouse, and he had breath that smelled like the wake of old cruise tugs down the Chesapeake.

"There is one job that might open up," he said, running his soft white hands up and down his black rooster tie. "Be a couple of weeks."

"Where's 'at?"

"Harborplace."

"Harborplace," I said. "That's where my wife works. What kind of job?"

He looked down at his desk and ran his hand across his thin white lips.

"That would be in your maintenance field," he said.

"The maintenance field. You talking janitor work? Trash collecting?"

"Well, some of that. It's a part of the special task force the mayor has instituted. The Baltimore Full Employment Brigade. Kind of like the old CCC camps. You know what I mean."

"Yeah, I got the picture. Let me try and paint it for you. My wife is working as a waitress in Weaver's Crab House, and she looks out the window and sees me, her husband, bagging trash, crab claws, and french fries people have thrown out. Picking up candy wrappers and ice cream sticks. You think I'm going to be able to hack that?"

Red Baker, Garbage Guy.

"Well, Mr. Baker, it's only temporary, and it pays two hundred a week."

"That's terrific," I said. "Is that it? That's all you got?"

"Mr. Baker, I wish there was something else. These are hard times. I'm sure your wife would understand."

"Yeah," I said. "Call me when it comes up."

This got a great big smile out of him. I half expected him to come out from behind the desk and give me a merit badge.

I turned around as he wrote a number on his card, and I looked at the two or three hundred other guys waiting in line for this exact same shit. Suddenly I wanted to pull a Henry and just rhino the hall. Sweat poured down my forehead like I'd just been walking in a hot summer rain. My ears felt as though they were flaming.

Nigger work for Red. Thirty-nine years old, working as a trash man.

A scream started inside of me, and I walked out of there, past the lines of huddled-up, dead-eyed guys. I walked out fast, hardly even speaking to men I knew.

Across the street I found the new mall bar. It was called the Angry Oyster and had a picture of a little demon oyster popping out of a shell with a rough-and-ready look on his face. The new Baltimore.

Inside the place was built like a schooner, with portholes and fake teakwood and waitresses pushing fifty done up in pirate miniskirts, black patches over their eyes, and rags wrapped round their heads. I looked at their varicose-veined legs and thought of Wanda and of myself, old sailors rotting away down on Pier One.

I knew that was horseshit, I was giving into cheap country music corn, but I felt like I'd been bludgeoned, hit with a belaying pin, and I staggered through the hanging plants until I found Dog in the corner, his head down on his arms and empty shot glasses surrounding him like fake jewels.

Some spittle dribbled from his mouth, and he snored loudly.

A waitress with a bleached-blond beehive came over and smiled at me. There was red lipstick on her teeth.

"You know this guy, hon? He's been at it for a whole afternoon."

"Yeah," I said, "I know him. Just bring me a double Wild Turkey. Okay?"

"Sure hon, but I hope there's not going to be two of you like that. We got our policies, ya know?"

I nodded, saying nothing, knowing if I did I might suddenly leap out of my seat and start tearing down the plants. I just watched her fat ass move away, and I sat there staring at knocked-out Dog, who snored loudly, ignorant of the cold news.

It wasn't long before the word came down. This wasn't your commonplace layoff; it might be six months before Larmel opened again. If they did at all.

I heard it from Billy Bramdowski one afternoon when I was food shopping while Wanda worked down at Weaver's Crab House. Felt weird prowling down the aisles of the Giant Supermarket like a housewife, doing my comparison shopping and thinking how damned embarrassed I was going to be when I pulled out our coupons for cereal, and sugar, and soap.

I was halfway down the breakfast foods aisle, pushing my big gleaming shopping cart, when Billy Bramdowski turned into the aisle and faced me.

At first I thought he was going to back up and get out of there, he looked that spooked. But then we both laughed and met there among the Count Chocula boxes.

"You hear what they got in mind, Red?" he said, rubbing the back of his hand over his cheek.

"No, what's that?"

"They're going to take the money they would be paying us, and they're going to sink it all into getting computers and stuff."

"Trying to compete with the Nips, huh?"

"Yeah," Billy said, sighing and looking down at his feet. "It's a hard one, Red, because when we do get back there, it's liable to be an all-new setup. Got to go to computer school to know how to use it. Seems like every which way a man turns, there's another wall."

"Well hell, Billy," I said, patting him on his square shoulders. "You can learn to run a computer as fast as the next guy. I can see you out there pushing those old buttons and yelling about warp factor one. A regular Captain Kirk."

This was a piss-poor attempt at humor, and Billy didn't even smile. I have a feeling he didn't even know who Captain Kirk was. Instead he just stared down at his shopping cart, which was filled with peanut butter and jelly, and crackers and cookies, and big bottles of Coke. Kid food.

"How's Jennie doing?" I asked.

"Fine." He smiled. "She's going to deliver in the summer. Number four.

"Kids are a blessing, Red. Just hope we can pay for this one."

"Hey, you'll find a way. Hang in there."

"Seen your friend Vinnie lately?" Billy asked.

"No, and I been losing lots of sleep over it."

Billy laughed and fooled with the zipper on his old N-1 jacket.

"That was some day. Thinks he's a badass. Well, gotta get home, Red. I'm head baby-sitter nowadays."

"Me too, Billy."

He tried another smile out and left me standing there staring at the oatmeal boxes. And feeling downright whiny and sorry for myself. Not to mention pissed off. Taking our pay and plunging it into fucking computers which would probably do our jobs for us when we tried to come back.

I wanted to take the shopping cart and run it into the big display of foreign crackers that was at the end of the aisle.

But I cooled it. I told myself that I was going to keep it together.

Take it one day at a time. Think about things carefully. Hunt down every job lead.

Act like a family man, Red Baker, keep your eye on the bright days ahead. One day at a time. . . .

Which is how I tried to handle it. Don't panic, keep it together, use the time off to see Ace. I remember a day not long afterward when Ace and his buddies were playing tackle football at Patterson Park in the snow. He was up early in the morning, and I had helped him with his helmet and shoulder pads and his old Johnny Unitas (number 19) jersey.

"Now don't break anything," I said. "Remember, you got to play basketball."

"Sure, Dad. I just hate to miss Saturday football. It's a tradition."

He poured half a bottle of milk on his fourth bowl of cereal, and I ran my hand through his hair.

"You're telling me? Listen, Doggie and I were in the first Saturday game. We played for five hours in the rain, but we won that sucker."

"No kidding, Dad? You played sports?" He laughed.

I shook my head. Sometimes he put me on like I did Dog. But I didn't mind it much. Hell, the truth is I loved it.

But he must have misunderstood my silence, because he started apologizing.

"Hey, Dad, I was only kidding. You know I like to hear about your old games."

Ace grabbed the pads from the kitchen floor, and I helped him lace them up.

"Is that the one that you threw to Dog for the winning touchdown?"

"Damn straight," I said. "I threw him a little swing pass, and he was headed downfield and three tackles were coming up on him. He just gave them a little bit of his leg, and he was gone. Doggie was some runner."

"All he does is drink now."

"Hell too," I said, "he's still in pretty good shape. He's just got a lot of worries, that's all. You shouldn't underestimate the Dog."

"Sure," Ace said. But I could tell he wasn't sure about Dog. It pissed me off a little bit because I know what a sweet and gentle guy the Dog is. I remember him pitching in around my house to help my old man when his heart was bad, without ever having to be asked.

"You play hard today," I said.

"You ought to come out, Dad . . . I'll bet we could beat you men if we tried."

"No way," I said.

"What's the matter, scared?" Ace said.

He laughed, and I gave him two left jabs to the shoulder. Then he hugged me and headed down the backyard steps to the alley and his friend Spence's house.

I sat down at the table, and in spite of everything I had to smile. Just seeing him dress up in that uniform, going up to play the same neighborhood game that I played so many years ago, gave me such pleasure. I could feel like we were part of something bigger than ourselves, our own small histories and traditions. Maybe it's corny, but seeing Ace in his uniform made me feel like I loved the whole damned city.

I guess I sat there at the table for quite a while, thinking about my kid (Wanda being out shopping with Carol), when I finally made my mind up to go watch him play. I pulled on my boots and walked out into the backyard. But I hadn't even made it down to our gate yet when something hit me in the arm. An ice ball.

I turned fast and saw Doggie hiding behind a telephone pole. He was laughing, sticking his head out like he was a kid.

"Red Baker's a whimp," he shouted.

I smiled and reached down into the snow as fast as I could, but he had another one aimed directly at me, and it burst with a hell of an impact on my shoulder, some of the cold ice spraying down my neck.

"You son of a bitch," I said, packing a hard one.

Dog came out from behind the pole, fired another one high over my head, and ran down the alley.

"All right, Doggie," I said. "You've had it now."

I started laughing like a kid and running after him. He was always faster than me, but he slipped on the ice, and I was gaining on him. I let go a snowball that got him on the back, just as he turned around the corner. I dug my boots in the alley snow and felt about a thousand pounds of fear and pain float out of me. I was fifteen again, chasing Doggie down the crazy street.

"I'm going to get your ass, Donahue," I shouted, feeling foolish but not caring who the hell heard.

But when I turned the corner he had stopped, not ten feet away, and looked at me with a strange smile on his face. His hands were stretched out, the picture of innocence.

"No weapons, Red," he smiled.

"What the hell's going on?"

Then I knew, but it was too late. Out from behind one trash can came Jimmy Silanski, and from another one Eddie Brandt, and another one Paul Wizniewski, and Chuck Mason and they all had snowballs in their hands.

"Ambush," they yelled, and I turned and began running like hell while snowballs went whizzing by my head, landing on my back, and splattering on my coat. I tried to turn to make a stand down by Wilenski's house, but there was a storm of snowballs hitting me in the chest, arms, face. I finally looked around at them all, drunk and laughing so hard they could hardly stand, and I tried like hell to fire back at them, but they were collapsing now, everybody pointing at me and holding their stomachs.

"Did that work or did that work?" Dog said, tears streaming down his face.

I looked around at them all. Every one of them an out-of-work father, come round to get me to go up and see the kids play.

"You sons of bitches," I said, laughing and punching Dog's arm. "I woulda never thought you were capable of anything so low."

Dog laughed and put his arm around my shoulder.

"The Dog is a sly one," he said, raising his eyebrows. "He has many unseen tricks."

He smiled and hugged me, and I felt such a warmth with him and all the other guys there that it brought tears to my eyes.

"Hell," I said, "let's get us a drink of whiskey at my place and then go see the kids."

"Shhh," Dog said, as he led us through the trees toward the park. "I think it's halftime . . . Yeah, be quiet. Goddamn it, Red, don't drop the bottle."

I giggled madly and picked up the Jack Daniel's and handed it to Jimmy, who was so loaded he was hanging off a pine bough.

"The Patterson Park devils will swoop down and attack!" he said, tripping and falling into me.

I began to laugh wildly, and all the other men began choking back their giggles.

Dog stopped and looked at us with a great seriousness.

"All right, men. Everybody have their snowballs?"

"Check."

"Okay . . . When I give the signal, I want you to pound across that field. When I raise my hands we attack. Are you ready?"

"I got to take a piss, general," Eddie Brandt said.

We all began to laugh again, but Dog shook his big head.

"Save it. All right, let's go."

Dog led us toward the Chinese Pagoda in the park. The kids were just on the other side of it, sitting around.

"Hey," Eddie Brandt's kid yelled. "It's our dads."

"Yeah," Bobby Mason said. "Let's challenge 'em!"

"Okay, men," Dog said. "Charrrrrrrrge!"

"They've got snowballs!" Jimmy Silanski, Jr., said.

"Ahhhhhhhhhhh," we yelled, slipping, drunk, throwing and falling down on one another, and getting up again. The football team was so astonished that for a second they didn't respond at all, and our snowballs hit them in a great, dense volley.

But they weren't long to catch on, and soon I was in the middle of the wildest snowball battle I'd had since I was a kid. I saw Ace making them as fast as he could and laughing wildly at me. He was firing his low, hard ice balls, which hurt like hell when they hit my back. I saw two boys team up on Dog, and I picked up a huge lump of snow and broke it over their heads. They fell to the ground, and one of them grabbed my legs, and then Eddie Brandt and Ace and two other boys piled on top of me. Dog tried to pull them off, but they tackled him too, and then some of the other men joined in and we were all rolling, head over heels along the fifty yard line, and there was shrieking and snow in my mouth, and somebody yelling "Don't break the whiskey, hell, don't break the whiskey," and I hit my head on the frozen ground, and felt the hand around my neck, and threw people off only to have two or three more jump back on, and I knew then that I would be sore the next day, but I didn't care at all, because this was the way I wanted it to stay, all tangled up with my friends and my kid, and all of us young and free and crazy on Saturday afternoon.

But suddenly in the middle of this wild-assed good time I heard a siren in the not-so-far distance, and when I managed to throw Ace off a little, I looked up and saw a black detective car screaming toward us. It stopped only a few feet away, and everybody got kind of quiet, and some of the men hid their bottles like they were fifteen again and might get taken in for drinking without cards.

The door to the cop car opened and out stepped Choo Choo Gerard. He was dressed in a tweed overcoat and had on a pair of expensive leather boots.

Behind him, still in the car, was Blazek, the guy they called "The Animal," Ed Blazek. I could see his mean round eyes focusing in on me. There was no love lost between us from long ago, when he hated me for taking away Wanda.

"Well, now ain't this something," Choo Choo said. "I get a call there's a gang fight in Patterson Park . . . and look what we have here."

"Sorry, Choo," I said. He spent too much money, and the word was he wasn't the straightest cop on the force, but me and Dog and Choo Choo went all the way back to high school. He'd stood up for local guys in court.

"Well, all I want to know is who is winning this match? You aren't letting these old dudes kick your asses, are you?"

The kids smiled and shook their heads.

"No way," they said. "No way."

"Hey, Officer Gerard, you want to help the men? It's the only way they're going to win."

Choo Choo smiled and looked back at Blazek, who sat stock-still with his big arms crossed in front of him.

"No way, I know better than to deal with you guys."

"All right," Ace said, laughing and reaching for the snow.

"Hell," I said. "You kids win. We're wiped out."

The kids gave up a great roar with that one, and Dog picked up the football.

"Go out for one, Ace," he said. "I believe this old arm is as good as it ever was."

Ace smiled and went long, and Dog cocked his arm and threw him a perfect spiral thirty-five yards downfield.

A couple of kids gave out with "whoasssss," and then somebody yelled, "Men against kids . . . yeah," and the men, holding their beer guts and taking one more good sip of Jack Daniel's, started calling for the ball and running out for passes.

I looked over at Choo Choo, who was laughing like hell. He had a good, kind laugh, which made it easier for him to run his numbers.

"Hey, great to see you, Red. Don't worry about this. A couple of old people over the other side of the park thought they were witnessing some urban blight."

I laughed and shook my head.

"How are you doing, Red?" Choo Choo said.

"Hanging in there."

"Yeah? Well, look, maybe we ought to talk, huh? Like to see more of you."

"Sure, Choo," I said.

"Gimme a call sometime, Red. Great kid you got there. Got a real future."

Blazek stuck his head outside of the car. "Hey, Choo Choo, let's leave these turkeys and go get some lunch, what you say?"

"Sure," Choo Choo said, winking at me. "Think you can beat those kids?"

"You know it," I said.

"Okay, Red, score one for me, and let's get together soon."

"Right, Choo," I said.

Then I ran back out on the field, and Dog threw me one of his perfect long passes. Ace ran toward it, leaped, but I managed to tip it away from him and made a hell of a two-fingered catch.

"All right, Mr. Baker!" Jimmy Silanski, Jr., yelled. "All right."

"Let's choose it up," somebody yelled.
"Yeah, let's go."

The rest of the day is like a great, boozy blur now. The men against the boys, like every Saturday I could recall long ago. And it was an even game too, Ace leading his team with his passing and Dog making a fantastic tipped-ball interception and faking out four of their defenders to weave and slide his way toward the winning touchdown. When the dark had settled on the field, we were all freezing cold and numb, but there wasn't one complaint from anyone, man or boy. This was the way it had always been in Highlandtown, and in spite of all that we had to face, on that day our neighborhood was connected, one generation to another, and it felt good and filled me with joy.

Now when I hear the cars slowing down on the dark street, I remember that day at the park with a kind of supernatural brightness, a picture with a fiery glow around it, and it lets me forget for a second just what might come down and how the world became as strange to me as it is to a beggar.

I remember how it was, feeling connected to all of them, knowing I wasn't alone in the world but part of Dog and Carol and their kids Lisa and Kathy, as well as Wanda and Ace. And when I sit here by the white lace curtains, staring out at the strange, alien moon, I recall a lot of days filled with the blood and muscle of friendship. Mostly times when we were younger, first married, and the kids were small, and Dog and Carol would come over the house on weekends, and we'd pull out a case of Boh, and fry up some oysters, and maybe play our oldies records underneath the red, yellow, and blue party lights Wanda and me would string up in the backyard. We'd sit out there in those green metal lawn chairs Ruth gave us, and under the bright moon we'd see the fires of the steel mill burning red and blue, the colors soaring above the flat rooftops from the south. Soon we'd be dancing, holding each other close while the kids played in the sandbox, or we'd do four-part harmonies on "Get a Job" or "In the Still of the Night," and afterward everything would be peacefully quiet, except the sounds of the crickets in the tomato garden down at the far end of our brand-new chain-link fence. And after the song we would all smile and feel the invisible rope which bound us together in something that must be like love. And then the lightning bugs would come out and dance through the black night air, their yellow, gentle lights making these beautiful patterns all around us, and I knew I was there, in the place I was meant to be, home.

But it's hard to hang on to these memories after all that has happened, hard now and, to be honest, hard even two days after the snowball fight, because that very next Monday I was faced with the same stomach-grinding facts—no job, not knowing where to look, my temples pounding and stomach churning just thinking of hitting the snow-slushed streets.

Maybe it was that day, yes, it probably was, that I started to slide, though at the time I told myself I was just lying in bed a little longer, waiting for Wanda and Ace getting ready to go off to work and school.

Up until that day I had been getting up with them, trying to keep everybody's spirits up, telling the kid that he was going to do great on his English test and assuring Wanda I'd get the food on the way back from the union hall or job hunting. But every day cost me, every day without work wore me down and made me think of Crystal and the open highway, every morning sitting alone in the house made me want to reach a little quicker for the bottle just to dull the ache.

This morning I didn't get up at all. And when they left I lay there, with two rose-printed pillows stacked up under my head, and felt my breath coming hard and a pain in my right side.

I stared up at the ceiling, at the cracks in the plaster, and thought of Dog over in his house, maybe doing the same thing, and Billy Bramdowski at his house, waiting for the new baby and scared shitless how he was going to pay for it all. And Henry and Babe down at Fells Point, sitting there waiting, and then it seemed like I could look into every home in Highlandtown and Dundalk, and they'd all be the same, the men sitting in their bathrobes, smoking cigarettes, staring at the morning game shows, maybe calling one another to keep their spirits up but having nothing to say, and finally even the sound of their buddies' voices, so hollowed out and defeated, made them feel more alone, so they stopped calling at all. And sat at white porcelain tables in their crowded kitchens under-

neath sunburst clocks, listening to the low drone of the TV from the
other empty rooms or the radio with its loud-mouthed wake-up
Balmere jocks.

I sat straight up in bed, my chest heaving with short, jerky
breaths, and I told myself to get a move on it. I'd been here before,
and I knew that late at night and early in the morning were the two
most dangerous times. Better by far to keep it rolling, get out in the
hustle, where even if it's tough you got the ability to get mad, to fight
back with anger, anything better than sitting stock-still, having ghost
visions in cracked-ceiling rooms.

After I made it to the bathroom I started to get undressed, but
found myself feeling a little dizzy, so I sat down on the bed and felt
the chill from the windows cutting through my bones. So I put on
my old terry-cloth robe, tied it right around me, and rubbed my
temples.

"Hey, it's going to be all right," I said out loud, but my voice
sounded like it was from somewhere else. And from something else.
The mechanical voice of a robot from one of those space pictures like
Star Wars.

I picked up the TV magazine and flipped through the rough pages
and saw suddenly that "The Honeymooners" was on. This was
something I didn't want to do, had told myself to avoid at all costs.
But suddenly it seemed (and I hate to admit this, it seems so lame)
that if I watched a little of it, with good old familiar Ralph and Ed, it
would cool me out, almost like talking to an old friend.

So I switched on the RCA ColorTrak we have on the gold tray
with wheels at the end of our bed, and right away I knew the episode.
Knew it? Hell, I'd seen it maybe forty times. It was the one where Ed
and Ralph buy all these pots and pans and cooking utensils which
they decide to advertise on TV. Old Norton is the Chef of the Past,
who uses this worthless old-time apple corer, and Ralph is supposed
to be the Chef of the Future, using their modern new equipment,
and the great scene, the scene that always cracked me up in the past,
is when Norton has this chef's hat on and he's fumbling with the
dull old apple corer and then he says, "Oh Chef of the Future, do
you know a modern way to core an apple?" And Ralph, who up to
now has been all cocky as hell and ready to knock 'em dead, Ralph
comes on with this new gadget. Only he gets stage fright, and instead of talking he starts mumbling "Ahummmmmmmmma

hummmmmmmmma hummmmmmmmmada," and sweat starts pouring down his great fat head, and he flails around like a baby rhino and knocks down the whole set, pots and pans flying everywhere.

Now, like I say, I've seen that show maybe forty times. In fact, it's one of my all-time favorites, didn't seem to matter how often I saw it, it always cracked me up. I'm talking about serious laughing, where you're holding your sides and you can't breathe right, and this time wasn't any different. I started laughing the second I recognized the show, and by the time the set was destroyed I was falling backward on the bed, yowling like a madman—only suddenly I couldn't stop laughing, and then my voice began to sound like the fat lady's screech at Gwynn Oak Funhouse, the place where Buck and Dot used to take me as a kid, and I saw the fat lady's mechanical mouth opening and her great, fat, geared jaws and those perfectly even, two-feet-long, filed teeth and the way she rocked back and forth like some crazed priest come to tell you about the everlasting pain of hellfire. And then I made myself stop, holding my chest and feeling like a fool and thanking God I was alone, but then another thought scared me almost as badly.

What if, when I was applying for a job, I got like Ralph and said, "Hi, I'm Red Baker, ahummmmmmmmada hummmmmmmmmmada hummmmmmmmmada," and I couldn't stop?

That thought sent cold chills through me, and I huddled up in the old terry-cloth robe, an act that usually settled me down. But it's a funny thing about terry cloth. You get yourself a fireplace, and a dog named Chief, and a good shot of Wild Turk, and your terry cloth, and it will seem like the damndest, coziest material on earth. But here, sitting in the drafty bedroom, my skin clammy with the fears, suddenly that terry cloth seemed cheap and threadbare and like everything else in my life—lousy, secondhand, something only an out-of-work bum would wear.

Suddenly I couldn't stand having it on me. It was the damndest thing, and I am ashamed to tell you these feelings, which I would ordinarily associate with a lunatic.

But it was me, Red Baker, who felt this way, and I knew the longer I stayed in that bedroom the closer I was going to come to heading down the booby hatch, so I threw on my street clothes, rushed down the steps, and set out looking for work.

I drove my old Chevy down Aliceanna Street toward Fells Point and stopped in front of Ruby's Play Lounge. Ruby was a black-haired, big-breasted woman who I'd known longer than Wanda. The truth is she and I used to do some parking out by Loch Raven Reservoir back when I was at Patterson. We'd long since stopped that kind of thing, but I knew she still liked me some, and since her husband, Jim, had died of a tumor last year, I figured she might need some help running her bar.

There is no place lonelier than a bar at ten in the morning. Only two old rummies sitting there at the counter, sipping their Four Roses and mumbling things to each other about Johnny Unitas and the Colts.

"I'll tell you if 'ey jest got Johnny U to play for 'em again, 'ey would never leave town."

"You said it. Get him and Raymond Berry. I'm telling you. 'Ey was great! Greatest combination of all time."

I looked at Ruby standing behind her bar, polishing the gold-edged mirror she'd put up. Behind me there were seven or eight dinner tables, with white tablecloths and flowers. It was a simple place, but she ran it decently.

At the bar was Ed Farmer, a milkman I know. He was telling Ruby about his new part-time occupation.

"Ruby, I tell you I started doing hair?"

"Hair?" Ruby said, catching my reflection in the mirror. "You're doing hair? Ed, I didn't know you were gay."

Ed Farmer's face puffed up like he'd been bit by one of them puff adders you see on "Wild Kingdom."

"It ain't like that. Goddamn it, Red, did you hear that?"

"Hell, Ed," I said, "it's nothing to be ashamed of. Some of the greatest men in history were that way."

"Goddamn," Ed yelled, pounding his fist on the bar so hard that the two old rummies down at the end almost fell off their stools.

"I am not a goddamned queer and never have been. In fact, I'm not even learning on women. I'm learning to cut hair on the dead."

"Hell," Ruby said, winking at me. "That must be easy. You don't even have to do the back."

This cracked me up, the first decent laugh I'd had in a week, but Ed didn't find it that amusing.

"Look here, it's a responsibility. You got the deceased's parents and family to face."

"Yeah," Ruby said, "I can see it now. 'Hey, my granny don't look like no Liberace.' "

"Well hell," Ed Farmer said. "You don't respect nothing. What do you do that's so great?"

"Well, one thing I don't do is cut no corpse's hair. You can't even ask 'em how they want it done. What kind of hairdressing is that?"

"Yeah, and they only come one time," I said. "How do you know they even like what you do?"

Ed Farmer took a deep breath, tossed off a shot, and shook his head.

"A couple of wiseasses," he said. "Well, how come you're not working if you're so damned smart, Baker?"

"Hey, I'm retired. Won the lottery, didn't you hear?"

"Smartass," Ed Farmer said. "World run by smartasses."

He picked up his milk bottles and clanged noisily toward the door, leaving Ruby and myself pounding the bar and laughing a little too hard. I mean, it wasn't *that* funny.

"Pretty rough on old Ed," I said, after a while.

"He's so damned dumb," Ruby laughed, "I can't help myself. Every time he comes in here I say to myself, 'Now this time treat him with some respect,' but then he starts in bragging about what a great provider he is, how some people don't want to work and all that other bullshit, and I just can't resist giving it to him."

I smiled at her, and she smiled back, and I thought of how we used to be, young and driving out in the country, the only worry whether we were going to beat Dunbar in basketball.

"You need a beer, Red?"

"Well, maybe one."

"Things pretty hard, Red?"

"Yeah. In fact, that's why I come to see you. I was wondering if maybe you had a job. I mean, I can make drinks or help out . . . anything."

She sighed and gave me the beer and then put her hand over mine. It was rough, scratchy, almost as raw as my own.

"Red, you need a little loan or something, I could come up with something. You know that. But, hon, I just had to let Steve the night kid go. To tell you the truth, what with the cutbacks, I don't see how

I'm going to make it through the winter. I got a plan, though. Before the money Jim left me runs out. Got a place all picked out."

She reached down under the bar and showed me a folder of a place called Deltona, Florida.

"I'm heading down that way by this summer, maybe sooner, Red. You can get you a Spanish-hacienda–type home down there for about thirty-five thousand dollars. Real nice and right on a lake. I know a little bar down there for sale. People down there got money too, Red."

I took a sip of my beer and looked at the folder. It had blue skies and palm trees and a young couple water-skiing and looking at each other like they were birthday cake.

I thought of Crystal and me down there. The thought ached through me, and I suddenly wanted to see her so bad, tell her I loved her and that we should leave now, just take off, head down the highway until we got to the land where the sun never quit.

Crystal and me in the moonlight, cutting through a midnight, black-water lagoon. Our boat nosing through the lily pads.

"Red, hon, you want another beer?"

"What? Oh no . . . I don't think so, Ruby. You really moving to Florida?"

"I don't know, Red. To tell you the truth, it scares hell out of me. I grew up here. I know everybody, but there's nothing left, Red. You can't live on memories."

"I know we don't see each other much, Ruby, but . . . well, I like knowing you're here. I mean . . . hell, you know what I mean."

She smiled at me softly, then leaned over the bar and kissed me on the cheek.

"You're a good man, Red Baker," she said. "I shoulda never let you go."

I didn't know what to say to that, so I just smiled and told her I'd see her before she left and headed back out into the sleet and wind and snow.

For three hours I drove around Highlandtown, past the old boarded-up National Brewery and up and down Broadway, past the Circus Movie Theatre, which was playing a picture called *Behind the*

Green Door, where I used to go see my serials like *Gangbusters,* and *The Rocket Man,* and Gene Autry in *The Phantom Empire,* and along with them would be two or three Woody Woodpeckers or Looney Tunes, and then a double feature. Saw my first 3-D movie in that picture house, *Bwana Devil.* Now it's all horny sailors from off the Greek ships down on Pratt Street, with newspapers on their laps.

And in the old days all of those pictures, serials, cartoons, and double features cost thirteen cents. 1948. When I was five years old.

This was Broadway, and on Easter people would march down this street past the Johns Hopkins Hospital, and they'd be dressed in their finest clothes, and the Navy and Marine color guard would lead the parade.

Now it was nothing but bars for artists and lawyers and a bunch of dead-assed stores, and not one of them needed help. I did hear from Jim Halenski that they might be hiring up at the soap factory, so I hustled over there and waited for an hour, waited in a gray room with one chair in it and the smell of old soap leaking from the walls. When they finally did come out they told me they'd cut back 34 percent of their work force. There wasn't even any point in filling out the papers.

I went out to the parking lot and sat behind the wheel of the car for a long time and thought again of calling Crystal. Fuck it, call her now, take off, get the hell out. I was forty years old. Maybe Wanda and Ace and I could throw a special party in the city dump, shoot and eat rats.

Oh, I knew I was falling prey to unmanly and unhealthy self-pity, so I kept moving, and after I had been turned down at Sunny Surplus and Bo Jangles' Biscuits I stopped by Smitty's Clam Bar, which is in the new market in the middle of Pratt Street. I have known Smitty since we were kids. He was a tall, thin boy with long hair when we were kids, wore it DA style and had hot rods. Now he was a stooped, thin guy with a few strands of hair left and hands that were cut a thousand times from opening his raw oysters and clams. Like Ruby, he was glad to see me, and before I could say anything he had stuck half a dozen fresh oysters in front of me and some hot sauce.

"Listen, Red, I did hear of one job might be open. It's over at Shaw's Mattress Factory. Yeah, you ought to get on over there soon. Might be something to tide you over."

"Jesus," I said. "That place . . ."

"I know, Red. I wish to hell I could give you some work here, but you look at this place. It's a tomb in here. I can't give this stuff away, and you know when people ain't eating seafood, they ain't eating."

I nodded and sucked out the last oyster, all covered with horseradish and cocktail sauce. It tasted so damned good that it picked my spirits up just enough to get out on the street again.

"Good luck, Red. You'll find something."

I shut the door and started walking across the street to my car when I heard something in the alley. I looked back in the twilight at the trash cans and soaked cardboard boxes and didn't see anything. Then I heard it again, a low moan.

Slowly I walked back there, looked to my right and left, knowing that it could be a trick, that any second I might get a knife in my ribs.

I saw what it was.

A man, maybe seven or eight years younger than me, lying in a pool of his own vomit. Next to him was some rotgut wine, and he waved his left arm at me as if he wanted me to come closer.

I didn't know what to do because the shock of seeing him made me stand still for some time.

He didn't have a nose. Just a pinched-up little scar and maybe half of one nostril.

"Think I'm ugly?" he said.

"No," I lied. He was the ugliest man I'd ever seen.

"Got it shot off in 'Nam," he said, and then he gave a small, cackling laugh that was close to a scream.

I don't know what it was, spending all that time roaming up and down the streets, hearing about Ruby leaving, but I suddenly couldn't stand it, and it occurred to me that he was me and I him . . . and I wanted to do something for him, wanted to pick him up out of there, get him to a hospital. But when I walked closer I saw he had a knife.

"You get near me you going to get the darkness," he said.

And then he began to laugh again, and stab weakly out into the winter snow, and I backed out of there, feeling the oysters sloshing around inside of me and wanting to throw up. I leaned on the brick wall for a second and looked back in the alley again and could see his torn boots and his raw, bare legs. Then I staggered back across the street and got in my car.

The mattress factory was like a building I saw in a nightmare once. I was running down a narrow cobblestoned street, and I was being chased by someone; worse, I think it might have been a friend, a friend with a knife, and I kept wanting to explain to him that he didn't have it right, I hadn't betrayed him, I was his friend forever, but I knew he wouldn't listen. He was coming after me, and my only hope was to get away. But up ahead of me was this building, big and square, with a million tiny windows, all of them covered over with black soot, and inside were things like people but with animal snouts and squidlike suckers coming off of their faces.

It was death from the friend or death inside the box.

I woke up and stayed alive.

But this wasn't any dream. This was Shawland. Outside was a big blue-and-white billboard of a blonde in a negligee sleeping with her eyes closed on her mattress. She was fifty feet tall above me, floating there above the snow like a sleeping angel. Underneath her was the potholed parking lot, leading up to the boxy building with the windows that looked like poked-out eyes. I thought of no-nose lying there in the alley.

I thought he had come in the night and sliced out the sight from those windows, from all who worked in that gray, filthy, soot-stained place.

I don't know how I got him and the factory mixed up, but I thought of him as I pushed open the filthy glass door and walked all the way down the gray endless hallway, by glass-partitioned booths that looked like places where doctors came to see if you were gone enough to work there.

There was a smell in that place too, like burned flesh, and puddles of water all over the floor, and I thought of death by electrocution.

Right before I got to the big steel EMPLOYMENT OFFICE DOOR, I stopped, took out my comb and slicked back my hair, and told myself to be ready. Look sharp, stand tall. Be a good imitation of Red Baker.

Then I walked inside. The secretary was a fat woman who was sipping a diet soda and reading a book called *Fury's Passion*. She wore a green dress with a ruffled collar that came up to her double chin. On the collar there was a sparkly, cheap turtle pin with rhinestones in its shell.

I gave her my name and told her I was looking for work. She gave me one of those Bible school smiles and looked back at her book.

"Mr. Porter will be back in a minute," she said, not looking up. "He just went down to the canteen. You can fill out this application while you're waiting. And please stand back from my desk. You're dripping all over my lunch."

I looked down and saw a brown paper bag sitting on the edge of the desk. I had gotten it wet. I moved back fast, trying for my friendly, boy-next-door smile. She didn't go for it.

I picked up the application papers and started filling out the forms with the Bic pen she handed me. It was nearly out of ink, and every other letter was faded and unreadable, making it look like I couldn't spell. I bore down twice as hard, but it was no good, and I had to ask her for another one.

"Some people applying for work would have thought to bring their own pens," she said. "That happens to be the last one. All the others have been took."

Her voice was like the lead paint chipping off the walls.

I finished writing out my application as best I could, and then her switchboard lit up.

"Mr. Porter, there is someone here to see you. Yes, a man who *claims* to be looking for work."

I could feel my adrenaline level pumping through me. I wanted to rip her paperback book in half, but I figured she already expected that of me.

"You may go back now," she said.

I nodded and made my way through the long gray halls to the employment counselor.

His door was shut when I got there, so I rapped on it and he told me to come inside.

When I walked through the door I stared at Peter Porter, a boy who was known as "Mange" Porter at Patterson. Of all the boys I had known in all my years at school, Peter Porter was the biggest whimp.

"Well, well, Red Baker," he said in a whistling yodel, looking up at me from behind his desk. "I don't believe it. Laid you off down at Larmel, huh?"

"That's right," I said. "Good to see you, Peter."

He smiled at me with his little yellow teeth and ran his left hand down his caved-in chest and then over his belly. He wasn't fat exactly—in fact, mostly he was thin—but he always had this beer gut. Your skinny-fat guy. He'd been the biggest suckass to all the teachers and had reported Dog for cheating once in math class.

They'd made him head of the safety patrol. I remembered him lurking in the halls, waiting to see if you were going to try and skip out early on Friday afternoon.

I remembered him getting caught jerking off in the boys' room.

I tried to recall if I had been hard on him, but it had been so long. He was the kind of person you forgot existed the second they left your line of vision.

"So what brings you to Shaw's?" he said in that same high, sticky voice I recalled from school. He took off his black glasses and tapped them on his wrist.

"I'm looking for work, Peter," I said. "I heard you have some jobs open."

"Well, isn't that interesting?" he said. "I mean, don't you find this an amazing turn of events?"

"What's that?"

"Just the fact that you're asking me for a job."

I shrugged and said nothing.

He got up, then rubbed his hand over his stomach and ran it around his jaw, like he was having some deep thoughts.

"Well, I find it an amazing coincidence." He whistled.

"Listen, Pete," I said, "I'm looking for work. I mean, I'd like to know if there's a job open or not."

He turned and stared at me, rubbing his right hand on his elbow and putting his left on his jaw, like The Thinker.

"I guess you would like to know about work. I thought at one time you were going to be a professional basketball player. That's what they said. Red Baker—boyhood hero."

I began to sweat a little then. I looked behind him at the high window which looked out on one of the three big buildings. Through their windows I could see people that looked like great hunched birds working away, moving slowly, bent in half as if they were in a dull, steady pain. I thought of my dream and felt the back of my throat get dry.

"What did happen to your basketball career, Red?"

"Nothing much. I wasn't good enough to play pro."

SWAMPSCOTT PUBLIC LIBRARY

He stopped and opened his eyes like one of those Japanese actors they got on public television.

"Red Baker not good enough? I don't remember it that way. It seemed to me you were always being touted as the best player Maryland produced in twenty years. I always wondered why you didn't go to college on a scholarship."

"I was married, had a kid," I said.

"Yes, I know," he said, walking back and forth. "I'm aware of that. But a man of your talents . . . they'd make excuses for a player like that. They would have probably given the newlyweds a house of their own."

I was starting to get uneasy. I didn't mind all the sarcasm, but he was leading me somewhere.

"Look, Pete, I don't see what this has to do with me getting a job, if there *is* a job."

He picked up a paperweight, one with Harborplace in a snowstorm inside of it. He shook it up and watched the snow settle on the small trapped city.

"I think it might have a great deal to do with it. It seems to me that I remember something about you and your friend, what was his name, the big, stupid one . . . Dog? Yes, I remember something about you losing your chance to get a basketball scholarship because of some holdup you were involved in. Isn't that correct?"

I sat still and put my hands in my lap. I took deep breaths and told myself to do nothing, to say nothing. Get it under control, Red, because I wanted to go for him now. I wanted to take his head and bash it with the paperweight a few times.

"There was no holdup," I said.

"No? That's not how I remember it, Red. This is no joking business I'm speaking of. If I hire someone who was in trouble with the law, there could be serious repercussions. People might think I didn't live up to the position of trust and authority the company has chosen to hand over to me."

I kept my breathing regular, looked him straight in the eye.

"I need work, Pete."

"Well, Red, I would be less than honest if I didn't tell you there is a job. It's in the stuffing division. Eight dollars an hour. But I'd have to know more about this . . . incident . . . before I could recommend that you be hired."

"I was eighteen years old, Pete. It was nothing."

"If it was nothing . . . why did you spend two years in the Maryland State Training School for Boys?"

"I was only there for seven months," I said. I sat perfectly still and looked at him. He was like a long white slug, staring down at me, still working his soft jaw with his flabby hand.

"I'd have to hear the story, Red, before I could recommend you."

I looked down at my soaked feet and back up at the gray sky, which pressed down on the building like a great lead shield.

"It was a gag. Me and Dog, we were drunk one night, just out tooling around in his old Buick, and we decided for a laugh to rob the Little Tavern. It was just a joke. We went in and told them to put up their hands. We didn't even take the goddamned money. We just stole all the hamburgers and sodas in the place and gave 'em out on the street."

His face lit up now, and his tongue curled around his lips. He rubbed his stomach like he was trying to trim off the fat.

"Did you use a *gun?*" he said in a high-pitched voice.

"Yeah, but without bullets. It was a gag."

"A gun," he said. He seemed to be off somewhere by himself, in one of his Pete Porter fantasies.

But he snapped back out of it quickly.

"That's all that happened? That's not the way I heard it. I heard you were involved in some other robberies. *Real* ones. I mean, I don't imagine they send boys to the state correctional institution for that kind of prank."

"You heard wrong," I said, and there was menace in my voice. He had finally drawn it out of me. In another minute I was going to be across the desk.

"*Red* Baker," he said, almost singing the words. "Reddddd Bakkkkker. Well, I'll tell you what, Red, I'm going to have to give this some thought. Yes, I'm going to have to give this some *careful* consideration."

"You are?"

He turned and smiled at me slowly. "Don't you approve of my methods? What do you think this is, Baker, high school?"

I didn't say anything. I knew he hadn't wanted to say that. He was enjoying playing the big man, but it had slipped out anyway.

"There's no job, is there?" I said suddenly, knowing it as sure as I know steel. It caught him off guard, and he gave a nervous little laugh.

"As a matter of fact, no, there isn't," he said with a look of surprise on his face. Then he started to laugh. A long, high whistle.

I got up slowly, feeling my heart beating, a hot red flush in my face, adrenaline pumping through me. I turned and started to walk toward the door, knowing that if I didn't go now, without saying anything, I wouldn't leave until I broke his head.

"Red Baker," he sang in a high-pitched whistle as I swung the door open hard and walked out into that gray, long, mud-splattered hall.

I must have been in a trance, some swirling blue fog, as I walked across the mushy lot to my car and climbed in, dripping on the frozen seat. I don't remember starting my car, don't remember much at all except going down Broadway past Lana's Lingerie, where they had something in the window for THE GIRL OF YOUR DREAMS, black-lace panties with an open crotch. Another nightie with buckskin fringe said SAVAGE. Then the light changed, and I was turning down Madison and stopping the car and getting out, walking across the garbage-littered streets, and suddenly I knew I was heading for Dr. Raines's.

I didn't want to be there, almost called it off, but once I was only a few houses away in the failing gray-slush light and saw the lines of men waiting there, I knew there was no turning back.

I needed what the dead-eyed croak had to give me, wanted to feel the white pill dissolving in my blood; let it make me fly, Lord, out of the last five hours.

No one knows what Dr. Raines puts in his pills, but it's clear it's the heaviest speed around. It takes maybe fifteen minutes for it to start, and then it can go either way, lift you out of the black-trash streets, give you the confidence to walk through walls, or it can turn against you, make you sweaty and clammy at the same time, cause a man to misinterpret the slightest smile or wave of the hand. Send you round the bend, oh Lord, yes. But now, with the day I had, I figured it was worth the risk. Ruby moving and the man with no nose and then Porter dumping on me, bringing up my criminal youth, working me like that, and me having to sit there and suck it in.

Though the Good Book tells us to be humble, I've never taken much stock in it. I wanted to wait outside the mattress factory underneath the sleeping fifty-foot blonde and grind Pete's face into the sidewalk. But then, what good would that have done me? The idea was a job, not revenge.

I stood in the line of men in the gray twilight, watching the cars slide through the slush, sending a spray of it up on our pants legs, covering the white marble steps. If there was one thing I was grateful for it was the gathering darkness, because I didn't want anybody to see me here. Nobody who stands in the Dr. Raines line wants to be there. No one can take his stress pills without feeling shame. But there were a hell of a lot of guys I knew trying to act casual about it.

"Hey, Ralph. Hey, Teddy, what's happening?"

Ten years ago when we thought we knew the world, these same guys were ready to kick kids' asses who were on dope. Commies, queers, scum.

I think we may have been right about some of it, even now.

I remember when the hippies said live for today, tear it all down, start a new world, we were the guys who screamed remember your families, remember what made the country great, remember who died in World War II to give you your freedom, but now we were in the dope line, and I don't know how it happened. Somehow we had all become the just-live-for-today guys.

Nobody understands this.

I stood in the line, the wind whipping over my soaked clothes, and I took out a bent, wet Marlboro, and Jackie Gardner in front of me cupped his hands around it while I lit up. Trying to stand there looking like a man. But it's hard to feel strong waiting in a dope line for thin, blank-faced Dr. Raines. I prayed that Ace wouldn't come by with his friends and see me here. Maybe he was getting to the age when he knew. Of course he was.

Whatever happened to me, don't let Ace come by here now, God.

"Hey, Bill, yeah, going up to see the old doc. Got a little flu."

I moved up another step, inch by inch, watching my buddies come and go, making quiet small talk, everybody with their hands stuffed way down in their pockets, guys looking down at the ground, shuffling their feet, pretending it's a voting line, a movie line, a nightclub line, a ball game line, anything but what it is, which is a dope line.

Shame moved up and down my arms, giving me the old electric tattoo.

Damned shame, like a shadow over the lie that promises you can forget the shame and pain itself.

I waited, the cold cutting through my coat, my teeth chattering. Lines, endless lines, and Porter playing with me, knowing about my record. Knowing all along, knowing that I couldn't even afford to break his head. Ruby leaving town, Crystal waiting for me, Wanda counting on me. Ace.

A black Merc pulled up to the corner. It was Choo Choo Gerard, and I put my head down in my coat further and turned my face to the snow.

But Choo Choo is sharp. He saw me. Called out my name.

"Hey, Red, you getting the health food diet?"

Blazek was with him. Broken nose and big split lips. He laughed, sending a spray of spittle out the window.

"Yeah, Red. You look a little fat."

"Why don't you get an operation and have a brain put behind your face, Blazek."

"You cocksucker. You junkie cocksucker. I should bust him right now, huh, Choo?"

Choo Choo reached over and touched Blazek lightly on the leg, and The Animal froze.

"Red, come on over here a minute."

"It's all right," Jackie Gardner said. "I gotcha covered."

I walked over to the side of the car. It made me jumpy to talk with Choo Choo. I felt like Wanda or Ace was hovering over me, watching my every move.

"So how's it going, Red?"

"It's going."

"You hear the news? They might not be opening up down there at all."

"I heard."

"Talks like a tough guy," Blazek said. "You a tough guy, Baker? Or just another junkie?"

"You might find out sometime."

"Shut up, Blazek," Choo Choo said softly. "You aren't talking to an asshole. Red is a friend of mine. Though I don't see him as much as I'd like. Listen, Red, how's Ace going?"

"He's okay."

"Hey, I know he's okay. I seen him the other day up to St. Mary's.

This is no shit. He played Bobby Mason. I mean, what's Bobby, three inches taller? And you know Ace beat him one-on-one by something like sixteen to seven. Ate him up. What's he, fourteen?"

"Sixteen," I said.

"Kid's good, Red. Hope you can hold it together so he can go to a good school. How's Wanda doing? Getting tired down the crab house, huh?"

I had had all I could take of this.

"She's not bitching. Look, see you later, Choo Choo."

"Maybe about ten tonight at Slap's? Buy you a few beers, keep Dr. Raines's pills knocked back. Say hello to the old croaker for me."

"Yeah, junkie," Blazek said. "I bet your kid would like to know that."

That did it. I moved for the car and grabbed his black raincoat.

"You fat cocksucker . . ."

But Choo Choo stepped on the gas, and all that was left was me and Blazek shouting at each other as they wheeled down the street.

I looked at Jackie Gardner, who moved up to let me back in.

"Fat piece of shit," he said. "Somebody ought to feed him to the fucking crabs."

"Thanks," I said, stepping back in line. I was trembling all over, tapping my feet, and my temples were pounding. More than ever I wanted to see Dr. Raines, and more than ever I felt sick at the thought of it.

I left Dr. Raines's with my package of white pills, feeling just like the piece of junkie shit that Blazek said I was. But that didn't stop me from going directly across the street to the Oriole Tavern, ordering a Wild Turkey and a Boh, and popping one of Dr. Raines's whites. As soon as it went inside me I thought of Wanda and Ace, and I suddenly wanted to go into the back of the bar and stick my fingers down my throat. Don't let it get into my bloodstream.

But I didn't do anything of the kind. I sat there and talked to Jackie Gardner, who was there for the same reason but fifteen minutes ahead of me.

"How you feeling, Red?" he said, smiling.

His eyes were lit up in a way that I knew mine would be in a few minutes. Feeling that speed, or whatever it is, pumping through you, giving you the charge. Taking you up to where your shame didn't matter.

"Not yet," I said.

He smiled and slicked back his black hair.

"Will be," he said. "Got to give it to the doc, stuff's got a ride to it, you know? Used to go to a guy down in Brooklyn, and the stuff made you want to go out and strangle puppies. Doc's got first-rate dope. People put him down, but I've always liked the doc, you know what I mean?"

"Yeah," I said. I was grateful for Jackie holding my place in line while I was talking to Choo Choo, but now hearing him rave on like that, just motor-mouthing off speed, looking glassy-eyed and dumb . . . he was ruining it for me.

I began to dread it coming on. Told myself not to just start yapping away, don't let it make me act like an asshole . . .

"Plant's going to open up soon. Things getting a lot better. You know what I'm talking about? Things gonna be all right, Red."

I looked at the deep lines in his face, at his slick-backed black hair and remembered when he played shortstop at Patterson, good little athlete and not a bad guy. Could turn the double play. Now he was into speed, screwing up, had an accident at the plant last year, mishandled a roll of red-hot steel, which about burned his left leg off.

I could feel the speed coming on, and I wished to hell I wasn't here with Jackie. I shut my eyes and held my hands to my temples and saw Porter staring at me, rubbing his jaw, and Choo Choo looking at me from the driver's seat.

"Hear about Billy Bramdowski," Jackie said.

"Sure," I said. "His wife's having a kid."

"No, not that. About Billy."

"What about him?" I said, putting my left palm on the bar.

"Killed himself this morning," Jackie Gardner said.

I felt like an electric prod had been jammed into my ears, right through my brain.

"What the fuck you talking about? I saw him, what, three days ago, shopping in the Giant."

"Well, you won't see him there no more. Did it with a shotgun, Red. Out back in his toolshed. His kid found him, came running out of the place with a garden trowel in her hands, blood and brains and shit all over it."

I felt my mouth go dry, the speed coming on. My hands got cold, and my neck muscles bunched up, sending this wild pain down my back. I drank the whiskey fast and asked the kid behind the bar for another one.

"I woulda told you in line, but I thought you knew," Jackie said. "It's already been onna TV."

"Billy Bramdowski?" I said, taking another hit of Wild Turkey.

"Yeah," Jackie Gardner said. "That was his name."

I tried to breathe but felt paralyzed. My nose has been clogged up for years from the dust down the plant, so I have to breathe through my throat, and now I couldn't swallow at all. I got up and walked shakily to the back of the bar, past the shimmering jukebox, which was playing George Jones.

The steam pipe was making a groaning noise, and I started thinking about Billy Bramdowski, shy Billy. I should have known the night I saw him at the Paradise.

I swallowed hard and threw water from the tap on my face and looked at myself in the dirty mirror again. My eyes were red, I could feel the pill working; it was too damned strong . . .

Jacking me up, jacking me way up . . .

I turned on the tap again, stuck my head under it, and took a drink. The water tastes better coming straight out of the pipes. I told myself it wasn't me, it had nothing to do with me. It was Billy. In the toolshed.

I wiped my face off with a paper towel and walked back out into the bar.

"Hey, Red, you all right?" Jackie Gardner said, smiling. "Feeling better now, babe? Dr. R's shit treating you right?"

"Yeah," I said. "Yeah . . . Look, Jackie, I gotta go. See you."

I started to pay for the drinks, but he wouldn't let me. He was sailing out there now, not even feeling Billy's death anymore. No job worries, no panic, no sweat.

I walked out of the bar and headed up the street. It was getting dark, and I could feel the speed shooting through me, and I kept seeing Billy's kid coming out of his toolshed with that garden trowel with Billy's brains hanging off of it.

I got into my car and wanted to scream, to start smashing my dashboard, but the pill was floating me up above it all, so I couldn't quite feel it. It was like . . . like television somehow, when you watch the crime news and see people being scraped off the street.

I tried to remember Billy. Blond. Heavyset. Pink face. Quiet. Good singer in the choir at church. Had a bass voice.

Liked to eat oysters. Balding. Went to Patterson, played baseball, I think. Not anybody I knew real well.

But always around. Somebody you were glad to see. Smiled, and the smile came from somewhere.

Good to his wife and kids.

I turned on the engine of the old Chevy and started out in the snow, not knowing where to go, too jacked-up to head home. Then I remembered it was rec day up at the high school. I could go play some basketball with Ace and his high school buddies.

I pulled a U-turn, went by the doc's, and saw the line there, twice as many now, guys with their backs to the street, hunched up against the wind.

By the time I got to Patterson, the pill was moving through my blood like a new Cadillac cruising through the traffic on its way to Florida. I almost stopped and called Crystal, but with my last ounce of sanity I didn't stop by a phone booth and make that call, or I sure as hell would have picked her up right in front of Vinnie's and been down the road.

Once those Dr. Raines's are in you, it's the little time-released capsules in control. Sending messages through you, like you are never going to die, never going to end up in a tan-painted, tin-roofed toolhouse with a gun in your mouth.

Inside the gym the lights looked weird to me. Strange glow coming off the tiles, and I thought of the unemployment office. Everywhere I went I was followed by neon and tile, and I couldn't stand that. Not here too.

Ace was down the other end of the court, putting up soft five-foot jumpers with his left hand and making them one after another. He was getting good with his left. Almost like it was natural for him. Focus on that. Get ahold of that.

I called out to him and threw my soaked sheepskin jacket over the parallel bars, the pocket with the pills in it safely buttoned up.

But what if he reached in there for something?

What if he could tell?

Don't get crazy. Don't get paranoid. Keep it together.

"Hey, Dad," Ace said smiling. "What chu say?" He dribbled up the floor toward me, let the ball bounce easy and natural through his legs. Something I could never do.

"Hey, kid," I said. "How's it going?"

I moved toward him but tripped over my own feet, and he caught me as I was going down to the floor and held me up.

"Hey, Dad, you all right?"

"I haven't been drinking, don't worry," I said, suddenly snapping at him and wishing to God I hadn't.

"Hey, I didn't say anything."

"Yeah, well let's just play some ball. That's what I'm here for."

My tone was harsh again, and I called for the ball and he gave it to me. Just shoot a few, get it down a few times and push Billy Bramdowski out of your mind. Fucking Billy Bramdowski. Shy, friendly guy, sitting in the Paradise talking about his new baby. Worried how he was going to pay for it all. Fucking pussy.

I shot the ball up and missed the whole goddamned thing. Pure airball. Then I ran in and got a rebound and dribbled to my left and shot it up again from the baseline, but it banged off the rim.

"Shit!"

"Hey, Dad," Ace said, retrieving it and putting it in softly, "take it easy."

"Yeah, take it easy. Who are you, Dr. Kildaire?"

He looked hurt now, and I wanted to go over and put my arm around him and tell him I didn't know what the hell I was talking about, but I still felt this wild pain shooting through me, and I didn't know what that was either, all the pill or Billy or Porter rubbing his skinny-fat stomach, and why didn't Billy put a bullet through *his* brains?

"Let's get a game up," I said as other kids drifted in. "Need a little competition."

"Hey, Mr. Baker," Rodney Hall said. He was a black kid on the varsity, built like a medium-weight prizefighter and the best ball handler in the school. He could float or sting you with his outside jumper, and at six foot five he could stuff the ball. He and Ace made the team go. I watched him glide to the basket and knew that I never had moves like that.

I was all muscle and banging on the boards and head fakes so I could get my jumper off. White-boy ball. But it worked. I could still score, and suddenly, now, it seemed important, more important than anything else, than Billy Bramdowski with his brains on the toolshed wall or me ever getting a fucking job, just let me score and score and score again, and let us move up and down the floor, running it, throwing it up, hitting the boards . . . and then we were out there, and Ace was bringing the ball up against Rodney, who let him fake going around him and then reached in behind and tapped the ball down low to Joe Louve, a tall kid nicknamed Cool Ray, and Cool flipped it downcourt to Rodney, who slammed it down in the basket, and I didn't want to say anything, it wasn't right, don't let it come out, but there it was anyway. "Hey, Ace, look for the pass. This isn't a one-man show." And Ace nodded and brought the ball up again, and this time I set a pick for him, and Rodney ran into it and let out a groan as he hit me, and my man, a big black-haired kid named Niles, went for Ace, and I stepped inside with a clear route for the give-and-go to the basket, but Ace tried forcing up the shot, and when it missed they cleared it and got another cheap dunk down court, and then I was screaming at him, "Hey, what is this, Super-man time or what? This is a team game. You got to pass. I put a few baskets in too, you know." Ace looked at me and shook his head, and I was sweating now, pouring off of me, and I got the ball on the inbounds and took it clean down the other end of the court and put my head down and went to the basket, and I made a blind side pass to Bobby Mason, who took it and gave a pump fake and then dumped the ball clean in. And I made a big deal out of slapping his hand and looking at Ace like he could learn a thing or two from Bobby, pure bullshit, which we both knew because Ace could take Bobby downtown anytime he wanted and passed better as well.

I don't know why I did it now, as I didn't then. I wanted to show him, to push his face in it, and it wasn't about basketball. Of course, I know that. It was about Billy Bramdowski and eating shit week after week and getting fucking old and Wanda and Crystal, and him floating out there, up, up and putting the ball down soft through the hoop, and even Rodney saying, "Oh yeah, atta way Ace babe, we gonna kill Poly this week, you know that, baby."

We got the ball again, and I made a dumb pass to Ace, who watched as Rodney stole it, went down, faked twice, and passed the ball off to Tony, who popped it home, and I started screaming at Ace then right there in the gleaming green tiles, and my voice going higher and higher—what if he looked inside my coat?—saying, "You got to come out and meet those passes," and Ace saying, "Jesus Christ, if you weren't so goddamned drunk . . . you'd be able to play," and me wanting to go at him then, not knowing what I wanted to do, break his nose (my son) or hug him and have him hold me, but just keep playing, keep playing, and when a young kid beats you, maybe hook him with your foot to show him that it's not fair, see it's not ever going to be fair, so why here, mutherfucker, why here?

"Mr. Baker, take it easy."

"Hey, come on, Mr. Baker, you're holding on to me."

And then Ace going up for a turnaround, missing it, grabbing the 'bound, and going inside with a reverse left-handed lay-up, and me screaming that he didn't pass to me, even though he made the shot.

"Dad, for God's sake, we're just having fun."

"Fun? You want to be a champion, you gotta take the game serious."

Talking like that. Talking shit I knew was garbage. Talking to keep from seeing Billy in the toolshed. Jesus, holding the smoking gun in his raw red hands.

"Well, maybe I don't want to be a goddamned champion, Dad. Maybe I just don't care about that!"

And then I turned and looked at Rodney Hall and Bobby Mason, and they were staring at the floor, and Ace looked as though he was going to cry or, worse, go for me, and I turned and walked toward the parallel bars and grabbed my coat, and it felt red-hot, like a bar of steel up on the twenty table.

If he looked in my pockets. If he knew. Blazek might tell him. If he did, I'd kill him. Break his head. Take *him* in the toolshed.

"Dad, are you all right?"

"Yeah, look, I'm sorry . . . I'm sorry as hell. I'm acting like an asshole. You go ahead and play."

"Dad . . . is it anything I can—"

"No. You just play, kid. You're doing great. Hey, see you later."

"Later, Mr. Baker."

"Bye, Rodney. See you, Bobby. Gotta get home. Let you kids play. Yeah, see you later."

I walked out the long hallway. Here in this tiled building I scored thirty-four points once. Here in this crowd Wanda and Doggie and

Carol and maybe Billy Bramdowski cheered my shots. Back then, when you woke up and put on your uniform and there it was. The touch.

By the time I got home I was soaked in sweat. Felt my jaw ache as I ground my teeth together. I chain-smoked cigarettes, stopped in Slap's and had two quick Wild Turkeys, standing at the bar. Everyone in the place was saying the same words over and over. "Billy Bramdowski. Four kids. Jennie's going crazy. Billy Bramdowski." I walked out of there and looked down at the harbor where they were building the new condos. Nice, smooth, poured concrete for nice, smooth lawyers with their hanging plants and sailboats. I kicked through the snow and saw a wire trash can with "Balmere Is Best" on it and picked it up and threw it with all my might down the snowy hill toward the docks. It bounced twice, slammed into a parked BMW, and then rolled on until it came to rest by a huge, impassable hill of snow.

Suddenly, even though the pill was still working in me, sending the electricity through my arms, legs, face, I felt wiped out. Dead, gone. I made it up to the house, fumbled with my keys, and then pushed the door open, and after throwing my coat toward the hanging peg and missing it, I fell on the sofa, facedown. The images flashed on in my brain, Billy and Vinnie and Ruby. No-Nose kicking in the trashy snow. Maybe he was there to warn me about Billy, but I hadn't known the signs, hadn't listened to what he said.

I knew this was drugs. This had to be drugs.

I wanted to blot it out, send it away, so I turned on the TV, but it was this new Spanish-speaking station, and in front of me were the Three Stooges speaking idiot babble and bonking each other on the head with lead pipes.

I shut my eyes, let the drug wear off some, felt my face and neck collapse, and fell into a nightmare sleep.

By the time Wanda shook me awake it was dark outside. There was crust on my eyelids, and my temples felt like someone had squeezed a pair of tongs around them. I looked up through the haze at Wanda, at her orange waitress uniform with cocktail sauce stains all over it, at her blond hair, which was falling down over one blood-shot eye, at the lines in her forehead.

"Red, are you all right?"

"Yeah, I'm fine. Better than Billy Bramdowski."

"I heard. Oh God, Red, isn't it awful? What will Jennie do?"

I shook my head without saying anything, and she suddenly fell into my arms.

"Red, hold me some, will you? I don't care if you've been drinking. I just need you now."

I held on to her, wanting to comfort her, but she smelled like crabs and her arms felt soft, the flesh hanging loose off of them, and suddenly I couldn't help but think of Crystal and that white road into the green leaves and the sun.

"How was it today, hon?" she said, nuzzling her head into my shoulder.

"Okay. Nothing yet, but something will turn up."

She reached up and held my chin with her raw, scratched-up palm.

"You look tired, Red. You're holding something back. Maybe it would help if you told me."

"Hey, there's nothing to tell, except I heard there was a job over at Shaw's and guess who the employment counselor was?"

She shook her head and rubbed her hand across my cheek.

"Peter Porter," I said.

"From Patterson?"

"That's right. He played a little game with me, brought up my record. Knew all about it, and then after he twisted it in for a good long time, he admitted there never was a job. Nice, huh?"

"Oh, Red, I'm sorry. Come here, honey. Let me make you feel better."

She reached down for my fly, and I jerked back as if I was bitten by a snake. I didn't want to do that. I'd fucked up badly enough for one day.

"Hey," I said, trying to make a joke out of it, "what if Ace comes in?"

"He's over at Spencer's house. He's having dinner there. He won't be home until later. They're studying for a test together."

"But, Wanda, I'm beat, I mean . . ."

"Red, I need you. I really do."

She fell into my lap then, putting her head on my knees, and I stroked the soft hair on the back of her neck, small golden curls of hair, which made me think of her like I did when we were kids, sweet and helpless and innocent, and suddenly I felt this old rush of affection for her.

"My girl," I said softly. "My lovely girl." She clung to me as I rubbed my hand down her back, and she started to sigh, "That feels so good, Red, so good. I thought of you today, hon. You know that I thought of you all day today."

"You did?" I said, holding her as the television flickered weird lights across the room and somebody sang about Pimlico being Balmere's best racetrack.

"I did, Red," she said. "I was on a break, and I thought about how you and I were in the booth of that restaurant out in the country, what was the name of it, where your supervisor Norman took us?"

"The Horse's Head Inn?" I said, and I knew the whole story and held her closer.

"Remember when we just sat there and Norman was talking about the plant . . . and I just looked at you and I felt myself getting so excited and you put your foot up under the table and touched my thigh . . . Do you remember that, Red?"

She was starting to breathe heavier now, and I felt icy, filled with dread.

"Do you remember what you used to say about my thighs, Red? How they felt? How they were hard and soft at the same time? Do you think they're still pretty, Red?"

She took my hand and put it under her dress, and I shut my eyes and felt like I was in the trash barrel, spinning down the street, smashing into the wheels of flashy cars. Billy Bramdowski in there with me, blood pouring from his eyes . . .

"Sure," I said, "I remember that."

"But am I still pretty, Red . . . ?"

"You know you are, Wanda," I said. "You know you are."

She sat up next to me, then rubbed her hand on my cock, and I thought of Crystal as much as I could, thought of her bending over, and I began to get hard.

"You still like me, Red?"

"Yes, Wanda," I said.

"Red, oh Red . . . is it going to be all right?"

"It *is* all right . . ."

"Red, take me upstairs. Right now."

I couldn't do it. I couldn't stand to see her breasts sagging and the way her stomach looked.

"Wanda," I said. "I feel . . ."

But she was gone now, rubbing me, moaning. "Red. Please . . . come on, baby . . . Red . . ."

I held my breath and thought of Crystal, and of Wanda in bed, her clothes off, wanting it to be romantic, and I said, "I want to make love to you right here, Wanda, right here . . ."

And I reached under her dress and put my finger on the inside of her pants and shut my eyes and thought of Crystal and kept thinking of her when Wanda unzipped my pants, and then we were sitting on the couch, and she was down on the floor in front of me, taking my cock in her mouth, and I felt embarrassed, I don't know why, just embarrassed, like I was too old for this kind of shit with my wife, and my cock just wouldn't get hard, and I brought her up to me, and she sat on my lap, and I thought of Crystal, and then finally it got hard enough to go inside of her, and she began to rock back and forth, holding on to me, and I could feel the tenderness in her and how much she really did love me. I could feel it, and I knew she had worked all day down there for me, and she smelled like fish, crabmeat, and it made me sick, but she had done it for me and Ace. This is your wife, Wanda, and you have to keep thinking of Crystal to keep it up and not Billy and his kid in the backyard, no, no way . . . And then she threw her head back and came and held her hands around my neck and put her head on my shoulder and said, "Red, you know I love you. We'll get through this together. We will, thank you, Red."

"Why are you thanking me?" I said, stroking her cheek.

"Because," she said softly. "I know you didn't want to do that. I just had to have it, that's all."

"I did too want to do it," I said.

"You don't have to lie. I know you didn't want to. But it's all right. Did you enjoy it just a little?"

"Hey," I said. "I loved it. You know I've always loved it with you. Remember down the Magothy on the company picnics?"

She smiled then and looked younger, and for the first time I knew I had faked my way through.

"Red," she said, climbing off of me. "Don't hurt me, Red, okay?"

"How? What are you talking about?"

"You know, with those girls you and Dog run around with. Don't let me catch you, Red, okay?"

"Hey," I said. "You're crazy. I love you, Wanda. You're my girl."

"Really, Red. You sure?"

"Hell yes." I kissed her on the nose, and she smiled.

"I better get dinner now," she said, climbing off and pulling up her pants.

"I know I don't look good, Red, but I'm going on a diet. I'm going to exercise. And jog with Carol."

"You look fine the way you are," I said, drawing her to me and hugging her. For the first time I felt her flesh, her own smells.

"Red," she said, "I have to tell you something. When I heard about Billy today . . . well, I got so worried. You'd never . . ."

I kissed her on the forehead and shook my head.

"No way."

"I don't mean do what he did, Red. I mean, you'd never go back into . . . you know . . . you wouldn't try anything crazy to get money, would you?"

"Hey, I'm done with that shit. I don't like jails a whole lot. They got these hard beds, and they don't have any good-looking women come home and make love to you."

She smiled at that and held me close.

"I do love you," she said. "I'm a damned fool for it, but that's the way it is."

I kissed her again and held her close to me.

"You're my baby, Wanda. You always will be."

"I better get us some dinner, hon."

Her voice was ten years younger, and she swayed softly as she walked out of the room.

I couldn't sleep for shit. I had started drinking, even though I swore to Wanda that I would lay off. I tried to for a while, but the daily grind of going out there in the rat drizzle or the snow, walking the narrow streets, running down leads for work that disappeared as soon as I showed up . . . well, it just started wearing me down, and in the mornings I would break one of Dr. Raines's white pills in half, pop it, knowing that it would only give me about five hours of feeling cocky and confident before it made me feel like there was a little man inside my head pulling the skin tight around my eyes.

Sweat poured off of my forehead, down my armpits, speed sweat, and my heart would start missing beats, and I'd have to throw down a couple of Wild Turkeys just to knock it back.

The booze helped at first, but by nighttime I'd be into full-scale weirdness, thinking that I was hearing messages from the television set, my eyes darting across the room whenever Wanda looked me in the eyes.

And I continued to give Ace shit, though I love that boy more than my own fucked-up, burned-down life.

Gave him a hard time about his homework, when he was a B-plus student. "Why aren't you getting A's?" Me, a goddamned straight-C student, and made a big deal about not playing his guitar seriously. I nailed him if he missed a night of practice. Or, even when he *did* practice, for playing the same shit over and over, which I knew he had to do to get it down right.

At night I'd put Wanda in bed, and I'd come back down to the cellar, sit there in the knotty pine basement, and start thinking strange thoughts, like the knots in the wood were eyes, all of them staring at me. I didn't know whose eye, maybe God's, watching what a complete asshole I was, not able to get any work. Walking from door to door, sweating even though it was freezing out, coming on with my shit-eating grin, and him watching me the whole time from up above, laughing at me like some gangster in "The Untouchables."

God with big lips and hard black eyes, just laughing at me with this great mocking growl.

My mom, Dot, saw to it that I got a full plate of religion, hustling me off to church every Sunday, enrolling me in vacation Bible school in the summertime. And for a while I tried to get with the program the way the preacher laid it down, because the old lady kept saying, "You'll see, honey. It's such a consolation when you get old. Such a consolation." That was just another lie—because the eternal-life part of it never took with me. Maybe they gave my portion of that to some other kid. What I remember is a Sunday school teacher named Mr. Hart sticking his face into mine and saying, "The thought is as bad as the deed. You even think about something evil, you better fall on your knees and beg Jesus to forgive you, 'cause he hears every word you say, and if your thoughts are impure, when you die you will never be rejoined with your mother and father in eternal life. No, you will burn for untold centuries in the black pits of hell." I remember sitting on a wood chair, staring out at the birds sitting on the telephone wires, wishing to hell I was up there with them and could fly the hell out of here.

And I remember Hart raving on about Job, old Job who got boils and about went mad trying to please God.

The very first time I heard that story it struck me funny.

Old Hart was holding up Job to us as some kind of illustration about how hard we had to try to be holy, but it occurred to me right then that Job was a pure sucker. I knew in my heart that God didn't give a shit about Job. Or Hart. Or me either.

That if he existed at all, God was nothing more than some Little Italy wise guy spitting down on the gutter from his soft blue heaven.

It killed me, I mean, they were telling me I was supposed to *be* fucking Job, break my ass to do right.

Like Buck used to say, "Don't piss on my back and tell me it's raining."

But the catch was, even though I knew their game and laughed at it, Hart still had me.

Because through his little stories and hymns he had infected me with the idea of goodness.

And once the idea of Christian goodness is there inside you, you can't shake it, no matter how hard you try. (And what with booze, broads, and drugs, I have given it a pretty good shot.)

Didn't matter how often you thumbed your nose at it, how many gallons of whiskey you drank, how many pills you took, the Jesus gang had their hooks in you all the same.

Like if you couldn't find work and support your family, it was because you were no goddamned good.

Even though you told yourself it wasn't your fault, it was the way things were for everybody, you still believed that if you had done something else, gone that one extra mile for Jesus, maybe you wouldn't be in this mess right now.

So night after night I would stay up late down the club basement watching reruns of "Star Trek" and "The Untouchables," the speed sending Jesus on a sprint through my veins and arteries, his pale eyes and matted wet hair wading across my blood, opening doors to the chambers of my heart, and falling through the trapdoors in my brain.

This was torture, nothing short.

I would doze off and then suddenly jerk awake, scared, knowing that tomorrow wasn't going to be any better but telling myself it wasn't true. It had to get better, had to, somehow.

And then one night Ace came down. Must have been three-thirty. I had drunk half a bottle of Wild Turkey I kept down in the liquor cabinet.

It had about leveled off the pill, and I was lying there with a half-day growth of beard, spittle coming out the side of my mouth, knowing he was staring at me. Suddenly I wanted to cry out, tell him that I knew what it was, that we had been cursed, that maybe the whole town had been cursed or we would have been somewhere else, somewhere in the sunshine, like Miami or Los Angeles.

But I said nothing, just tried to smile at him a little. He sat on the steps, looking over at me as I lay there half gone in the old rocker. My daddy Buck's rocker, which still smelled of his Prince Albert.

"Dad, you all right?" he said, putting his knees up and resting his chin on them.

"Fine."

"You sure, Dad?"

"Yeah."

"What are you thinking about?"

"Just was thinking about Dog. Worried about him a little. He's getting crazy on me."

Ace smiled and scratched behind his ear.

"Dog's always crazy."

"Why do you say that?"

"Well, you know, he's always getting you in trouble with Mom."

"Well, I don't know about . . ."

"Dad, how come you hang out with Dog so much?"

"He's my best friend."

"Yeah, but like you always tell me to be careful who I become friends with."

"That's true. You become friends with people without getting to know them a little bit first, well, then it's hard to get out. You get trapped by how much you care about them. You see that?"

"Is that how it is between you and Dog?"

"Hell no . . ."

But then it occurred to me that maybe this was true. I had never thought of it before and had given the kid this speech all my life.

I didn't want to think of it that way and felt myself ready to snarl at him again.

"You have to know more than you do before you can understand Dog and me."

"Like what?"

He said it softly, not a smartass but really wanting to know.

"Ah hell," I said. "You don't want to hear about that."

"Yes, I do," he said.

"Well, then, I guess maybe I could give you one little example."

Now he was really grinning.

"This happened when I was just a boy. You know I wasn't always big. That happened sort of like it's happening to you, all at once. But when I was a little kid and me and my folks were living over on Foster Avenue. I was one of the smallest kids in the neighborhood. And guess who was the biggest?"

"Dog?"

"Nah! He *was* pretty big, yeah . . . but the biggest, and the meanest, was Vinnie Toriano."

"Fat Vinnie?"

"Yeah. He was the King of the Block, and if you didn't do what he told you, or gave him any shit, he had some cute tricks."

Ace's eyes were getting big, he was wide awake now.

"Like what?" he said, holding on to the railing.

"Slow down," I told him. "I'm coming to that. You know where the parking garage is now? Well, that used to be a lot with a hill, where we played cowboys and Indians, Civil War, stuff like that . . . Well, I was over there with the little kids one day and Vinnie comes by. Me and this other little kid, Jimmy Finnegan, were playing ball."

"How old were you?"

"I guess I was about nine or ten. Anyway, we were playing catch and Vinnie yells over for us to throw him one. I tell Jimmie not to because I had seen this trick before. Vinnie never gives the ball back. He likes to stand there on a weed clump in the hill, just tossing the ball up in the air, over and over . . . while the little kids beg him to give it back. But it was too late, Jimmie threw it to him, and, sure enough, he smiles at us and says, 'Thanks, I can use a new ball.' I just couldn't stand it that day, so I said, 'Listen, fat ass, give us the ball back or I'll get you for it, I swear to God.' "

"You said that?" Ace said.

"Yeah, which shows how smart I was, because it was a hot day and I guess old Vinnie was feeling kind of mean. He came over and grabbed me, and I tried to hit him in the face, but it was no use . . . He was bigger than me, you know? He picked me up and carried me down the hill there to the corner and got one of his pals to hold me, who just happened to be Joey Capezi, the same boy who works for him now. Then Vinnie puts his big ugly face right near mine and says, 'You're going to wish you never opened your big mouth, Baker.' Then he gets down in the street and pulls the sewer grating up, and with me screaming and kicking, Joey and him stuff me down there and replace the grate . . ."

"He did that?" Ace said, his eyes getting big.

"Oh yeah. And the whole purpose of this game was to make me cry. Sometimes if you cried he'd let you out. Other times he'd keep you down there anyway. I remember looking down at the sewer pipe —it looked like a huge black mouth—and then he started laughing at me and saying that pretty soon the rats were going to come through the pipes and eat my legs, and Joey opened his mouth, and I could see all his gold fillings, and he nodded and said, 'Yeah, the rats, Baker, the rats!' And I knew that if I thought about that I might start to cry, so I looked back at him and I said that I knew all the rats and they were pals of mine . . . besides, they were better than Vinnie. This really pissed Vinnie off. So he starts spitting on me, and I can't even duck down, I'm so afraid of the rats, and then he's telling me that the rain'll come down the sewer and I'll drown, and I'm saying to myself, I can float, I can float on the rats . . . but I won't let him make me cry, no way . . . and then he said if I asked him real nice he might let me up, but I wouldn't do it. I looked at him and said nothing, just stared at him and thought about ways to get even. Thought about setting his house on fire or sneaking up behind him with a piece of rope and gagging him . . . and I tried putting my hands through the grate to pull myself up, but I couldn't budge it at all . . . I was down there, and I heard something then

down in the pipes, and I knew it *was* the rats, huge gray rats. I could
hear him coming to get me, so I started sort of mumbling, 'Squirrels,
it's squirrels,' and Vinnie heard me and started laughing at me and
calling me 'Squirrelly,' and by now a lot of kids were there, and they
were all looking down at me, and it was getting dark, and the gutters
were running brown water down on me, and then I looked down into
the black sewer and there it was, the goddamned rat staring right at
me, its eyes open and red, and I kicked at it as hard as I could, but it
dodged out of the way and made a high shrieking sound, while above
me I could see Vinnie's fat gut shaking up and down, and then the
other kids started saying he oughta let me up, but he told them to
shut up or he'd put some of them down there if they didn't like it,
and he waited until I tried to push the grate up again, and then he
stepped on my fingers. I could feel the tears coming down my face,
and God I hated him for it. He'd about broke my hand and scared
me to death with those rats, but the worst thing was he made me cry
like that . . . So finally Joey and he pulled the grate off and walked
off, laughing and calling me 'Red, the squirrelly son of a bitch,' and
some of the other kids helped me out, dragging me through the
goddamned old candy wrappers and wet leaves . . . I acted like it
was no big deal and went home. It wasn't until I was up in my room
that I went nuts. I started ripping my bed to shreds, pounding it and
screaming that I was going to kill the son of a bitch . . . My old
man didn't know what the hell to make of me."

"God, we oughta get that bastard, Dad."

"Yeah, that was what I thought."

"But where does Dog come in?"

"Right about here. The next weekend was the St. Dominic's Carnival, and I was going with Dog's younger brother, Tim. See, Dog
was older by two years, same as Vinnie. Anyway, I had once helped
out his younger brother when some kids were pushing him around
when we were playing marbles. And Dog had always kind of liked
me. So the night of the carnival he comes around with Tim and he
says he wants to take us up to the church. Now Dog was a lot bigger
than me then, and I didn't hang out with him much. I was still a
little kid. I was real surprised by this, but I went along, and he said
to me, 'You know what we're going to do tonight, kiddo, we're going
to have a game, a little competition between us, called Knock Down

the Clowns.' That was a softball game where you threw balls at these milk-bottle clowns with blue fringe all around them."

"I know that game," Ace said. His eyes were lighting up. And I was feeling pretty good myself, for the first time since I could remember.

"So, we get up there and I figure since Dog is a lot bigger than me, he'll be able to knock down every one of those milk bottles, but he turned out to be the worst damned pitcher I've ever seen. He doesn't even come close to hitting any, and the nuns are there laughing at him, and he's going into these Bob Turley kind of windups and letting the softball go and hitting everything in sight, the roof, the backstop, Christ, he was even hitting the *prizes,* but not one damned clown. I beat him easy and won myself this bamboo cane. And Timmy and I were kidding Dog about it because he had bragged all the way to St. Dominic's about how good he could throw. Then we split up. Dog went to talk to Carol, who he knew even then, and Timmy and I were wandering through the parking lot, playing the games and eating cotton candy, when suddenly I see Vinnie with Joey Capezi. They're walking toward me, laughing and nudging each other, and I felt my heart jump into my chest. I was scared. I was mad as hell too, but I knew if I did anything to either of them, they'd gang up on me, and they were about maybe two feet away, and they're laughing and starting in, 'Hey, Baker, you like it down the sewer? You like it, Squirrelly?' And I was so goddamned mad, you know, going nuts, but suddenly from behind me, before I know what's happening, someone takes the cane out of my hand and kind of bumps me aside, and I look up and see Dog. And then he flicks out the cane and catches it right around Vinnie's neck, you see? And yanks him toward him with a fast jerk, smacking Vinnie's forehead into his own. I mean hard. Like walnuts cracking. And then in this low voice Dog has when he's really pissed, he says, 'I heard you fooled around with my man, Red here. Maybe you want to fool around with me now, huh, fat boy?' Joey Capezi took a step forward, and I couldn't resist it any longer. I jumped up off the ground and took a swing and smacked him right in the nose. He started bleeding like hell. Fell right on his ass. He couldn't believe a ten-year-old kid had hit him like that. And then Vinnie makes a move, but Dog kicks him right in the shin hard, and he falls on the blacktop crying, and then little Timmy, Dog's brother, kicks him in the ribs. That was really wild . . . I mean, this was a little kid, three feet tall, but 'bang' right in the ribs. Two, three times, and then Dog said, 'I ever hear of you bothering Red or any of the other neighborhood kids again, I'll put your fat Wop ass down the sewer and leave you there for good.' Then Dog turned to me and said, 'Hey, I told you two we were going to knock down the clowns. And we did. So let's go the hell home, huh?' "

"That's great," Ace said, laughing, "that's fantastic. Dog did that? Wow!"

"Probably shouldn't have told it to you."

"Why not, Dad? That's great. 'Knock down the clowns.' Yeah, that's fantastic. All *right,* Dog!"

"Yeah, Dog never lets Vinnie forget it to this day. Whenever we see him and he starts coming down on us about how rich and successful he is, Dog says, 'See you up the carnival, Vinnie.' Sends Vinnie into a fit even now."

"Great, great," Ace said. He was rocking back and forth now and banging on the cellar railing. "I love it. Wow!"

We both started laughing then; hell, I loved it too. But I knew how much Wanda hated me to tell violent stories to Ace. So I had to cut it off.

"Going to wake up your mother. Get on up to bed now, Ace."

"Sure, Dad, but aren't you coming?"

"Be up there presently," I said. "Get going."

"Dad, I almost forgot this. I just wanted to say that I know you'll get a job, and I wish you wouldn't worry so much about it. Okay?"

"Yeah," I said. I got up out of the chair then and came over and gave him a hug and felt the damned tears coming down my cheeks.

"Get on upstairs," I said. I didn't want him to see me like that.

"Okay, come on up soon, Dad. It's late."

He headed on up to the dark kitchen, and I picked up my bottle and my cigarettes and the ashtray full of butts and threw them in the garbage.

Then I had the weirdest thought of the night. That Vinnie was God, that these were Vinnie's eyes looking at me through the wood, laughing at me, mocking me, knowing that in spite of that day at the carnival he was still hanging over me, laughing because he knew something I didn't. Something about being good.

Something about how it didn't matter.

That thought scared me more than any other, and I turned out the light and thought of my kid's face as I went through the dark up to bed.

It was near the end of the second month when they cut off my benefits down at the unemployment. The first couple days the check didn't come I figured it was just held up in the November mail— people sending Christmas packages and all. But by the fifth and sixth days I knew there was no mistake. I called the office at nine in the morning, but the phone was busy. It stayed busy for the next three hours, but I was damned if I was going to go down there when I didn't have to.

Finally, at two in the afternoon, I got ahold of Miss Motown, who gave me the good news in her high Bible school voice.

"Mr. Baker, you *had* an appointment on November 11 at nine sharp for your audit."

"Audit? What audit? I sent in my cards every week so far, with signatures on them. In case you don't have the picture straight, we're in a recession. There isn't any goddamned work."

"It's no use in you cursing me, Mr. Baker. We didn't receive your cards for the last week, and we sent you a letter to that effect. In this letter we advised you that we had to review your case and see if you were legitimately looking for work. Since we didn't get any reply from you, we have been forced to cut off your unemployment benefits until you're able to get three character witnesses to write letters for you, and we can schedule a hearing."

I heard this sitting on the edge of the couch. The words pushed me back, and I gripped the sofa arm so hard I could almost feel it melt.

"I never got any letters, Miss . . . Miss . . ."

"Torrance, Mr. Baker."

"Miss Torrance, I never got *any* letter. I've sent in the cards every week just like you asked. I swear it."

"Mr. Baker, I'm sorry, this matter isn't in my hands any longer. We understand the importance of this check to your family and yourself, and we don't wish to deny you your benefits, but there are laws."

"Laws, hell," I said. "I played by the laws. I sent in the cards, and you cut me off. What about that? You lose the goddamned cards over there, and you make me and my family pay for it. Is that what you call the laws?"

"Mr. Baker, I'm not going to get into a shouting contest with you. Why didn't you respond to our letter?"

"Because I never got any letter."

"Mr. Baker, I doubt that. Perhaps you misplaced it."

I took a deep breath and ground my teeth together.

No money. No goddamned money coming in.

"Look, Mr. Baker, just as soon as you get your three character letters we'll have the hearing, and you can be reinstated. It could happen in, say, two weeks."

"Two weeks. What the hell do I do meantime?"

"I'm sorry, Mr. Baker, but you should have thought of that before you failed to send in your cards."

Her voice was like a needle cutting through my head.

"I'll get the witnesses. Who should they be?"

"Well, Mr. Baker, I would assume you would try to get the most upstanding people you know."

There was a real backspin in her tone when she said that. Miss Motown was enjoying this. She hadn't forgotten the scene Dog and I made in the line, and this was her way of paying us back.

I put down the phone and felt as though the room was swirling around in front of me. A carousel at a cheap bayside park.

I picked the phone back up and called Wanda and told her the news. She was cool, God bless her.

"Don't worry, Red, I can get Rev. Davis to write a letter for us, and the manager of Weavers, Bruce. If we could get one more person—"

"Wait, I know," I said. "Tom Lusinki, the president of the union. I got to go over there this afternoon for a meeting anyway. I can get him to write the letter. Then I can take them down there personally and make them give us the hearing earlier."

"We'll make it, Red. Now don't do anything crazy. Promise me."

"I promise. Don't worry."

"I love you."

"Yeah, me too."

I hung up the phone and stared down at our worn, fake Persian carpet and felt something die inside of me. Something like a shadow falling away, down through the floorboards to the dark cellar below.

I took a deep breath, threw on my sheepskin jacket, and headed out into the cold, dripping morning. Close to flat broke.

Tom Lusinki was a big guy with a huge red forehead with a big knot on it from where he ran into a forklift once. Lucky he didn't break the prongs right off the mother.

I stood over at the union hall in his office, which was a lot like my basement, all done up in knotty pine. On the wall behind his desk was a deer head. Tom was a big hunter, always talking about guns, canoeing, blowing the hell out of small animals.

"Now listen, Red, there's nothing to worry about. I'll get the letter written this afternoon. You can come pick it up tomorrow."

"Thanks, Tom," I said, sitting in the chair, twisting and turning as though chiggers had gotten under my skin. I stared at his old goose-necked lamp and at his big wide nose. And at the green-and-brown-spotted duck on his desk.

"These damned unemployment people are giving our boys hell," he said. "But we're going to deal with them. Got a bill we're working on in the meeting tonight, you hear about it?"

"No, what's that?"

"Well, a lot of the guys are afraid if this goes on much longer, the repossession boys are going to be coming around taking their houses and cars away. We're giving this bill a big push. Going to ram it through in Annapolis, Red. It'll say that for the entire year no guy in our union has to pay his mortgage or his car payments in full, just the interest on them. You see? Bill 212."

"That's good, makes sense," I said. "But do you think we're going to be out of work the whole year?"

"Hard to say, Red. But we're working on it. Meanwhile we got to get you taken care of. You stop by tomorrow, and I'll have that letter for you. Oh, and Red, listen, I know of a job, nothing much, I wouldn't even mention it, but it might tide you over. It's at the L and S Parking Lot down there on Eastern Avenue. You know the place?"

"Yeah, I know it."

"Yeah, well, it's not much, couple a hundred a week. But you might look into it."

"Parking cars," I said.

I looked at him behind the desk, fat, with one of those big white plastic penholders with seven different colored ballpoints.

"Best I can do now. See me tomorrow. Have that letter for you. Oh yeah, there's one more thing. Wait here a minute."

He got up and walked by his Kiwanis club plaques on the wall and looked outside the door.

"Darlene," he said, calling to his secretary. "They started on the line yet?"

"Yes, Mr. Lusinki. Just starting now."

"Much of a crowd?"

"Not yet."

"Okay, go get a box for me. Tell them I need it. Personally."

I sat still, holding my hands in front of me, telling myself that no matter what happened don't go back to Dr. Raines's, don't pop any of the few pills I had left. I looked up at the plaques, Man of the Year. Highlandtown Softball League, a team I'd been on five years ago.

Big Tom, Heart As Big As All Outdoors. He'd busted at least three guys' asses I knew personally to make it as president of the union. Now he had his office, and his big chair, and his duck-hunting weekends down in Trappe, while I sweated it out with Miss Motown.

The Meek Shall Inherit Miss Motown.

He came back into the room now, a big cardboard box under his arm.

"Here, Red, you don't have to stand in line."

"What is this? A fucking CARE package?"

"Hey, don't take it like that, Red. You know I always liked you, son, but you got the bad attitude. This here is just something we're doing to help out. Cut the costs. Got some good food in there. Chicken, tinned ham, powdered potatoes, that's all good stuff, same as you'd buy in the store. Just to tide you over, ya know?"

I looked down at the box, which now sat like a rock in my hands. I started to laugh then, shaking and laughing like I had been inhaling shit from the chem plant all day.

"Fucking CARE package. Too fucking much."

Tom looked down at me now with his beet-red face.

"Look, Red, I try and do you a favor . . . you sit there and laugh at me. You want the letter or not?"

"Hey, take it easy, Tom. I'm sorry. I gotta go. I'll get back tomorrow. Thanks for the job tip."

"You gotta watch the attitude, Red. You screw yourself with the wrong attitude."

"So I've heard."

I got up with my box of food and walked out in the hallway, down to the other end; the men were lining up again. Some looked as they had in the dope line. Heads bowed down, hands deep in their pockets. One more piece of their hearts torn off and tossed down the sewer.

I think it was on Broadway, about two blocks from Ruby's Play Lounge, that I got my bright idea. The rain was coming down harder, and the alley was dark.

I walked back slow, holding the box out in front of me, suddenly realizing he might not even be there anymore at all or, worse, that he might be waiting behind one of the trash containers, hidden under the old bedsprings and walls of refuse.

I got to the end of the alley, and then I saw his place. He'd fixed it up some. There was a great new packing crate, and he'd punched a hole in the side of it for a window.

I held my breath, holding on to the food, and then suddenly I saw him looking out at me from his window. His head was shaved now, and he kept what was left of his nose just below the sill so I couldn't see it.

He said nothing, but he stared at the box.

He looked like he'd been plugged into a wall socket.

I nodded and stood very still.

"I want to leave this here," I said. "For you?"

He stuck his head up a little and looked at me. I could see what was almost his nose holes.

He was shaking now, and I saw how thin his wrists were.

I ripped open the box and took out the chicken and then the potatoes and the cheese and bread.

"You're an asshole for coming back here," he said, but there wasn't much anger in his voice. Tears ran down his noseless face, dripped off his lips.

"Are you Him?" he said.

I shook my head and backed away.

He nodded to me very slowly, his eyes opening wide, his face suddenly looking like a child's.

And then, looking at him there, it occurred to me that I knew him. That he was somebody I knew from way back, but he was too young for that, some friend of Ace's . . . but that wasn't possible either.

"Don't come back again," he said. "The next time I can't tell you what it'll be like."

I backed out of the alley. Overhead there was some thunder, and the rain kept moving faster. When I was on the street I saw him scamper out of his drenched hole, pick up the canned ham, and hold it in his arms like it was a tin child.

Then he turned and ran back to the crate, out of my sight.

I turned and headed on down the street, told myself that I'd have just one with Ruby, since she was leaving soon. Just one. Maybe give Crystal a call, and then I'd get home, change, and make it on down to the L and S Parking Lot and grab off that job.

It must have been around four when I hit Ruby's. In short order I downed maybe six Wild Turkeys. And half a Dr. Raines's, just to get me over the hump of having to go down to the parking garage.

I thought I was handling it all, but then there was that call to Crystal, just hearing her small voice and laughing with her about what an asshole Vinnie was. He'd hired a guy to be a knight down at Mona Lisa Pizza. Made the son of a bitch wear armor all night while he stood there near those pizza ovens, which were almost as hot as the steel mill.

It wasn't like I was cutting out on Wanda, or it didn't seem that way. It was just that I had to hear Crystal's voice to stay even with the flood that was pushing me down, sinking me to the bottom.

I needed her laughter. Though I know that's wrong. It was me, living with the likes of me, that killed all the laughter in Wanda, and now I was like a monster from one of Ace's vampire movies, bleeding all the laughs out of another, younger woman.

She sounded so young and up, and she talked about Florida to me again, the way the trees looked and the way the birds landed on the beach at night, their wings lit up by the moon.

And then I called Dog, and we talked, and the pill and the booze was working; I hadn't seen him for so goddamned long . . . Dog, Doggie, Yo Dog, we got to get out and kick a little ass tonight . . .

It seemed like some small mercy from God that I had beat Wanda home. I made it upstairs, wrote out a note that I had a lead on a bartending job and had to go scout it out. I wrote it fast, pretending it was some other person who was lying to his wife, even making Wanda herself up in my head as a different person than the one I knew her to be—Wanda the Witch, who wouldn't let me alone, who killed me with her kindness and understanding, Wanda the Goody-goody, who didn't understand that I had to raise hell, that I had to get away from it . . . Wanda the Dummy, who knew nothing about where I really lived . . . the booze and pills made it easy, so easy, until she came in, caught me on the way down the steps, the note in my hand.

"Hi," I said, feeling the shame wiping over me again, knowing that it was the drugs and the dope and Miss Motown pushing me out, wasting me away. That and my own blown-up pride.

"I got the letters, Red. You can get down there tomorrow."

"That's great," I said. "I got mine too. But I also got two leads on jobs. One tomorrow. At the L and S Parking garage. It's crummy, parking cars . . . that's why I hope I get this one tonight. Bartending job down at this place called Cap's, down on North Point Boulevard . . . Got Dog coming by to pick me up . . ."

I may as well have saved my breath, but now that I'd played the card I had to keep on raising the bet.

"Wrote you this note. Look, I gotta talk to the guy, might be a little late getting in."

"Red," she said, dropping her knit handbag onto the couch and staring right through me. "If you go down the Paradise tonight to see one of those whores, I'm going to be gone when you get home."

She turned and walked through the dining room into the kitchen.

I followed her in, furious and feeling like she had cut it out from under me, all the glory I'd worked up for the night.

"Goddamn it, Wanda, I'm telling you it's a job. This place called Cap's. You want to call there and ask about it?"

"No, Red, I don't want to embarrass you. I know you feel rotten about us getting taken off unemployment."

"Hey, I don't feel rotten, I feel goddamned angry. It wasn't my fault."

"I told you three days ago, Red, that you had a letter from them. You said you'd take care of it."

She had opened the refrigerator and was already cutting carrots up into a bowl.

"You didn't tell me anything of the kind," I said.

"Yes, I did. Twice. It's upstairs on the night table next to your bed."

I sunk down in the kitchen chair and put my head in my hands.

"Christ, I'm sorry. Look, I screwed up. But one of these jobs are going to come through. Besides, Dog—well you know how he's been lately. So goddamned moody. You know? He needs to talk some stuff over with me."

"I know Dog's been depressed, Red. Carol told me. But you're not his doctor. What about Ace and me? I haven't hardly talked to you all week. Look at me. I'm getting old. I smell like goddamned crabs. Men grab at my ass down there, and George the cook, he's screaming at us all the time . . ."

"I'll break his head for him if he bothers you," I said, touching her arm.

"No, you won't," she said, starting to cry. She threw herself down at the table and gave a low moan, like that of a child, and I felt so torn and rotten, wanting to comfort her and wanting to bolt at the same time.

She sobbed deeply now, and I reached over and touched her hair. It was still soft, and I was overcome with tenderness and love, which cut right through the booze and dope.

"I just want you to try, Red. I just need to know that all I'm going through means something to you. I've got to know it's worth it. Does it matter at all?"

"Of course," I said. "Of course it does. Christ sake."

I held her to me, patting her on the back.

"It's going to be all right," I said. "You gotta trust me. I'm going to have a job by tomorrow. I swear it . . . No matter what."

I held her chin up with my hand.

"It's you and Ace that matter to me. I won't let them push us around much more. I mean it."

"Will you stay home tonight? I'm so tired . . ."

I wanted to say I would. I wanted to . . . but then I heard Dog's horn honking outside, and I could feel the surge shoot through me. It was like a light going on inside my head.

"Look, I won't be late. I already made these plans. But I won't be late. Okay?"

"Sure, Red," she said, and then she gave me the saddest, tiredest smile in the world.

"I mean it, Wanda."

I kissed her on the head, balled up the note I'd written her, and slipped it into my pocket.

I should have stayed home. I know it. She deserved that, Christ, and much more. But it was like a ghost had come over me, brought me back to life, and if I stayed in that kitchen for one more minute, I'd lose it. I felt that shadow come over me again. Sucking me dry. It was lame, cowardly, and wrong, but if I hadn't left just then, I would have felt like the man with no nose. I couldn't tell what would happen. What I might break. It had gotten like that.

When I hit the street I expected to see the down-and-out Dog I'd talked to on the phone the last few weeks, a mumbling, snarling drunk with a personality like a wolverine.

Instead I got the Dog of old, the ass-kicking, crazed-party Dog, with his new Levi jacket, black corduroy pants, clean-shaven and bright-eyed. He had his tape deck on too, Merle Haggard singing "I'm a Lonesome Fugitive," and he was wailing along with it.

"Down every road there's always one more city. I'm on the run, the highway is my home . . ."

"For Christ's sake, Dog," I whispered, giving a half look back at the window to see if Wanda was checking us out. "I told Wanda you were down and I had to go talk it over with you. Turn that god-damned thing down, and let's get the hell out of here before she comes out the door."

"Hey, hey, don't remind the old Dog, amigo," he said. "I just started feeling better about an hour ago. I can't figure out why, but something just told me that things are looking up. Way, way up."

He gave this crazy laugh with his head thrown back, which made me laugh but sent a shiver down my back too. He was crazy as hell, I could see it, and I knew, I guess, even then, that as high as he was, he would soon fall just that low.

But I tried not to dwell on that. Hell, I needed a night off from it all, needed to drink some and see my sweet Crystal and just set it aside.

So we took off, with old Merle blasting away and both of us hitting the Wild Turkey, and I even popped a quarter of a Dr. Raines just to keep it moving in the right direction.

It was snowing like hell, snowing and sleeting like it had for days on end, making Highlandtown into a frozen world, icicles hanging off of Rev. James T. Carter's African Black Nondenominational Church, and Bill's Foodtown, but now, with the music going and Dog yelling "Oh yeaaaaaaaah, having a party," it didn't seem bleak to me at all because it didn't seem real. Instead I felt like we were two miniature steel men being moved by an invisible hand, exactly like the little men I used to push around in my Christmas train garden when I was a kid. I'd sit there for hours and hours as the Lionel trains went round, moving my "men" to the post office, and the department stores, and the boats by the dock, and I felt protective toward them and happy for them, knowing they were all right, because I was there to keep them from harm.

And now, riding and yelling and drinking until we were out of our own flesh, I had become one of those little men, safe and happy, and crazy as hell.

"I've been thinking, son," Dog said, squeezing my thigh. "I been thinking that it don't really matter if the mill opens or not. Hell, I can do a lot of stuff, Red. Work as a short-order cook, if I have to, do some carpentry, be a stone mason. I ain't going to worry no more. Lord, I know it's going to be all right. The Dog feels it, Red. Yes."

"I know you do, Doggie," I said back. "Red feels it too."

Oh, he was way off the ground. That's the stone truth of it. He was flying over the rooftops of Charm City, and after a few more hits of the Wild Turkey I just wanted to be up there with him. Let me fly, fly, fly, leap out of this tired and wrinkled skin, fly up there with the smoke from the trains that circled us like some warm, secret coil, holding us all in that cozy, snow-covered village where no one ever cried and a man didn't ever get old.

I had gotten so far deep into my own thoughts that I didn't even notice that Dog wasn't headed for the Paradise.

"Hey, where you taking us?" I said.

"Going down the kennels," Dog said. "Got to take me a quick peek at Sadie . . . Grady's training pups now."

"Oh no," I said, "we're going to the Paradise."

"Now now," Dog said, squeezing my arm until the blood stopped, "don't get yourself into an uproar. I just want to see my new babies."

There was no use arguing with him. Dog got his name because of his love of dogs, any and all dogs. When we were kids he had eight of them at one time. They tore up his backyard, pissed in his parents' house, and raised hell with the postman, but no one on this fair earth could get him to give them up.

Now we turned off the North Point Boulevard and headed down to Grady's Kennels, Dog smiling and raving on as though he had all the confidence in the world.

"Yessir, Red, I been thinking, when this is over I might go in with old Grady down here. Raise hunting dogs . . . If I could just get a stake. Need a couple grand to become a partner."

"I thought it was more like ten grand," I said.

Dog smiled as we turned up the gravel road. Suddenly there were big trees hanging over us, oaks with icicles on them, frozen like phantom hands with long brittle fingers. I felt a pressure released inside of me. Doggie smiled to himself and began to hum in a quieter, less crazed way.

We drove over the rough, bumpy road, shining our lights into the snow-covered bushes. Then we saw Grady's old house. It always amazed me that it still stood. Only four miles away from all our brick row houses, a taste of the country.

"God, it feels like we're in another world," Dog said. There was a clearness to his voice, and he held his head up and looked around him as we pulled to a stop.

In front of us was the farmhouse, all lit up and cozy, like something in a children's book. We could see Grady's outline leaning against a porch post, his long, lean body dressed in hunting boots and his shell vest, a cigarette hanging from his mouth.

Dog got out of the car fast and crunched across the snow. Suddenly the pointers in their running stables came out into the cold, and I heard Sadie begin to give a loud yelp. She knew Dog even in the dark.

"Hey there," Grady said. "What you doing, boys?"

"Hey, old-timer," Dog said. I walked behind him. I'd been anxious as hell to get down the Paradise and see Crystal, but there was something about this old place. I knew why Dog loved it so . . .

An uncommon stillness hovered over Grady's place, shut down the voices clanging together like the raw machinery down the plant.

And Grady himself was part of it. He moved slowly, not like an old man but like a person who knew how long a time he needed to take to get somewhere.

"Well, Sadie's doing fine, and them puppies are looking good. Couple of 'em might even make real bird dogs."

He smiled like old creased leather, and Dog smiled back at him, looking somehow younger and calmer, as if Grady had rubbed a magic cloth over his face and washed away his fears.

"Come on down the kennel," Grady said. "Going to feed them babies right now."

We tracked across the snowy ground, toward the white concrete building surrounded by the cyclone fence.

The dogs were out in the run now, yelping and jumping up, pressing their noses to the frozen fence and jumping back as the ice nipped them.

Dog turned to me and smiled, and in the half light from the moon, I saw what a sweet, cheerful look was on his face.

He loved it here. It suddenly occurred to me that he was living the wrong life, that his family should have never come up from the country down in Marlboro. He would have been happier on a tractor somewhere or out hunting birds under a cloudless sky.

We walked into the bare-bulb kennel, the wet, dripping concrete reflecting the hot yellow light. The dogs came racing back into the kennel, barking and yelping, and Dog smiled and hung on the fence.

"Damn, they're getting to be big little buggers," Dog said. "Look at that one there, Red."

He pointed to a lemon-colored pointer with the saddest eyes of the bunch.

"You two just tourists or you want to help feed these guys?"

Dog smiled again, softly, and I thought just then that there was something between him and these animals. It seemed to me that their brown-eyed gazes were aimed at Dog and Dog alone, as if he had some calm and loving bond with them that I would never understand.

Dog picked up the big sack of Jim Dandy as Grady opened the cage.

When he went inside, all of them crowded around him, even Sadie, who usually growled if anyone else got near them. Dog reached down and picked up his favorite. The dog began to suck on his fingers, and Dog stroked her softly and I watched his whole frame relax.

"Tough little bugger."

"She'll be a hunter," Grady said. He reached into his shell jacket and pulled out his thunder whistle as Dog poured the Jim Dandy meal into the bowls.

The dogs went for the meal, and Dog smiled at them again.

"Ain't a bad life, huh, Red? Chasing birds and eating?"

I smiled at him and thought of the way he had set the little dog down softly on the ground. As the dogs ate, Grady blew the thunder whistle three or four times in short, startling bursts, to teach them to get used to noise.

Two of the puppies jumped back and coiled their heads to the ground, and Dog and Grady smiled.

"Got a ways to go, babies," Dog said.

He picked up the old cap pistol with the steer on the plastic handle, and popped three or four rounds.

Again the dogs jerked a little, and Sadie looked up at him, curiously, then went back to eating.

"They coming along pretty good," Grady said. "Getting used to the sound."

Dog smiled again and sat down against the kennel wall. For a second it occurred to me that he was going to eat out of the dish with them, and I got the crazy idea that not only was he a city boy by mistake, but that maybe by mistake God in heaven had made him a man.

"Dogs doing damned good, Grady," Dog said, running his hands through his thick, tousled hair.

"Pretty well," Grady said. "We going to get some hunters out of them."

"Think you'll get another Bruno?" I said.

Dog's face softened, and he shook his head. "There will never be another Bruno."

Dog had hunted with Bruno for eighteen years. A big black Labrador, Bruno was the greatest hunting dog anybody in these parts had ever seen. He had died three years ago at the age of twenty-two, and Dog still grieved over him.

Sadie finished her meal while the pups squealed and fought for position around the bowl.

Sadie came over to Dog and lay at his feet, and Dog took out his bottle of Wild Turkey.

"Hell," Grady said, smiling at me, "it's old Doggie, the King of Beasts."

"Hey, girl," Doggie said. "Used to beat your ass, didn't I? But she knows how to hunt. Never seen this old girl point at no rabbit yet. Yeah, good old Sadie."

He shut his eyes and ran his fingers over her back, and two of the pups came and began to bite at Dog's shoe. Two more ran over his plaid jacket, and Dog touched each of them gently with his huge hands.

Grady lit a cigarette and shook his head.

"Hell, ought to get a picture of that," he said.

Dog's eyes almost closed, and he looked up at me.

"We ever get us some money, this is where I want to be," he said.

Doggie smiled at me and tossed the pint of Wild Turkey up to Grady.

"You boys on a tear tonight?" Grady said, taking a sip.

"Maybe a touch of one," Dog said. He got up slowly, the pups jumping off of him and clustering around his boots.

Grady took a swig and started to hand the bottle back, but Dog shook his head.

"You keep it."

He looked fresh-faced, the lines smoothed out under his eyes. When he locked the kennel, he stood for a long while just staring in at them.

"Okay," he said, after a while. "We got to get going. The night is young, and the girls are waiting."

"Wish I was fifteen years younger so I could go make a fool of myself too," Grady said.

Dog turned and put his arm around Grady's shoulders.

"The Dog will drink three extra whiskeys tonight in your honor," he said. "I'm coming back on Sunday. Want to work some of these babies with you, okay?"

Grady smiled and shook his head.

"Sure," he said. "But don't come early. I got me a lady friend spending the night."

Dog squeezed him tightly and cuffed his head.

"Hell," he said. "This is the life."

Inside the black-velveteen-walled bar, we smelled the smoke and heard the men yelling encouragement to Miss Dolly James, another of Vinnie's dancers, who was bumping and grinding to one of those disco songs I can't ever name. All I know is they have a lot of bass and a beat that sounds like a Nazi military march. Half expect to see people start goose-stepping all around the horseshoe bar.

The place was filled with hard hats from Bethlehem Steel (those of whom were left working), a couple of college kids from down the Community College, and old-timers trading bullshit stories about the O's.

Down at the end, where the girls and Vinnie usually sat around, I saw Crystal. She looked up at me and gave me a big, warm-faced, loving smile, and I felt my whole body ease up. Lord, I loved her, not like Wanda, not with history and muscle and bone, but like something new, some bright flower found somewhere, or maybe something seen only once and suddenly, like the sight of a covered bridge at sunset in western Maryland.

Now Dolly was revving it up, moving and shaking, while the old-timers drank their cheap bar whiskey and the college kids with their Big Cat hats on (so they'd look like workers) yelled too.

"Shake it, honey."

"Tell the *truth* now, girl."

"Whew . . . go baby . . . go for it now!"

Dolly smiled her gapped-tooth grin, bouncing her breasts up and down while giving them all a little tongue action.

"Everything I got the Lord gave me, boys!" Dolly yelled down, and then she turned fast and showed everyone her blue panties. The crowd of guys screamed, and Dog banged on the bar.

"Oh yes, love Miss Dolly James."

I left Dog at the bar and walked down toward Crystal and Vinnie, who looked up at me and gave me a nice, hateful smile. Sometimes there is nothing to add juice to your life like seeing an enemy. He had on his green-checked gangster-special leisure suit tonight, and his thin, greasy hair was conked up on top of his head, like black whipped cream.

"Hey, look who it is," Vinnie said in his bad Godfather imitation. "My old friend. How you doing, Red? They made you president of the Maryland National Bank yet?"

He laughed in his actorish way and turned to Frankie Delvecchio, who had on so many gold chains I wondered how he held his head up. Frankie opened his mouth and showed me his noiseless and joyless smile.

"Bank president," he said. "This bum as a bank president."

"That's real good, Frankie," I said. "Say it again and Vinnie'll give you a banana."

"Hey, fuckface," Frankie said, stepping forward, "you want something?"

"Not me," I said, taking Crystal's hand. "I'm a lover, not a fighter."

"Lovers got to have money," Vinnie said.

"Don't worry about us," Dog said, coming up from behind me and putting his big friendly hand on my back. "We doing fine."

"Yeah," Vinnie said. "I can see that. Hey, but I heard about a job you two aces could get."

"Gimme a break," I said, squeezing into the barstool next to Crystal.

"Yeah," Dog said, sipping his whiskey and Boh back. "Break it off, Vinnie, it stinks some."

"Hey," Vinnie said, opening his arms, palms up, "I'm serious."

"Do that again for a minute," I said quickly.

"Do what, Baker?"

"Open your arms again, like you just did."

"What? What you mean, like this?"

He opened them wide, grubby palms up.

"That's amazing," I said, winking at Crystal.

"What?"

"When you do that just right, you look exactly like Wayne Newton. I'm not shitting you, Vinnie. Listen, this time do it and start in with a little 'Danker Shane.' "

This brought a big laugh from Crystal and Dog, two fine Wayne Newton haters.

Vinnie looked around at Frankie and then back at me. His lips were bunched up like curled worms.

"Hey, you think you're putting me down?" he said. "But I was in Vegas last year with Darla, and it just so happens we took a personal tour of Mr. Wayne Newton's estate, and I'm here to tell you he's one classy guy. He's got more class in his pinkie ring than you do in your whole fucking empty head, Baker."

"That hurts a lot, Vinnie. All the years I been coming in here and you can say a thing like that."

Crystal and Dog laughed again, and Frankie looked like he was dying to reach into his coat.

"Hey, but listen," Vinnie said, "I know a couple of jobs you guys can get. Some Dots are opening a curry joint downa road, and they need some assholes to slaughter the goats. The two of you clowns hurry up, you might start whole new careers."

"A couple of what?" Dog asked, staring down at Vinnie like he was looking at a large roach.

"Dots! You know, Indians from India. They got them things . . . them dots on their heads."

"Christ, that is ignorant," Crystal said, putting her arm through mine. "Jesus, Vinnie, they are very cultured people."

"If they're so fucking cultured, what are they doing in Baltimore?" Vinnie asked.

"Hey, they happen to know a great town when they see one," Crystal said.

"Yeah," Frankie said, grabbing a beer, "and besides, it's a hell of a lot better than living in teepees."

This wisdom stopped *everybody* cold.

"Say that again," Vinnie said. "I musta not heard it."

"Teepees," Frankie said. "What you stupid or something? Everybody knows fucking Dots live in fucking teepees."

"Aww shit," Vinnie said. "Man, that's American Indians. These guys are from the other side of the world. Dots are India Indians, you know the kind that are into snake charming and voodoo and shit."

"Voodoo," Crystal said. "Indians aren't into voodoo. That's what people from Haiti are into."

"Hey," Vinnie said. "You ever been to India?"

"No," Crystal said.

"Then shut the fuck up. What would you know about voodoo? Snake charming and voodoo is the same thing."

"Bullshit," Crystal said. "Voodoo is when you make little dolls of people and stick hatpins in them, and they start to look like Wayne Fucking Newton."

Well, this got the biggest laugh of the night. Even the sailor on the other side of Crystal cracked up over that, and Vinnie was really pissed.

He started in with his defense of Wayne Newton, but nobody could hear him because we were all roaring. Especially Dog. He had his head back and was holding his gut, and tears were streaming down his face.

"Hey," Vinnie said, "what the fuck you laughing at? You're just a fucking welfare man. Just like the niggers. 'Whoa suh please gimme my check.' "

"Hey, cool it," I said to Vinnie. "We're just having some fun."

"You cool it then," Vinnie said. "I don't want to hear one more word in the denigration of Mr. Wayne Newton, who is a great performer and a hell of a guy."

"Great," I said. "A great guy."

But Dog didn't say anything. He just stood there, staring blankly past Vinnie, as if he were dreaming of pointers sectioning off a green field of tall grass and high above them a pheasant streaking toward the sun. Then he blinked and looked around, and I could see it happening to him again, his dream being wiped out by the bar, the sound of the cash register, and the dull hardness of Vinnie's eyes.

"Shut up, Vinnie," he said in a voice that was deathly still.

Vinnie looked at him with as much meanness as he could muster up, but there was something gone in Dog's face that scared even me.

"Hey, Doggie," I said, "come on now. Let's get us a booth over there."

"You better have money, Baker. This place don't run on credit."

Dog stood very still, his hands rubbing the bottom of his jacket.

"Shut up, Vinnie," he said again in that same silent way.

Vinnie swallowed hard and walked toward the other end of the bar.

"Come on over and sit down with me and Crystal," I said, tugging at his arm.

"No, want to think some," he said, sitting down on the stool. "I was just remembering Bruno. That was one hell of a dog."

He smiled at me with such pain in his face that I squeezed his arm.

"We're right over here if you want to talk," I said.

"Yeah," Crystal said, "don't go into one of them funks now."

Dog nodded, but I could see he was already headed down into it. The black sewer, covered with twisted, wet leaves.

I looked over at the barmaid, Julie, who gave me a quick glance. I knew she'd keep an eye on Dog. Then I followed Crystal over to the booth.

"I hope Doggie's okay," I said. "He's worrying me. Keeps changing moods."

"He's just tired, hon," Crystal said to me. "It's a strain, you all been going through. But tell me what you been up to, Red. Where you been keeping yourself?"

I slid into the booth and relaxed a little. Always been a booth man since I was a little kid. Booths are like quilts, you don't feel anything bad can happen to you long as you're in or under one.

"Well," I said, "I been looking for work, that's about it."

"You know how to use a pay phone, don't you?"

"Honey, it's only been a month or so."

"Only a month, and what am I supposed to do, stay home and knit two purl one?"

"Hey," I said, "gimme a break . . . goddamn I'm so glad to see you I can hardly stand it, and here you are getting angry on me. But I bet I know what it is."

I reached over and took her soft chin in my hand and stared directly into her big green eyes.

"I'll bet you were worried when you got your hair cut short like that I'd be upset, and all I want to say is you look prettier and younger and more sexy than ever . . . I don't usually like that shag haircut on most women, but on you, well, it just makes you look like an innocent kid."

Her face got all soft, and she put her cheek in my palm and sighed deeply.

"You're a bad man, Red Baker. You really are."

"Hey," I said. "I'm just doing the best I know how, honey."

She smiled a little, that curious half smile that always cut straight into my heart.

"And damn you, that's pretty fine. Am I going to see you tonight?"

"Sure," I said. "We can go down your place after you get off."

"I wish you could stay all night, Red. I get so damned lonely. I mean it, I could just cry."

"I'm sorry, Crystal, I really am. You know I miss you too, honey. All the time, every day."

"No, you don't, Red. You miss me, but you have Wanda and Ace. There ain't any point in you pretending you don't love her, because I know you do."

I just smiled and shrugged at that one. There was something about being with Crystal that made me feel like I could love a lot of people. I don't mean screw them, I mean love them. She saw this in me, this largeness of heart and spirit, and I saw her seeing it and kind of picked up on it and felt that way when I was with her. That I was this big, kind man.

It wasn't the worst way to feel.

I reached over and rubbed her cheek again, just getting set to let some tenderness float over to her, when I was crushed by a three-hundred-pound wrecking ball of flab who slid into the booth next to me.

"Hey," he said, "what you two doing?"

On "doing," Henry's voice went up just like Andy Devine playing Jingles on the old "Wild Bill Hickok" show.

"Well, we were getting ready to go over the top-secret nuclear bombing strategy for NATO," I said, "but I guess we can let that wait."

Along with Henry came a huge hero sandwich, about the only thing Vinnie's kitchen knew how to make.

Henry, as I have mentioned, is a big man, not your basic slob. He's just big all over, though he could probably benefit looks-wise if he dropped a couple hundred. Much of his girth is due to subs, of which he is way too fond. He also enjoys describing the making of these great sandwiches, whether you are in the mood (and no one ever is) to hear about them or not.

"Look at this beauty," he said, rolling his eyes, pressing up against me, and driving me into the wall. "Custom-made job. I had Robinson make it for me special. It's got cappicola and turkey . . . see right here."

He opened the sub and pried back a couple of layers of cheese.

"Got American and Swiss too . . . Robinson says he don't like Swiss cheese, but that's the way it is with niggers. Anyway, yeah here it is, cappicola and ham . . . and turkey. Yeah, three kinds of meat. They add up to this one kind of taste. Home, Babe makes these for me just right, but Robinson, he's got this special sub oil, which I have never been able to duplicate, and he just will not tell me what's in it. Does that to get even with me cause I won't give him Babe's donut recipe . . ."

"That's extremely interesting, Henry," I said, my bones being crushed and wanting like hell to have more time alone with Crystal.

Henry smiled at Crystal and me and then took a huge bite of his sub, smiling again while he was chewing and managing to drop a good deal of it down his plaid shirt and green work pants.

"Ummmmmmmm ummmmm, is that good or what?" he said. "You want some, Red, Crys?"

"No thanks, Henry," I said. "But that does look good. Yessir."

"Well, it's hell of a lot better than a crab-cake sub. Robinson thinks he can put crab cakes in this kind of roll. I told him fifty times that you eat crab cakes on saltines with mustard and a little horse-radish. Only assholes eat 'em in sandwiches . . . That's the truth. I swear to God."

"No doubt about it," I said. "What else you been up to, Hen?"

"Nothing, 'cept I got me a job today."

"No shit? Where?"

"Vinnie here gimme one. Darned good one too. I'm the new bus-boy for the Mona Lisa Pizza."

"That's great," I said.

"I don't know," Henry said. "He's making me wear one of them outfits, you know, to look like I'm out of one of those Charlton Heston movies or something. I got to stand around a lot with a spear, but it's damned hard work, I'll tell you. Man, Vinnie does a business there, you know that? I mean, it seems like people keep eating pizza and drinking beer no matter what."

"I guess ole Vinnie's paying you pretty good too," I said.

"No, not that good yet. Paying two bucks an hour. Babe is making more'n that over at the mattress factory. It's just a temporary thing."

"Yeah," I said, "well, it's better than what I got. So far I'm batting a giant goose egg."

"You been looking hard?" Crystal asked with her half smile again.

"Sure I have," I lied, but she started laughing at me right way.

"What's the matter?" I asked.

"I can always tell when you're lying," she said. "You rub your nose every single time."

"Nah, bullshit."

She reached over and touched my nose real soft and smiled again.

"Ev-er-y sing-le time," she said in a slow, sexy voice.

"Okay," I said. "You got me. But I am going to really start tomorrow. I needed some time to get over the shock of getting dumped. It's just that the jobs I hear about are such shit."

"Yeah," Henry said, "I'm thirty-eight years old, and they got me busing tables. I feel like an asshole. You know?"

"Yeah," I said, "I do know . . ."

Before I could say anything else there was a nerve-splitting sound of smashed glass.

I looked up in time to see Dog picking up his beer bottle and hurling it full force at Vinnie, who ducked barely in time to avoid getting hit square in the face.

"You son of a bitch," Dog screamed. "You come up the god-damned carnival, Vinnie. You hear me? You come up the carnival."

"Oh shit," I said.

I tried to get out of the booth but had to wait for Henry to vacate his place, which took maybe thirty seconds, way too long to stop Dog, who was running full tilt the length of the room and knocking people off their barstools in the process. Vinnie was backing away fast, holding his short, fat arms in front of his face.

"Dog," I yelled. "No . . . wait."

But it was no use. He made a flying leap toward Vinnie and grabbed him around the throat. Vinnie stepped out of the way just enough to avoid having his head torn off, but Dog still had him around the neck and was choking him down. They were like two lumbering bears in slow motion, and then Frankie came up and smashed Doggie in the ribs and knocked him down next to the Pac Man game. He started kicking him, but I had managed to get around the bar myself by then and leaped on Frankie's back, grabbing him around the throat and pulling him behind me. Joey Capezi was moving forward, but Henry jumped in the way and pushed him backward.

"Hey, who the fuck you working for?" Vinnie screamed at Henry. "You fat fuck."

"I just don't want to see anybody get hurt, Vinnie," Henry said. "Dog's just drunk, that's all."

Joey Capezi pushed past Henry and tried to get a kick in at Dog, and I stepped forward and grabbed him, but he turned quickly and hit me in the forehead. It was like being struck by lightning. My eyes went dark and I fell backward, and I saw him coming straight at me, so I gave him the only defense I could think up quick, which was a good sharp knee right in the nuts.

This sat him down next to Dog, who woke up and hammered him once in the face with his fist.

"You crazy mutherfucker," Vinnie screamed. "What the fuck is wrong with you? Baker, you get that crazy-assed son of a bitch out of here, or I'll have him taken downtown, I swear to God. One more time like this, I'll have his ass. He's fucking psycho."

Suddenly Vinnie reached down and grabbed Dog by the chin.

"You hear me, you psycho fuck. You ought to be in Meyer Clinic. No wonder they fired your ass. You're a bag of shit, you hear me?"

Dog started to grab Vinnie by his gold chain, but I smacked his hand away, and between Henry, Crystal, and myself we got him on his feet and started for the door.

Vinnie was full of himself now, screaming and ranting as we left.

"And you're going to get a fucking bill for all of this, whacko, and you better come up with the bread. I mean it, or you're a dead mutherfucker, you hear me?"

"Fuck you," Dog said, turning his head around, though his feet were dragging. "See you up the carnival, asshole."

Outside I got him into the truck and gave Crystal my sheepskin jacket. It was cold as hell, and the snow was getting deeper. Big, fast flakes covered her face and hair.

And suddenly she looked strange, like a ghost of her own youth, and I felt a chill come over me.

"See you guys later," Henry said. "I got to get back in. Cold as hell. He going to be okay?"

"Yeah," I said. "Thanks, Hen . . . I'll take him home."

Henry waved and hurried back to the red door.

"Well, what in God's name started that?" Crystal asked. "I mean, Vinnie was down the other end of the bar."

"Jesus, I don't know. He's been like this for a month or so, maybe longer. He keeps changing on me. I think this layoff thing is really nailing him, but it's been coming on a long time too. He and his wife are just about through, the two girls side with her . . . I don't know, shit . . . everything coming down on him. I got to get him home, Crys . . . Damn, I wanted to come over tonight. You know that, don't you?"

She huddled close to me and held me around the waist.

"I know," she said. "You couldn't just drop him off and then maybe come over for a while? I don't finish here for an hour more."

"I want to, honey. But I think I better stay with Dog. You know?"

"Sure," she said. "Go ahead, but after he gets to sleep, I mean."

"I don't know, honey. I mean I go out then, and Wanda hears what time I left from Carol . . . well, you know."

"Oh shit," Crystal said. "Goddamn it, Red, I'm sick of waiting around here for you. Jesus Christ, you got loyalty to everybody but me. I'm getting damned tired of it. I don't have to play second fiddle, Red. You think there's no guys . . . lots of guys who want me? Huh, guys coming in there every damned night?"

"I know there are, honey," I said, feeling so cold and so damned tired and old.

She walked away through the snow, then stopped and turned around.

"I'm sorry, Red. Call me tomorrow, will you?"

"First thing," I said, "and I'll make it up to you. I promise. We'll go down Bud's Crab House on Thursday . . . How's that?"

"Sure," Crystal said. "Sure, that'll be great. But I won't hold my breath."

Then she threw me my jacket and ran back across the parking lot to the bar.

I got inside and looked over at Dog. His face was covered with blood, which was running out of his nose, and he was moaning and holding his ribs.

"Get me home, Red, get me home."

"I will, partner. But first we're going by Hopkins emergency ward. I think you might have a couple broken ribs."

"No, man. No . . . just get me home. That fuck Vinnie. I just wanted to do it, you know? I couldn't look at that cheap fuck any-more. I couldn't stand it, Red, you see that?"

"Hey, I see it, Doggie, but take it easy, will you? Don't worry about it now."

"You hear the shit he called me? He said I was a sack of shit, that I was nothing. You hear that?"

"I heard it. You know it's all bullshit."

His big hand came over and touched my leg. He put his head down next to my lap, and started to cry.

"No," he said. "No, it's true. Vinnie's right, Red. I'm nothing. I got nothing and I'm going nowhere. Red, it's all true. It just hurts to hear it from a fuck like Vinnie. Shit. Shit . . . I went down for a carpenter job today, Red, but they didn't want me. Nobody. Nothing."

He began to sob deeply. I put my hand down on his head and patted his hair. It was covered with snow and sweat and blood.

"It's bullshit, Dog," I said. "You're the best man in town. You believe that shit and you're nuts. Don't ever say that, you hear me?"

"It's fucking true," he said again and again. He sobbed deeply. I took my hand off his head long enough to turn on the truck and shift into reverse. The tires skidded as we hit the highway, and I held on to him as we drove slowly through the blizzard down the dark, dangerous highway toward the emergency ward.

At the Johns Hopkins emergency ward I waited for Dog to get his ribs X-rayed and taped up. It turned out Frankie had managed to split two of them pretty good, and even though he was in considerable pain, the Dog talked about getting even with a vengeance, but with the same wild-eyed moon lunacy that I'd felt coming off of him earlier. I mean, he fairly shined with craziness.

"I tell you what we do, Red. After I get these old ribs taped, we head back down there and wait for Vinnie and Frankie to come out, and then we fucking waste them, man. I've eaten that fat Wop's shit for the last time. You know what I mean?"

I stood there looking at the doctor's face as he tried to hold Dog still long enough to get the tape around him.

Every once in a while he'd look over at me and raise one eyebrow. Finally he took out a needle and gave Dog a shot.

"What's that for, Doc?" Dog said. "You a friend of Vinnie's? Maybe slipping in the old hypo on me, huh?"

The doctor assured him it was just a little painkiller to help him relax, but suddenly Dog grabbed the doc by the lapels and began to pull him down toward the table.

"Maybe I don't want to fucking relax, asshole, you ever think of that?"

A nurse named Miss Pritchard, a beautiful brown-haired girl with big green eyes, looked at me as though she were going to scream and ran to get an attendant, but the doctor reached out and grabbed her by her thin tanned wrist.

"I'm on your side, Mr. Donahue," the doctor said calmly. "Now lie still and rest. Nobody can bother you while I'm here. The medicine I gave you is already starting to act. Do you feel better? You do, don't you?"

Dog looked up at the doc, his mouth hanging open and a strange puzzlement in his eyes. He began to laugh a little, and spittle drooped from the corner of his mouth.

"Feeling better. Like a warm hand coming over me, Doc. Got that old soup running through me, right?"

"That's right, Mr. Donahue," the doctor said, letting go of Nurse Pritchard's arm.

"You with me Red?" the Dog said.

There was a child's panic in his eyes.

"Red, you here, Red? You still with me?"

I grabbed his arm, and he looked up at me through the cloud behind his eyes.

"I'm with you, Dog."

"Yeah. You my buddy, Red. You and me kick their asses . . ."

"You know it."

He shut his eyes then and drifted off, and the doctor and I let him go. Looking at him there, silent and breathing easy, I envied him that peace.

When the Dog was asleep I asked the doctor to come to talk with me for a minute. He nodded and took me into a narrow room filled with bottles of blood that dangled from gleaming steel hangers.

"What is it, Mr. Baker?"

"It's my friend, Dog. He's out of work, like me, but that's not what's worrying me. It's more his moods. I don't know who's going to show up when I see him—Dr. Jekyll or Mr. Hyde."

"He has rapid and seemingly unmotivated mood swings?" the doctor said, running his hand through his beard.

"I guess you could say it that way. Yeah, one minute he's up, I mean flying, and then a second later, like tonight, he's heading across the room ready to kick ass."

"You say he's out of work?"

"Yeah, and he's forty-two and he thinks his wife maybe has an eye for other guys, but still this is different. He had a tumor about a year ago, too . . . in his neck. But he seems to be okay from that."

"Your friend may need psychiatric help," Dr. Swartz said. "There's a condition controlled by a drug called lithium . . . The condition is called mood swing, and it can happen due to a variety of reasons, some physical, some psychological. I'd suggest you get Mr. Donahue into therapy at Meyer Clinic."

I looked around at all that plasma and thought suddenly that the whole world was nothing more than a sea of the stuff, running in our bodies, trapped inside our veins. And that Dog's was bursting to get out . . . The strangeness of the thought made me sit down on a stool. After a time I looked up at Dr. Swartz.

"Look, Doc, Dog's an old-fashioned guy. He won't go to any headshrinker."

"I think maybe he has to," Dr. Swartz said. "I could talk to him if you like."

"Yeah . . . but not tonight. Let me bring it up first. We're old friends, maybe I could convince him. Except he doesn't have any money now either."

"You pay on a sliding scale at Meyer," the doctor said. "Look, Mr. Baker, you don't have to be crazy to need help. But your friend is showing all the signs of somebody who could get in some serious trouble, hurt himself or someone else. You ought to really give it a try."

"All right," I said. "I'll talk to him soon."

"Good. Now I've got to get back to my less interesting patients. Just your average gunshot wounds and stabbings."

We both managed a smile at that.

I got a prescription for Dog from the doctor for pain pills and sat in the waiting room, staring at the patients—a black man who dripped blood from his right arm and kept saying "Mercy, Lord, mercy" and a young girl whose face was black and blue, held up by her mother, who lectured her on "seeing that no-good bum Frank again." And winos and hookers, one red-haired, her right arm dangling like a broken chicken wing, and then at the back of the room I saw him there too, the Man With No Nose.

He wore an old Army jacket and a blue knit cap on his head. When our eyes locked, he cocked his head to the right like a puppy, as though he knew me but couldn't remember from where.

The sight of him there, with no apparent injury other than that of his gross ugliness, scared me through to the bone. I turned back toward the front and waited, waited for his hand to come up behind me, touch my cheek.

I knew him. I was sure of that. Knew him like I knew Wanda or Dog or Ace.

I knew what his fingers would feel like. I knew that he'd lightly touch my ear. I knew I wouldn't be able to bear it.

Slowly I turned to see him again.

But the seat was empty. He had slipped away. Out into the dark night, back to his home in the streets, his narrow alley guarded by the great, drenched pile of trash.

The next morning was so quiet around our house that it felt like Wanda was already gone. I didn't even try getting up and explaining; it wouldn't have done any good. She hadn't even been awake when I got home around 2 A.M., didn't grill me about where I'd been, but just lay there asleep or doing a damned good job of faking it.

Either way it scared the hell out of me. When Wanda's screaming at you, or crying, or just telling you how it is, well, you know you're still in the ball game, but the silent treatment is something else. Lying there that night I felt that I was dead and buried as far as she was concerned. Or, like the Man With No Nose, something not quite human.

If I had any chance of holding my family together I had to find a job, and I had to do it today. If it was the parking lot, then I'd have to hack it no matter how pissant low it made me feel.

As soon as Wanda and Ace were off to work and school I put my new checked shirt on, some cleaned and pressed corduroys, and my work boots and headed out down ice-covered Aliceanna Street.

On the way down to the lot I told myself it was going to be a snap. I'd have the job in no time. Hell, I knew Mr. Morris, the fat guy who owned the place, had known him since I was a kid, and there probably weren't that many guys going for the job anyway.

Dead wrong again, because by the time I'd gotten down there, eight guys were standing around in that white cement underground tomb, five of them white guys I knew from the mill, and three blacks, only one of whom was over twenty-one.

Something must have already gone down too, because the blacks and whites were standing off in little separate clumps and were staring holes in each other. I saw one of the guys I knew from down the mill, Spike Ladd, and he told me that Morris was picking three new guys on account of he just fired his whole parking team for slamming the cars around.

"Buncha spades," Spike said under his breath. "You know, they all think cops are chasing 'em when they go up those ramps. We got a good chance to get this job, Red."

"Great," I said. "What's it pay?"

"Three bucks an hour."

"Jesus Christ. With this and three more gigs I can maybe buy a can of Spam."

"Know what chu mean," Spike said. "You going to the union meeting Friday?"

"Sure," I said, but I wasn't thinking union. I was watching the black guys looking us over, staring at us with all this fire in their eyes. I'm no racist, but frankly these young black dudes scare the shit out of me. They don't know nothing but television, and a lot of 'em think if they shoot you, they'll get up and walk off and be right back after the commercial.

"Hey, look at all these white boys," one of them said, a big black cat with a scar across his cheek.

"Old mutherfuckers too," said a little one next to him, wearing an Army jacket.

"Yeah, too old to be parking cars," the big guy said. "Why don't you dudes do something else, man? Leave these jobs to the men who know how to drive."

Spike shot the big spade the finger. "Sit on this, asshole!"

"Hey, man," the black guy said. "You want to get fucked up? You come down here to get fucked up? 'Cause I can fuck you up. You know what I'm saying? I don't want to hurt you 'cause you an old, feeble mutherfucker, but you give me any shit, and you could go home in a ambulance."

Spike stepped forward, but I grabbed his shoulder and gave him a good jerk back.

"Hey, let me go, Red. This coon don't scare me. I'll stick his head up his ass for him, you know?"

"Yeah," I said, "I know. But you ain't down here to get in a battle, man. You think Morris is going to hire you if you're in a brawl?"

"Yeah, okay. But I hate to be pushed around by any fucking nigger."

I looked over at Ray Barnes, another one of our boys; he had a screwdriver in his hand and was whacking it back and forth in his palm.

"Ray, put that son of a bitch away."

"Man, you going to have that up your nose, you don't get rid of it," another big black guy said. This was the only adult in the gang.

He moved forward, and I stepped out in front.

"Hey, man, look, this is bullshit. We're all down here to get jobs. For Chrissakes, think of that."

The black guy looked me up and down.

"How's that jump shot?" he said.

"What?"

"You Red Baker, ain't you?"

"Yeah."

"Leroy Carter. I played summer ball over Patterson Park with you. You was on the Ramblers, weren't you? Good jumper, man. Hurt us in that game. I'm on the Jive Bombers."

"Hey, yeah," I said, taking in a deep breath. "But I'm not talking to you today, Leroy, 'cause I don't hang out with guys who kick me in the shoulder when I go up for a bound. It's embarrassing."

"Shit," Leroy laughed. "Hey, man, I didn't want to start no trouble here today, it's jest hard times, you know?"

He looked at Spike and put out his hand.

"Let's forget it, man, huh?"

"Yeah," Spike said, but he sounded too goddamned surly. I personally wanted to slam him in the head for that. Leroy was a good man. The truth is blacks are probably better guys on the whole than white people at forgiving shit.

"Yo be playing this summer?" Leroy said.

"Hey, if I don't get a gig I may be too weak to play this summer."

"I hear you, man."

We slapped hands, and I thanked God for my jump shot.

A tense half hour later Morris showed up and got out of his car. He drives a big-assed Lincoln Continental, and he's got this huge gut, which he hides under a two-hundred-and-fifty-dollar overcoat, with some kind of fur around the collar. He's got these tiny little feet, and when he walks he sort of bounces around. He looked at us, and when he came to me, his eyes opened wide.

"Red, what you doing here?"

I felt a hot flush of shame, and right behind that my breakfast flipped in my stomach. Forty fucking years old, oh man, I just wanted to run out of there.

"Just need a job, Mr. Morris" was all I was able to come up with. I sounded weak and puny, like Ralph Kramden after he's realized he's treated Alice like a shitheel.

"Well, Red, come over here a minute, will you?"

I shot a look at Spike and Leroy and walked over to his car with him.

"Red," he said, "this is a job for niggers. You don't want this."

"You're right," I said. "I don't want it. But I need it bad, Mr. Morris."

"Yeah, I heard about the mill. They're not going to reopen, are they? Red, you need to make some long-range plans. You're not a youngster anymore."

"Don't I know it. Look, Mr. Morris, you own the market, some other stuff, is there anything you can help me with?"

He shook his big shaggy head and looked down at his well-polished shoes.

"Red, I'm laying people off. I'm only hiring here because the last boys were hot-rodders. You know how to drive carefully, right?"

Jesus Christ, I thought. I was starting to sweat, sweat just pouring off of me. I felt like I couldn't breathe and that there was witches' fingers clawing at me from the inside.

I told myself I wasn't having a heart attack.

"Yes, I can drive very well, Mr. Morris."

"You used to be a kind of wild kid yourself, Red. Remember stealing the ham from the market?"

"Mr. Morris, I was seventeen then."

"There's a saying, Red, once a thief . . ."

"Mr. Morris, look, I'm honest, I'm straight. That was a long time ago."

"You walked in with that friend of yours, what was his name?"

"Dog Donahue," I said.

"And he's laid off too, isn't that right?"

"Yeah, but he's straight. We were just kids. You know."

I didn't know what else to say. Sweat was pouring down my face, soaking through my shirt. I felt my breath coming in short, hot spurts.

"You two waltzed right in, took the ham off the hook, and walked right out. I guess you thought that was funny."

"No, Mr. Morris. We were too dumb to think about it at all. It was a stupid thing to do. I don't do things like that anymore."

He looked me up and down.

"You're sweating, Red. It's cold in here, and you're sweating. I have to think maybe you're sick. Maybe you have that flu that's going around. Then I have to ask myself if I should hire a sick man."

"I'm not sick, Mr. Morris."

"No," he said and smiled a little, "I guess you're not. Maybe you're nervous. Maybe you're scared, huh?"

I said nothing again. I prayed quietly for the Lord to give me strength not to pick Morris up by his collar, turn him around, and bash his head over and over again into the trunk of his car.

"Okay, Red," he said. "You got the job. I tell you what, I'll make you the boss of the crew. You pick the other guys. And meet me here tomorrow. I'll show you the ropes. I have a meeting now."

"Hey," I said, "Mr. Morris, I don't want to pick those guys . . ."

"No?" he said.

He stared down at me and smiled. He had yellow teeth, and his lips looked like they belonged on someone else's face.

"All right," I said. "All right, for God's sake."

"Don't take the name of the Lord in vain, Red," he said. "I need three guys. One of them has to be a nigger, or I'll have trouble with the goddamned NAACP. Take your pick. But don't let me down."

"Thanks, Mr. Morris," I said. "What about my hours?"

"You work seven to three one week and three to eleven the others. Just make sure you show up. And don't steal nothing. I'm taking a chance on you, Red, a big chance. I'll tell you what, since you're the boss, I'll give you four dollars an hour."

He sounded so delighted with himself that I was surprised a sled with reindeers didn't arrive to take him away. Four dollars an hour. It occurred to me that one summer, when I was seventeen, a pal of mine and I went out to Guilford to the posh houses, with front lawns. We had a couple of mowers and some clippers, and we cut grass for four bucks an hour. This was in 1958, and I was fifteen.

Morris got into his big Continental, backed out of the garage, and left me standing there to face the others.

"Well," I said. "It's like this, boys. I need three guys. I'm picking guys I know, who I figure I can trust. There's no more to it than that. I want Spike, Ray, and Leroy. The rest of you guys I'm sorry about."

The black guys mumbled "shit" under their breaths and gave me some bad looks, but sort of wandered out of the garage into the cold. You could tell that both of them hadn't really expected to get a job anyway.

But the other guys from the mill—Jeff Foreman, Harvey Miller, and Steve Malachek—just stood there looking at me. I had known them all for years, though none of them were really in my gang. Still, they looked pissed, and who could blame them?

"Hey," Harvey said, "you chose this black mutherfucker over us? Man, what the fuck is wrong with you? How could you pull a stunt like that?"

"I had to," I said. "Mr. Morris told me one guy had to be black."

"Bullshit, when did Morris become a bleeding heart?"

"When the NAACP come down on his ass, that's when!" Leroy said.

"You coulda talked him out of it," Jeff said. "I know you, Baker, and you could talk a crab right out of its shell. Maybe you didn't want to, huh? Maybe you and this nigger are real close pals. Basketball buddies."

Now Leroy stepped forward, but I stood in his way.

"Get out of here, Jeff," I said. "There's nothing here for you."

"I won't forget this, Baker. You fucking nigger-loving asswipe."

He turned around and walked with Harvey and Steve out of the building. Spike and Leroy stood there looking at me. Ray put his screwdriver back in his pocket.

"Well," I said, "that was great. Two shifts, morning and night. I'm taking one of the morning shifts this week, who else wants it with me?"

"I take it if nobody cares," Leroy said.

"You got it then," I said. "You two guys work at night. Don't wreck the cars, all right? We got to all meet Morris here tomorrow, but we might as well get a head start. Come on in the office, and we'll look at this ticket-punching stuff."

They followed me across the parking lot.

I had a job. Parking cars.

Ten days of parking people's cars in that white, ice-cold, walled maze, and I felt as though I had never known anything else. There was no escaping it, even at night, when I would dream of being driven blindfolded in chariots, spiraling around and around, and knowing that somewhere, just around one of the bends, there wasn't going to be any more concrete, and I would fall off the edge of the world.

On nights like that I'd sit straight up and let out a cry that would wake Wanda, make her hold on to my waist and pull me back down.

I started taking some of the money and buying a pint of Maryland rye. Wild Turkey was too damned expensive, so I fell back on the booze I'd started with as a kid, that oversweet rotgut that burned holes in your stomach.

All day trapped down there, eight hours a day, taking shit from my own neighbors, some of whom were guys who once looked up to me and felt both bad and superior to me at the same time.

"Hey, Red, playing any ball lately?"

"Hey, Red, can you hurry with my car, I got these theatre tickets."

"Baker, what the hell were you doing up there, jerking off in my car?"

And me and Leroy answering politely, smiling, taking it all in like it was a joke. When all the time I wanted to bust heads, break ass, take their BMW's and Volvos and smash them into the ramps, break off doors, and stick burning rags into their gasoline tanks and watch them blow the hell into a million pieces as they headed out into the slush-covered streets.

I don't know when it was, maybe the third week, when I started getting the shakes in the daytime as well. Leroy noticed it though, and one day when we were eating lunch in the miserable, freezing-cold office, he smiled at me and shook his head.

"You're a good ball player, Red, you know why?"

"No, you tell me."

" 'Cause you play the game in here." He pointed to his head. "I watch you, you one step ahead of the other guys, moving without the ball, setting up your shots."

"Yeah," I said. My right arm had started to jerk in the bicep, and I had become embarrassed by that and didn't want him to see.

"Red, you mind if I say something?"

"No, man."

"You got to do the same thing here, you see? You got to be one step ahead of the mutherfuckers. You got to see that they don't even really know what chu about. They just like their cars, man, these people. I mean, they machines, mostly out of whack, needing work. You look at 'em like that, see, out-of-control machines, you can laugh it through."

"Is that how you do it?" I said, eating my egg salad and reaching into my hunting jacket for my rotgut.

"You bet . . . Ain't no fucking machine going to make no toy out of me. I got basketball to play this summer. We got a new kid coming out. Vertical leap about forty-two inches . . . Make Dominique Wilkins get tired, man, you know?"

I looked at him there, sitting across from me, smiling, and suddenly I felt that I was going to start crying. It made me so fucking furious that I got up and locked myself in the men's room, turned on the water real loud, and then smashed both my fists against the sink over and over, until the bottom of my hand was raw and red.

When I was done, I went back outside. Leroy looked at me dead on.

"You cool?"

"Yeah. Thanks, Leroy."

We slapped five, and somehow that day went a little better. I could feel the rage in me burn a little less bright.

But I also knew that it would take less than nothing to turn it up again. I wasn't long for that place.

I didn't know what I might do, how bad I might hurt somebody. Red Baker, an out-of-control machine.

But even the worst of times aren't all bad.

Some days at home I managed to keep it together, and Wanda and Ace and I would be like we used to. Kidding around, going out to Patterson Park to take a walk, Ace and me passing a football, or some nights down the cellar, pulling out my old Gibson F-hole guitar and playing some country duets, with Ace doing the leads and singing high harmonies. Wanda would sit there on the steps watching us, smiling, and I knew that I had to hang on, that we'd get through this somehow.

And yet I dreamed of Crystal. Only now it wasn't us on the highway to Florida, but she and I jerking around in that twisting, turning cavern of a parking lot, in a car that ran by itself, no brakes, no steering, smashing into the concrete walls, Crystal burying her head in my lap.

And I worried about Dog too, who called up from his bed at his house and who was convinced I was pissed at him, which was partially true. Not that I wanted to be, but maybe I'd strapped on all I could take for now, didn't know how to deal with his madness, the wild light in his green eyes.

But I owed him too much to stay away for long. Loved him too deeply to not give it a shot. So one dead-black night I sucked it in, hit myself up with a good belt or two of Four Roses, and made it around the block to his house on Foster Avenue.

Though we lived in almost identical red brick row houses, Dog's is different in that he has an iron sculpture of a dog screwed into his front door. Wanda made it for him for Christmas two years ago, and Doggie loved it to death. It's a little corny if you want my opinion, but Dog smiled and shook his head happily every time he opened the door. Unlike me, it doesn't take confusion to make Dog feel alive.

Our houses are decorated differently too. We have mostly old furniture, granted, but Wanda has a way of making everything seem homey and comfortable. Carol, bless her soul, has never had the homemaker's touch. So when she wanted to fix up the house, she just went over to Sears and bought all this blond Danish Modern stuff, the kind that shines out at you. Dog didn't like it worth a damn, said it looked like the kind of stuff you saw in porno flicks, but Carol said that it was all the rage in New York City, and what did Dog know about the art of interior decoration anyway? So there they had it—couches, chairs, coffee table, bedroom set, all of it hard blond and sending out these dentist-office glares at you.

It was unpleasant to sit in Dog's living room on the best of days, and this was a hell of a long way from that. Doggie's ribs were still bandaged—I know about rib injuries from football, and when they're bad you just pray to God you don't develop a cough—his hair was messed up, he wore his faded, old Colt T-shirt (number 19), had a can of National Boh in his big right hand. He was surrounded on his yellow couch by both his girls, Lisa and Kathy, and all three of them were staring at a TV cartoon cat with a menacing grin on its wide black face.

"Well, it's almost four-thirty," Lisa said. "And we are turning this trash off so we can watch Lana Turner in *Imitation of Life.*"

Kathy crawled over Dog, who shook his head at me and rolled his eyes.

"No, we're not," she said in a singsong voice. "We're watching cartoons."

"I am not going to waste my time arguing with you," Lisa said, standing up and heading for the television. "I have to watch Lana because she's a great movie star and I intend to learn all I can from her."

"Daddydaddy," Kathy wailed, "she always gets her way."

She threw herself down on Dog's lap, her shoulder hitting his ribs. Doggie groaned but managed a laugh and patted her head.

"Seems to me you already watched enough of them cartoons. You ought to go work on your coloring a little. Or read that book . . . *Black Beauty.*"

"But the Roadrunner's coming on," Kathy said.

"The Roadrunner is an imbecile," Lisa announced, switching channels.

"Don't you talk about the Roadrunner that way, you . . . you orange-headed creep!"

"Now calm down," Dog said, looking over at me and rolling his eyes.

"You wish you had hair as beautiful as mine," Lisa said, running her hand over her recently peroxided locks. She had attempted to turn her brown hair into gorgeous technicolor blond like Lana, but it had come out sort of dried out, like orange weeds in an old, parking lot.

"Ha," Kathy said, "some joke . . . Orange-headed creeeeeeep!"

"That's about enough of that, you two," Dog said in a soft, firm voice. "Lisa gets to watch Lana Turner today, but tonight Kathy can see whatever she wants for an hour. That's the deal."

"Oh great," Lisa said. "We'll have to watch about a million hours of 'Family Feud,' which is the dumbest show of all time. Next to the Roadrunner!"

"I don't want to hear any more out of either of you," Dog said. "I mean it now!"

Lisa sighed and sat down heavily next to her father.

"I just have one thing to say, and that is I hate this house, I hate this street, I hate this city, and as soon as I am of legal age I'm going to take a bus directly to Hollywood, California."

"Now that's enough!" Dog said loudly. He'd begun to sweat, and his breath came hard. "You don't go around bad-mouthing your hometown. Balmere, Maryland, is the finest city in this country. We're second to none. Ain't that right, Red?"

"Damn straight," I said.

"Come on down the cellar," he said. "Cooler down there. Been trying to fix our old fan."

I was shocked to see Dog's workshop. Ordinarily he had a place for everything—hammers, saws, files, screwdrivers. He took a hell of a lot of pride in being handy and in the perfect order of his work-shop, but now tools were lying around everywhere. Saws sitting in the corner in his old overstuffed chair, hammers lying in sawdust piles on the floor. Bent nails lying on top of the old, dead radio.

"Looks like a cyclone hit this place," I said.

"Yeah, I just haven't had the energy," he said.

Doggie shrugged, then picked up the old Air Kool fan and started unscrewing the back. His hand trembled a bit, and I pulled the bottle out of my pocket.

"Want a hit?"

"Yeah."

He took it and wiped off the cap with his hand, and suddenly I remembered him making the same gesture when we were both bright-faced kids over at Patterson Park. The sun shining, a baseball bat in Dog's hand, and an Orioles cap on his head. Wiping off the quart bottle of water, drinking from it, and passing it around.

"Any luck looking for work, Red?"

"You didn't hear I was parking cars?"

"Oh yeah, I guess Carol mentioned it. Good future in that."

He went back to work, taking the grill off the fan, and sweat poured down his face.

"Just temporary. Gets me out of the house."

"Well, I ain't doing it," Dog said. "And I don't guess I'm going to goddamned computer school either. That's what I heard down the union hall the other day. They're maybe planning to send some guys . . . the *smart* guys . . . to computer school, 'cause it looks like the steel mill isn't going to open again."

As he spoke his voice got tense, and suddenly he stopped working on the fan and sat down on top of it.

"Gimme that bottle again, will you, Red?"

"Sure."

He took another long pull and shook his head.

"You know, Red, I'm sorry about the other night. I just went crazy, I guess. I been thinking about it . . . I can't quite figure it out. Suddenly, I just couldn't take any more of Vinnie's shit, you know?"

"Yeah, I know."

"I'll tell you what, staying home's getting to me too . . . and I got something else on my mind. You keep a secret?"

"Come on, who you talking to?"

He dropped his head down, and I saw the sweat pour off his thick, hairy neck.

"It's Carol. I think she's screwing this guy over to the Big Burger. Dickie Nellis, the night manager. She's been coming home late, him driving her. When I asked her about it, she says they're taking inventory. It's inventory all right, you know what I mean."

I took a hit of the booze myself. Dog picked up a ball peen hammer from the workbench and began to swing it back and forth between his legs, bouncing it off the fan's grill.

"Hey," I said. "You're going to break that if you don't watch it."

"That ain't all I'm going to break. I swear, Red, if I find them together, I'll kill them both. No bullshit."

I walked around the room, the hammer clanging on the fan echoing in my head.

"Dog," I said, "will you stop that for a minute?"

"Sure."

He dropped the hammer on the floor and looked at me with such a sadness that I wanted to put my arm around him.

"Look, Doggie, we been friends all our life. Not just you and me, but Carol and Wanda too. I just know she isn't dicking around on you. She isn't like that."

"You don't really know what people are like," Dog said. "You think you do, but they find ways to turn it around on you. Down at the job, here at home, it's all the same thing. You can't count on nothing anymore."

"Doggie," I said. "Look, I'm worried about you. You're not yourself. I mean going nuts like that with Vinnie and now suspecting Carol . . . Look, maybe you ought to go down there to Meyer Clinic and talk to one of the . . . guys down there."

Dog's eyes widened, and he stood straight up, like I'd sent an electric current through him.

"You mean talk to a headshrinker? What the hell you talking about, Red? There ain't nothing wrong with me that getting my job back wouldn't cure. You know what it's like staying home with the girls every day, like some damned cleaning woman? God help me, I love those two more than anything in this world, but just today I thought if they have one more fight, just one more, I'm going to slap their faces, both of 'em. And I have never so much as laid a hand on either of them."

"But that's what I mean," I said, "you're upset . . . you're not yourself . . ."

"Goddamn your ass, Red, I thought you'd understand. It's not my head, it's my goddamned life . . . They've taken away what I love, Red, and I'm going outta my skull. I ain't no genius like you. I'm a steel man. That's it. Period. That's what I do."

He sat back down on the fan and stared at me with a little smile on his face.

"You got a lot of fucking nerve, Red. Coming over here telling me I should talk to some goddamn headshrinker. Who the hell are you anyway? How many times I pull your ass out of a fight? How many times I seen you drunk as hell? Who the fuck you think you are talking to me like that?"

"But this seems different to me . . ."

"Yeah, 'cause it's *me*. If it's you, it's okay. I think you better get outta here now."

"Hey, Doggie, don't take it like that."

"That's how it was said, and that's how I'm taking it . . . Go on home. I mean it now."

"I'll come around in a couple of days, maybe you'll feel better."

"Don't," Dog said. "I don't need no help from you."

It wasn't any use, I could see that. So I turned, went up the steps and outside into the snow.

Out on the street the slush was starting to come down again, and I walked down Dog's block under the big, pink, blinking sign for Sardino's Subs, and I felt as though the sleet and drizzle and gray slime was going right through my skin, filling me up from the inside. I wanted to rip out one of those marble steps in front of me and hurl it in Sardino's window. I didn't know why.

I wanted to go back and kill Dog. Crush a pillow in his face and put him out of his misery. Throwing me out on the fucking slush-covered streets. But that feeling went by fast, and then I was over-come with a kind of mood swing myself (maybe this shit was catch-ing). I just felt cold and empty, and my chest was tight, and my hair was matted to my head, and I felt dizzy too, very dizzy, like I was having some goddamned heart attack.

There was something I was supposed to do, I knew it. It was lying there in the back of my head, but everything was swirling too quick, everything was too drenched and cold and dead for me to be able to pluck it out of the whirlpool.

I took a right and saw Slap Horton's bar and started for it, but I stopped and took a deep breath.

"Take it easy. Take it easy," I said to myself, talking out loud just to hear a voice.

"Hey, Red, what you trying to do, catch pneumonia?"

I looked at Horton's black doorway and saw Choo Choo Gerard leaning there smiling, a toothpick between his teeth. I always do my best to avoid Choo Choo, but just then I was never so glad to see him in my life.

The one thing about Choo Choo, you see, was he was consistent. You could depend on him to be a cheerful slime.

"Get in here, man, I'll buy you a drink."

"Right," I said, knowing "wrong" was the right answer.

But a few minutes later I was sitting at a table with him, drinking Jack Daniel's with a tall National Bohemian beer back, and I could feel the tension and fear and rage draining out of me. My neck muscles started to unbunch, and my fingers got a little heat back in them. I was so relieved to be away from the goddamned car lot, and Dog, that I let myself forget Choo Choo's games.

"So, Red," he said, "can you believe the Colts are gonna leave town? That mutherfucking Irsay!"

"Yeah," I said. "It's a shame."

"Goddamn criminal is what it is," Choo Choo said. "Just when Kush had them playing better too. They weren't lying down. They're going to be back in the playoffs soon. But in Indianapolis. Damn, I can't believe it. Remember when they had Unitas? Now that was *the* team."

"Yeah," I said. "Ole Johnny U."

"Yeah," Choo Choo said. "We had fun going to the games in them days. Dog and me and you. I tell you the truth, I miss going to games with you guys. We ought to be better pals, Red."

"Hey, you know how it is. Wives, kids . . ."

"Yeah, and work. Time waits for no man, huh, Red? You know, when you got that nice job in the mill, I thought, well, that's one thing he can always depend on, steel. But these days, I guess even steel is shit, you know? I might have the only job in the world they're going to need for good. But it gets you down, working with low-scale guys like Blazek, though this is strictly between me and you. Plus, the pay ain't shit. Cops in New York City, they live like fucking kings compared to us. We deal with the germs all day long, and they pay us dick. It ain't right."

"Yeah," I said. "But from where I'm sitting, having your job looks pretty good, Choo."

"I guess it does, Red, I guess it does. It all depends which side of the street you're on. Like the geniuses say, it's all relative. I got my debts, I got my alimony, I got my child support, and I like to live maybe a little higher than I should. The way I figure it, you're here for a short time, you know, what with all the shit in the air and the heart attacks and the goddamned poisons in the food, you might as well make the best of it."

By now he had gotten me my second drink, and I was starting to feel kind of warm toward old Choo Choo. After all, we did play ball together, and really, he wasn't the worst of guys.

"Listen, Red, I hear you're working over at the parking lot. That must be tough."

"It ain't so bad, Choo Choo."

Choo Choo smiled and shook his head.

"That's why you're a good man, Red, you don't bitch and complain a lot. That's why you got a good rep. You're a man people can depend on. They did a damned stupid thing letting you go down the mill."

"Yeah," I said, downing the drink. I don't know why, maybe all the tension in the day, but those two drinks hit me hard. I never have been a big drinker anyway, but right then I was beginning to feel very relaxed. And maybe a little sorry for myself too.

"Twelve years down the fucking drain," I said to the table as much as to him.

"It ain't right," Choo Choo said. "Puts a strain on a man. And you with such a great kid. I hear he's going to be the best guitar player in the state."

"Yeah," I said, "if we can afford to get him into Peabody. They got these scholarships, but they tell me he could only get a partial one. Still, way too much money."

"Yeah, but Peabody, that's the best, right?"

"Yeah," I said. "I want him to go to the best."

Drink number three had come from old Slap One-Eye, and I was already halfway through it and working on my third beer. I still couldn't understand why I was feeling so loaded, then it came to me —I had taken a little of Dr. Raines's pill that afternoon, right before I got off work, figuring it would get me up to talk to Dog.

"Red, listen, I know how you feel about me," Choo Choo said, "but I'm a friend of yours. You should know that."

"Hey, I know that."

"No, don't bullshit me. You think I'm bad news. But we all got our problems. Listen, I got something you should consider. If you don't want to hear about it, though, you just say so and we'll drop it. Because I like you, and I don't want to jeopardize our friendship. But this is a good thing. Nobody gets hurt, and the people that lose, well, maybe they deserve to."

I could feel my heart pumping faster again. I remembered the times Dog, Choo Choo, and I had pulled a couple of small jobs when we were kids. Nauronski's Candy Store, which got us sixty bucks. And the Music Mart, where we mainly took records. The Little Tavern and then the job at Sears, which messed up my record.

"Look, Choo Choo, I appreciate the drinks and the offer, but I can't do anything that would screw up my family, man. It's not the same as when we were kids, you know? I mean, my son, if anything went wrong, it would kill him. You hear me?"

Choo Choo nodded his head and reached into his bag of cheese curls. A couple dropped on his lap, and he swept them away onto the floor into a puddle of cold shoe water.

"I hear you, Red. But I know how it's been for you. Christmas is coming up too. This is a walk, I mean it. And we could net maybe fifteen."

"Fifteen hundred?" I asked.

"Thou, Red. There's one more guy, so we're talking a minimum of five thou apiece. We're talking maybe an hour. Minimum danger. I cased it already. A walk."

When I heard that, my mouth got dry. I drank down my beer and called for another drink and tossed that one back, and then I was drunk, tired, and tingling in my hands.

"I need to know in two weeks, Red. That's all. You got plenty of time. If you're interested, call me at the station, we meet here, and we'll run it down."

"Who's the third guy?" I asked.

"You in?"

I wondered if he could hear my heart beating. It was that loud in my ears.

"No," I said.

"I'm sorry to hear that, Red, but I'm a determined man. There's other guys I could get. They'd be lined up for this, but the reason I haven't ever been nailed, and don't plan on being, is I only work with guys I trust. You call me if you're in, okay, Red?"

I nodded my head and finished the last whiskey and beer, and then a worse panic overtook me.

"Holy shit," I said. "What time is it?"

"Lemme see. I got seven forty-five."

"Christ, I got to get to Ace's recital tonight. He's got this jazz band at the school, and I have to make it. Jesus, if I don't, I'm a dead man."

"Where's he playing?"

"Over at St. Bart's, you know. Christ, that's thirty minutes away by cab, and with the goddamned snow, there's no way."

"Yeah," Choo Choo said. "You could maybe get there by cab at say . . . nine."

I jumped out of my seat, drunk and shaking.

"Shit," I said. "I'm fucked."

Choo Choo smiled and got up too. He looked over at Slap, who shook his head. Choo Choo hadn't picked up a tab in this lifetime.

"You're going to be there by eight-fifteen, partner," he said. "Let's go."

"You're kidding."

"Hey, Red," Choo Choo said, "what are friends for?"

Then we were swirling through the narrow row-house streets, the siren blasting and the red light flashing, me drunk and afraid and hating Choo Choo for roping me into goddamned Slap's in the first place and half loving him for riding like a bat out of hell so I might just possibly make Ace's part of the program. As the snow came down in bigger and bigger flakes and Choo's cruiser fishtailed around the corners, smashing into the back ends of parked cars and narrowly missing people crossing the street at Broadway, I gave up a little, silent, drunken prayer that Ace's band wouldn't go on first.

But on top of all my worries, I have to admit that it was exciting being in the car with crazy, big-lipped Choo Choo, hearing the police radio reports and watching all the cars pull over to let us by.

"Son of a bitch, ain't this it?" Choo Choo said, stepping down on the pedal even though the streets were getting to be pure glass.

"Jesus, watch out for that kid," I said.

"No problem, Red," he said, as cool as he could be and power gliding that baby right past this teenager whose mouth hung open in pure terror.

"Reminds me of the old days, Red. Remember the drag strip out there by Westport? That's what I always wanted to be, you know? A stock car guy. Man, let me be old Fireball Roberts booming around Daytona. That's the life. Only became a cop 'cause it seemed like the next most exciting thing after I got married. See, shoulda gone with my first instinct, 'cause now Martha is living in Syracuse and I'm stuck here on the force. Got to go with what you're best at, Red. You know that?"

"Right," I said, looking at the clock on the dash. Eight-thirteen and we were still five blocks away. Long blocks, filled with cars stalling, horns honking, but old Choo Choo didn't even seem to notice. He hit the siren even louder, sending shock waves through my eardrums, and when we got to the gridlock he just took that son of a bitch up on the curb and drove half tilted over, screeching and sliding and fishtailing his way until the street was open again in front of us, and then, somehow, seventeen minutes later there we were, sitting half turned around in the street at St. Bart's.

By this time I was in such a daze and so loaded I could barely walk.

"You getting out or what?" he said. He was laughing now, and so was I, a wild, crazy laugh, which I had no more control over than Dog did his.

"Jesus, thanks, man. I'll see you."

"Call me soon, Red," he said. "We're a real good team. I'd come in with you, but I got a feeling Wanda might not like it too much."

"Thanks again," I said, pumping his hand, and then I was out the door, falling down in the street, right in a puddle of slush, so my whole front was soaked and old Choo Choo was laughing at me so hard he could hardly breathe.

He turned the cruiser around in mid street, gave me one more blast of the siren, and pulled away.

I opened the big wooden doors to St. Bart's, pulling my plaid shirt out of my pants at the same time. It was going to look bad coming to my son's recital dressed like a wino, but I figured it was better than looking like I just pissed myself.

St. Bart's is this old, huge Catholic church with high arches and fantastic stained-glass windows and little concrete statues of saints all down the side where the devotional candles are. In the middle are these long rows of pews, and from my distorted and half-crazed perspective it looked like the pews went on forever. Up front, where the priest did his hocus-pocus, they had cleared things away, and there was a band of students and some older guys, one of whom, Joe, was Ace's music teacher in school. Everything was a great blur to me, and I stood in the back for a few seconds trying to get my focus right, to see if I could spot Ace in the band.

When I finally was able to see through the musty, half-yellow light, I saw that Ace wasn't up there, and of course I then went into a deeper panic thinking that his group had already played. I took my deep breaths and tried to think of some halfway decent-sounding lies about having to talk to Dog, but I knew that Wanda would check up and find out I'd left there in plenty of time to make it here, and before I could come up with anything else, Wanda was turning and staring at me through her glasses with her dead-faced you've-done-it-again expression. The worst part was that she was way up front and had saved me a seat, so I had to tiptoe up the aisle, covered with slush from head to toe like some slime monster from the horror flicks.

I heard people giggling and laughing, and I could hardly blame them, because I must have looked like the original Big Foot of Baltimore. But I kept on creeping and the band kept playing, and I finally squeezed in, dripping water all over people as I went.

"He's on later, right?" I said with as hopeful a voice as I could muster.

Wanda turned and gave me her grim mouth, thin lips pursed tightly together, and her eyes narrowed to tiny slits of light.

"Christ, I'm sorry," I said. "There was a problem over at the lot. Some guy lost his car keys and we had to get a locksmith, and I had to get back there because the other guys didn't know what to do."

"Sure," she whispered to me. "If you don't have the decency to come to your only son's recital on time, at least don't ruin it for the rest of these people by lying all the way through it."

"Hey," I said in as small a voice as I could, "it's the truth. Anyway, I didn't miss him yet, right? He hasn't played, has he?"

"Shut up, Red, for God's sake," said a voice. This wasn't Wanda but Ruth, her mother, who lived three blocks away and who I avoided at all times like the plague. I hadn't even seen her sitting next to Wanda, I had been so intent on getting seated, so now I had to give a sweet little smile, which didn't fool her at all.

"He played in the opening song," Wanda said, looking straight ahead, "but he's on for two more. So you can hear him and then tell him about all your problems at the car lot."

I was still drunk as hell, and I was freezing to boot from the cold water all down my pants, but I figured I deserved that; hell, I deserved whatever she threw at me, even Ruth being there, because I had been such a jerk with Choo Choo.

So I sat stock-still and listened to the jazz band playing something by John Coltrane, a great favorite of Ace's.

People say that rednecks hate Negro music and only like country and western, but this isn't true a little bit. I like all kinds of stuff, especially good old groups like the Rolling Stones, but this modern jazz stuff always makes me feel stupid.

It always starts with something recognizable and then seems to go off into outer space, and I guess the idea is to take you on a "Cosmic

Journey into the Realms of the Musical Stratosphere," as the black
jazz DJ once put it on Ace's portable radio.

The thing is, it's not that I don't like it, so much as I am afraid of
it. I mean it, and after all that's happened to me, I might as well just
tell the truth.

I fear the Musical Stratosphere. For me, earth is about as much as
I can handle, what with the Dog turning into a madman, and Choo
Choo offering me deals, and Crystal waiting for me to call her. And
thinking about the parking lot and how I got to go back there tomorrow, and the horrible number that is going to go down after the
concert, and turning forty. See what I need is a music that sort of
keeps me hanging in there.

Maybe it just comes down to I am too old for the Musical Fucking
Stratosphere, and that's that.

Anyway, the whole thought of being sent out there with no hand-
grips just makes me nervous as hell.

But Ace, he's young, and he's not afraid, and he's got this ear for
stuff that his daddy never understood, and who the hell knows where
he got it, which is one of the only nice surprises about living, that
your son or daughter suddenly becomes this other person with these
talents and tastes that you don't have, and you can kind of say,
"Well, I did all that shit so they could go on and hook up with the
Musical Stratosphere, even if I can't."

And damn, if this kid couldn't.

Because soon after I got there his group came on, and it too was
made up of part students and part teachers, but Ace was clearly the
kid they were featuring, and they played something called "Green
Dolphin Street" first, which I had heard Ace practicing and which is
still in the lower part of the Musical Stratosphere as far as I'm concerned. Because I could follow it, sort of, and by God my boy could
play. Up and down the scale, and here a soft patch, like green grass
in western Maryland, and there a kind of floating bit, like clouds
over Beaver Dam, and then this faster part, a duet with the horns,
which sounded really fine, kind of trading off things, playing the
same notes, really "cooking" (as Ace says), and Ace has this look on
his face like he's just soaring around, and then once near the end he
looked right at me, and he smiled, and I don't know what happened
to me, maybe I really was getting as crazed as the Dog, because I
started crying, just a little, but it was all I could do not to break out

in this great, gasping sob. I felt so proud and full of love and terrified
. . . I had to suck it back, take these little breaths, and grit my
teeth, and I wanted to take Wanda's hand so badly, and finally I did,
but just as I knew she would, she pulled away from me, so I had to
sit there and watch and keep myself in check.

And that was hard because he was so beautiful up there, played
like an angel, but not soft. No, he was strong and tender at the same
time, and he was off out there in whatever lovely and scary space he
had chosen for himself, filling the great black holes with music, and I
had never been so proud or so in love with him in my life.

He was my son, and nothing I had ever done in my whole life,
including playing basketball, was as good as what he was doing right
there in St. Bart's Church, and I felt like it was a miracle, a real
miracle, and I didn't care if I was wet anymore, or cold. I was still
shaking, but it wasn't from the weather, it was from love and admi-
ration for Ace.

The trouble was that everybody was so damned mad at me that I
couldn't just run up to him afterward and throw my arms around
him like I wanted to. No, instead I had to act like Humble Joe and
let Wanda and Ruth go up first and hug and kiss him, while I stayed
in the rear, dripping wet, hair matted to my face, literally twiddling
my thumbs and feeling like a fool. Which was fair enough, since
that's what I had acted like. All the other mothers and fathers, some
of whom I knew, kept away from me, like I was some kind of plug-
ugly who'd just happened to stumble in here hoping he'd cash in on
the powdered donuts at the end of the show. A guy I knew from
down Bethlehem, Paul O'Brien, who was still working, looked me up
and down and smiled one of those some-assholes-never-learn smiles,
which made me want to grab the son of a bitch, run him outside, and
stick his head down in the street mush.

But I only nodded back to him and kept my eyes on Ace, who was
accepting congratulations from Father Mulligan, the short, toupee-
wearing priest. Finally, when the crowd had thinned out some, I
walked over to Ace.

"God, Dad, what happened to you? You have a car wreck or
something?"

"No, just slipped on the ice trying to get here, son. Couldn't get the car started and had to get a ride. Old Choo Choo got me here fast, the siren was blasting . . . you shoulda seen us."

None of which I wanted to say. I wanted to tell him how he had it, how he was on his way, and how I'd get him there somehow. Somehow I'd get him off of Aliceanna Street to places where people could hear him play, because he was that good, and I was proud of him and loved him more than my own life.

But I was able to say nothing more, and Ace gave me that curious smile, the one I'd been seeing too much of lately. Like he didn't believe me, like he was just starting to know what a liar I was.

"Well, I'm just glad you made it, Dad. I hope you liked it."

There was something cool and distant in his voice, and I thought this kid is fifteen and I got to be straight with him.

"I loved it, son," I said. "I really did, and don't you worry, you're going to get to go to Peabody or wherever else you want."

"Sure, Dad," Ace said, smiling, and the disbelief in his voice just about killed me.

He turned away from me then, and I thought of how just two years ago anything I told him, any story at all, he believed it, and he looked at me with these great big eyes, like I was Brooks Robinson or something, but now . . . now it was like he was drifting out there with his music, away from me, and I thought of losing him, how it was going to feel, and I wanted to reach out and grab him and say something that would make it all like it used to be, just one magical moment that would make us father and son, like we were when he was little and I would take him to O's games, and he'd say, "I bet you could field the ball like Brooks when you played, huh, Dad?" God, I know that was corny, but it killed me to have him know I let him down.

And I had. I had let all of them down.

Ruth was tight-lipped, and Wanda stood with her arms folded, and then finally, after what seemed like a long, terrible hour, we walked out of the church and caught a cab going home.

"Hey," I said when we got to the house. "Let's make some hot chocolate and maybe pop some popcorn and watch a little tube."

Ace looked at me and shook his head.

"Nah, Dad, I got to get up early tomorrow for school. Got to study my history and then get some sleep. See you tomorrow."

I went over to hug him, but he gave a little wave of his hand and went up the steps real fast.

Wanda sat on the couch and stared at the TV, though there was nothing on. That made me so nervous I turned it on and stared directly at the face of Ted Koppel, the news guy with the wig. She took one look at it and walked upstairs, slowly, not so much as blinking at me when she left.

I sat there staring at soundless Ted for as long as I could, and then I got up and turned him off. He was still out there in the world somewhere, being serious, but I couldn't use the world's sorrows to relax me tonight.

Instead I went upstairs, expecting Wanda to be crumpled on the bed, still dressed in her church clothes.

Instead, when I opened the bedroom door she was standing there in this short little Chinese robe that came just about halfway down her thighs. She had combed her long blond hair straight back, and she turned and looked at me with bright green eyes and her rich full lips. Except for the worry lines in her forehead, she looked as young and slender and hot as when I first met her back at Patterson years ago.

I looked at her thighs, and I realized that they weren't so bad at all. She'd always been able to lose weight just like that, and now she looked young and slender, and suddenly she smiled at me in a way that took away my breath.

It caught me off guard, but then women always have.

This was Wanda, Wanda who could drink me under the table when we were younger, Wanda who once leaped out of a speeding car when she found out I was fooling around with another girl and damn near broke her collar bone, Wanda who drove every boy in the school half crazy . . . Now she turned around, not facing me, staring at herself in the full-length mirror.

"I don't look that bad, do I, Red?" she said.

"No," I said, barely able to get my breath. Her legs were strong and long, and I thought of the way they felt wrapped around my back. And how I couldn't throw that away.

She turned back to me and smiled. She knew she had surprised me again.

"I've been thinking, Red, thinking a lot. I was going to give you a long speech, but I don't think I need to anymore. I'm tired of hearing my own voice. Just look at me a minute, Red."

She pulled the black silk rope, opening the Chinese robe, and I stared at her beautiful breasts, at her rounded, full nipples, at her stomach, which was still flat. Flatter than mine.

"What do you see?" she said, smiling at me.

"I don't know what you mean?" I was paralyzed.

"I'll tell you what you see, Red. You see nothing. You forget how it used to be. I almost forgot it myself until lately. Then I started working out, looking at myself again. I was like those girls you ran around with once. I was young and tight all over, but I'm still not bad . . . even with the goddamned crab-meat smell sticking to me and thirty-six years and being a mother, which I sometimes get so goddamned sick of I could die. Even with all that I'm not so bad, am I, Red? I can see it in your face. You're turned on . . . Well, let me tell you something, you aren't the only one. When Ace and I walk out of here, it won't be that bad. You hear me? There's plenty of guys that would like to have Ace for a son, you hear me? Plenty of them that wouldn't have to chase after Crystal Lewis down at the Paradise when they had me at home."

I stood there staring at her. She smiled at me, and in her fury and anger she seemed years younger, like another woman entirely. I wanted to go slap her in the face, the words hurt me so badly, and yet I was paralyzed because she understood where I lived, understood it only too well.

"Am I making you mad, Red?" she said, laughing a little and running her hand through her blond hair. "Too bad. Just like it was too bad you couldn't make it to Ace's recital tonight."

"Wanda, I'm sorry . . . I didn't mean it."

"No, of course you didn't, Red. But it doesn't matter a hell of a lot any more what you mean or don't mean. What matters is what you do. And you do nothing. You've lost your guts, and I've begun to hate you, you hear me. I'm an old-fashioned girl. I get used to you abusing me. All the women in my time are like that, but when you abuse Ace, when you show up drunk and looking like a bum, then I say fuck you, you hear me . . . ? Fuck you and your goddamned, two-bit, asshole friends . . . You bastard!"

I thought she was going to run after me, but all this was delivered in a flat tone of voice, as if she were talking to a ghost.

"Wanda," I said. "I'm sorry, baby. You got to believe me. I'm sorry."

She smiled at me.

"Good old Wanda, huh, Red? She'll always understand."

She ran her hand over her breast, something she used to do when we were first married, something so bold that I felt myself getting excited, and I moved toward her. Then she let the robe slide to the floor.

"Wanda, come here."

She smiled again and stepped back so I could see her back and ass in the mirror.

"You don't want me, Red. You don't want Ace or me. You want to live with Dog. You and him being boys forever. Well, maybe you'll get your chance real soon."

The tears came down her face, and she tossed the hair out of her eyes, and then I was on her, wrapping my arms around her, kissing her shoulders, smelling her natural sweet skin.

"Wanda," I said. "You can't leave. You can't . . . I love you . . . Goddamn it."

"Red," she said, "fuck me. Fuck me one more time."

So I did. I took her there on the bed, lying across it, and she dug her fingernails into my back and bit my shoulder as I rammed my cock into her, and it was like it had been at the Benjie's Drive-in all those years ago, when I couldn't get enough of her and thought about her all day in class, dreamt of her breasts and her neck and the way she cried out when she came. She turned over, and I fucked her up the ass, and she reached back and pulled my hair hard, and I bit her neck and she screamed out, "Red Red. I want it. Come on, Red," and then finally we were both spent and lay there as the globe lights came on in the cold, wet street.

When we were finished she looked at me and smiled with that sexy corner-of-the-mouth grin that had always excited me in the past.

"I won't be here much longer, Red," she said. "You know that, don't you?"

"Don't say that. I love you and Ace, and you know it."

She shook her head, putting her long, strong legs over my own.

"I used to think that, Red. I used to think you were better than the rest of them, but it isn't true. You've just got more charm, but that's not enough anymore. Not for me *or* Ace."

"Goddamn it, that's a lie," I said. I wanted to slap her, bite through her skin. She lay there in bed, looking at me, wrapped in my arms, half laughing, mocking me, and half crying. And I was amazed. I hadn't known how much of her there was or how strong a spell she still held on me.

Finally she fell asleep, but I lay there awake for a long time. Her words had stung me badly, I could feel the welts rising inside my chest and arms. Was I like the rest of them? All charm and bullshit?

Long after Wanda had fallen asleep I lay there, my heart pounding, thinking how it is a man knows he believes certain things, but he slips a little here and slips a little there, and eventually he looks the same but he's not even a man at all. He's just a liar, and that means he's nothing, and I tried to turn that over in my head—was it true, was I just a liar, and how could I be anybody at all anyway, with no job and working at the parking lot . . . ? It didn't seem possible, and then this terrible sadness came over me, and I figured that there was somebody I once was, young and pretty damned good, and this guy, this other guy believed in the future and loved his wife and kid and took them out on walks and bought his wife flowers and his son toys and came home after work and fixed the house and thought about having more kids and getting a better job at the mill, and then he began to see it all slip away. But he thought that it was still all outside of him, that even if the mill was going under, and even if he hung out with the guys too much, and even if he started whoring around and doing drugs, and all the rest, even if he was doing all that shit, underneath he was the same guy. It was like being on vacation from himself.

Except up the Sunday school they used to say "by your acts ye shall be judged," and I have never forgotten that.

And my acts now were pretty much those of a no-good bum.

But it wasn't only your acts, was it? A man dreamed things and felt things and wanted to be good. That had to count for something.

But maybe it only counted to him. Maybe only he knew, and so the Bible was right. It *was* your acts you should be judged by.

Except it was all well and good to come on with noble stuff like that if you were a priest or somebody who had the inside track with Jesus. Me, I was a steel man without a job and no goddamned money. What kind of good acts was I likely to pull off even if I wasn't such a fuckup?

I thought of Choo Choo and the fifteen thousand dollars.

I got up out of bed and walked to the window and looked out at white, snow-covered Aliceanna Street, and it was real pretty, all covered over, and I thought if I were a kid tomorrow I'd go sledding over in Patterson Park.

But tomorrow I'd be back down in the white-walled, dead-ass, cold garage, water leaking out of the pipes, guys screaming at me about their goddamned theatre tickets, and I wouldn't be one step closer to getting my life together than I was now.

Still, I had to try. I loved my wife and kid. Wanda was wrong about that. I was a selfish bastard and a fuckup, but I couldn't take it if they left.

I had to try to keep it going.

I owed it to them, and to Doggie too. Yeah, he had thrown me out, but he wasn't going to get rid of me that easily.

These were my people, and I was stronger than most of them. Damn, I had always known it, and I wasn't going to just sink.

I'd get another job, and I'd really start spending time with my family. I'd keep it together somehow.

And then, right in the middle of this new resolve and all these warm thoughts of Wanda and Ace, right on the spot I started thinking about Crystal's tight little ass and the way she looked out on the parking lot the other night, and God how I wanted her.

I lay back down in my bed and tried not to think of her and how she too was threatening to leave me. And goddamn, I couldn't stand that either. I needed her, the way she made me feel.

That was the trouble again. I needed everything at once, and I shut my eyes and sent up a little prayer to a God who might or might not be hanging out there above the row houses, and I said, "Let me do right, and keep those I love, and not want everything in Baltimore."

For the next two weeks or so I kept a tight rein on myself. I knew things around the house were right on the edge of exploding and that it would take both Wanda and Ace one hell of a long time to forgive me for screwing up at his recital.

I stopped worrying about getting back on unemployment and tried to forget about the steel mill altogether. I told myself that for now I was a car attendant, that there was nothing shameful in it, that it was just a temporary thing, and I'd handle it like a pro.

I even gave myself little pep talks in the morning, cornball stuff like "Okay, Red, so you're a parking lot attendant. Well, you son of a bitch, you're going to be the best goddamned parking lot attendant in Baltimore."

Then I'd nod to myself in the mirror and head off down the cold, snow-blown streets to the garage.

But God, just seeing the garage entrance, dark and underneath the ground, like a mouth waiting to swallow you up. I thought of Jonah every time I went in there . . . down in the belly of the whale, freezing my butt off, with only Leroy for company. Some days, driving the cars around the ramps, I'd begin to think that I was trapped in a maze, and that I'd never get out but go down lower and lower, and down at the bottom something was waiting for me I couldn't name.

When that would happen my heart would race, and my head would get light, and though it was cold, the hot flashes would start me sweating right through my flannel shirt. And I'd silently pray, "Don't let me die down here, God. Don't let me, please." And then I'd look around and realize that maybe I was two stories down, and I'd think of Vinnie putting me down the sewer, and the idea that God and Vinnie were partners came into my head, and I was ashamed of it and hoped He wasn't watching me and didn't know . . . A man's not really responsible for what thoughts come into his head, is he?

I thought that they had put me down the sewer as a child and they had let me come up, Vinnie and God, let me come up for a hell of a long time, just to trick me into thinking that I was out of there forever. But now, at forty, when a man wants to start thinking about his future and preparing himself for his older years, they had put me back down it again, only this time . . . this time, it was for good.

They had tricked me into thinking I was free.

But why? What had I done? Was it because I'd screwed around

with Crystal? I couldn't believe that. Was it because I hadn't been a perfect father? Or that I didn't go to church anymore?

Or was it like Job, a test of some kind? And if it was like Job, what was the point of all that I had learned in church school as a kid?

What kind of a God would put me down here in these cold circular roads which burrowed into the earth, water from the cracks in the pipes dripping on my head?

What kind of a God would snatch away the job I loved, let Billy Bramdowski, who never hurt any man, blow his brains out in the toolshed? Was he like the gods I read about in high school, those old Aztec lords who were made of gold and bronze and needed human sacrifices?

Was he hungry again, having eaten Billy's brains? Maybe now he was calling for mine too?

Would it be a heart attack down on the Green Level, falling crumpled over some lawyer's Mercedes?

Or would he drive me crazier, day after day, down these circular, mazed, underground streets, where the air got as flat and as dead as the eyes of the people who asked for their cars?

Or would he send people, was he already sending the bastards, to stir up my anger and my pride?

Like the guy one morning who accused me of stealing the bottle of vodka he left on the backseat?

"I never took your vodka, mister. I don't even drink the stuff."

"I didn't say you drank it," the guy said. He wore a long tan raincoat and horn-rimmed glasses and had a pointed needle nose. He seemed to be sniffing at me as though he couldn't quite tell if we were both men.

"Maybe you took it and sold it for a few bucks. Or maybe your black friend over there swiped it."

I stared at him, down there on the third level, and thought how easy it would be to grab him by the collar, turn him around, and just run him into the wall. How, just then, I would have enjoyed it more than anything in the world.

But I kept my peace.

"No one took your vodka. We don't steal in here."

I spoke with as much calm as I could muster.

I think he heard me then, because there was a spooked look in his eye. He stared bug-eyed at the white walls, the huge basement, empty, and the only sound that of the dripping pipes. And he nodded and looked away from me, then got in his car and pulled out, blowing the exhaust in my face.

Or the guy who accused me of putting a dent in his fender, a dent I'd seen that morning (there were so many of these bastards that you tried to remember the condition of every car). I had to actually threaten him to get him to leave.

Leroy saw me flipping again.

"Hey, man, cool out. Maybe you need a drink."

But he was wrong about that. I didn't need one drink. I needed a hundred drinks, a thousand, nothing less would do. One night at the Paradise could finish me off. I'd be on the road to Florida with Crystal, heading down to those bright sands . . .

And late Tuesday, after Wanda and Ace had fallen asleep upstairs, I poured myself a long, stiff drink and dialed Crystal's number on our living room phone.

I half hoped she wasn't home.

But she was there, half asleep, and when I heard her sweet, smoky voice, groggy and a little scared, a tenderness and warmth cut through me. Emotions so strong they almost brought me to my knees.

"Crystal, it's me, honey."

"Red? Red, is that you?"

"Yeah, babe, it's all right. It's fine."

"You scared me, Red, what time is it?"

"Three o'clock."

"Red, are you in trouble?"

"No, I'm fine. Just fine."

"Where are you, Red?"

"I'm downstairs at my home," I said, whispering and looking up toward the stairs.

"Red, are you crazy? I don't hear from you since Dog gets beat up, and now you're calling me from your house? What if Wanda wakes up?"

"It's all right. She's a deep sleeper. I just had to talk to you, that's all. I miss you, honey."

"I miss you too, Red, but I wish you hadn't called me."

"Why, babe?"

She started to cry a little, and I began rubbing my nose, feeling like such a fool.

"Because I told myself that I wasn't going to see you anymore, Red, that's why. I didn't sleep good for a week, up all night thinking about you and wanting to call you. You don't know how many times I almost called your house. And then, about three days ago, I just started sleeping a little . . . and now, now you call me at 3 A.M., and I won't be able to go back to sleep all night."

"Yes you will, honey," I said softly. "Look, I'm sorry, I really am . . . I just wanted to hear your voice, that's all. I miss you and want to see you."

"Sure. Just like the night we were supposed to go to Bud's for crabs. That was Thursday a week ago. Remember?"

She caught me up short on that. I had completely forgotten about it, what with all the excitement concerning Dog and practically being thrown out of my home.

"God, I'm sorry," I said. "I really wanted to do it. It's just been hell around here. Dog has been acting nuts, and my kid, Ace, he needed to see me. Crystal, I don't know what to say. I just want to see you soon."

There was a long silence, and she cried some more. I could picture her, lying there alone in her bedroom in her little apartment down on Pratt Street overlooking the harbor.

Underneath her quilt, with her cat, Alfie, lying at her feet. Her short boy's hair and her big green eyes and all curled up like a kid.

I loved her then, more than I ever had.

"Crys," I said. "Listen, I could come down and see you on Tuesday night. I could stay real late, and we could go get those crabs, and drink some beer, and make a night of it."

"No, Red, I don't think so."

"Crystal," I said. "We'll hear your new records and turn down the lights. Just the two of us."

"Red, you idiot, I can't stand this. You hear me? I love you, and I can't take this anymore."

She never said that before then, and it felt like someone had turned a warm shower on my face.

"Red, I wanted to tell you in person. I hate to say important things over the telephone, but you might as well know, I don't think I'm going to be around much longer."

"What do you mean, honey?" I said, feeling cold and fearful.

"I'm leaving. I'm moving to Miami."

"Miami?" I said. "You can't do that."

"Why shouldn't I? What's keeping me here?"

"Honey," I said. "You got friends here, people who care about you. Down there you don't know anybody. That's a bad town. Full of crazy mental-patient Cubans Castro sent over on the Looney Boat. They got drug wars down there too. I read in the papers just the other day that they had to hire a bunch of new ice cream trucks and convert them to morgues, just so they could scrape the cocaine dealers up off the street."

She laughed a little at me and then sounded like she was starting to cry again.

"That's why I shouldn't move? You came up with every reason except the one I wanted to hear."

"All right," I said, breathing hard now. "I love you, Crystal . . . Goddamn it, I can't stand it if you leave."

"You don't mean it," she said in her little girl voice.

"Don't tell me I don't mean it," I said, raising my voice and then dropping it again.

"What about Wanda and your son, Ace?"

"What about them?" I asked, stalling.

"What about them? Are you ready to leave Wanda for me?"

"Crystal, they're my family. They need me."

"Red Baker, Old-fashioned Guy," Crystal said.

"Yeah, in some ways I am. But Crys . . ."

"Well, you weren't so old-fashioned the first night we met at the Paradise. You wanted to jump on my bones the first second we met, and when I refused you told me I was acting like a prude. You remember all that talk, Red. 'Don't let a good moment like this go by, Crystal. Think of all the people who are afraid of life and miss out.'"

"Crystal," I said. "I don't remember all that. I only know I mean what I just said, I love you, honey. You can't leave Baltimore."

"Oh, Red, I don't know. I don't know if I can believe you anymore. That's the worst of it. It's not waiting around, it's that I might have been wrong about you. That you might be a liar like all the others."

When she said that I sagged against the couch, just as though somebody had punched me hard in the gut. Could lovers read each other's minds?

Maybe it was true. Maybe I was no good. Maybe I had fallen that far. And if she left, if she left me, that proved it, didn't it? It was another reason to never let her go.

"Crys, you know that's not true. You know it."

"I *used* to know it, Red."

I heard a bed squeak upstairs. I looked across the darkened room at the chest of drawers with the gleaming, moonlit artificial fruit on the top.

"Crys, I got to go. I'm tied up for three days, but I'll come see you Thursday night, all right?"

"Sure, Red," she said, but her voice was flat, like she was already talking to somebody she used to know.

"Believe me, Crystal, I love you, I do."

"I love you, Red. I always will," she said, and then she hung up.

My heart was beating wildly. I heard another shuffle from upstairs, then Wanda's voice.

"Red? Are you all right?"

"Yeah," I said, gripping the edge of the couch. "Just couldn't sleep. Had a drink of juice."

"You better come up to bed. You have to get up in four hours."

"Sure, honey," I said. "I'll be right up. You go back to sleep now."

I heard her sliding back to the bed. The sound of her slippers over the rug, like an old woman.

Soon we would both be there. Old and broke, Ace gone off somewhere—but not college, because I didn't have the money to send him —the three of us like flies you swat on the screen door in summer.

And Crystal gone too . . .

Gone to that white beach and crashing ocean surf, singing "Misty" to men with money.

The next day all hell broke loose, and the thing is I should have seen it coming. I hadn't slept better talking to Crystal; instead I just laid there staring at the ceiling, thinking about how things had come down.

At seven I was flat out, and the only way I was going to keep it going was to take a Dr. Raines's white, something I had avoided since the night of Ace's recital.

The pill came on fast, taking me up for a hard-edged, rough ride, and I knew within fifteen minutes that I had to stay away from people. Meaning everybody.

But that's the evil in Dr. Raines's pills. Even when you know you're going around the bend, you can't help yourself. You want to talk to people, even if it's just to cut them up.

I started on Ace at the breakfast table when he mentioned he needed money for his music teacher, Joe Lawrence.

"He'll get it when I get ready to pay it," I said, ripping a piece of toast in half and stuffing it into my mouth.

"Hey," Ace said, "we owe the guy three back payments. He's not a millionaire, you know."

"Yeah, well tell him he can come over here and pick his money off our tree out back . . . Hell, we got so much to spare, tell him to bring friends."

"God, Dad, what'sa matter with you? He gave me the lessons. We owe him."

"Red," Wanda said as she slid an omelette onto my plate, "Joe Lawrence has to eat too. He's got a right to ask."

"Yeah, I know that," I said, turning on her. "I'm not a god-damned moron, you know?"

"Hey, nobody said you were," Ace said. "I mean, it's embarrassing for me to go in there and ask him to keep giving me lessons when I don't pay him."

"Is that right?" I said, suddenly thinking of Crystal leaving for Miami. I had an exact mental image of her behind the wheel of a U-Haul and driving down the highway, leaving me standing there in the snow.

"You think you got problems? You think that's embarrassing? How about working like a nigger every fucking day down at the parking lot? You think that's a party?"

"I know, Dad," Ace said. "It's just that I'm worried about losing Joe. He told me that if we didn't pay soon, he'd have to drop me."

"He did?" I said, jumping up from the table, though I knew I was acting like a fool. But Dr. Raines was sending electricity through my veins. I didn't want to hold it back any longer. I didn't want to cool it. Let it come down now. Let it blow down the house, that black poison from my mouth.

"Maybe I ought to go over there and talk to him some. Maybe he wouldn't be so anxious to drop his best student, the two-faced asshole."

That sent Ace out of his chair. And I knew it would, God help me, I knew it.

"Great, Dad. Be a big man. Go over and break Joe's hands why don't you? That's just what we need."

"You think I couldn't?" I said. "You think I couldn't? Fucking fancy hot-shit college-boy guitar teacher."

"Red," Wanda said, grabbing me by the arm and spinning me around. "What's wrong with you? He's a friend of ours."

"Goddamned whimp," I said. "Goddamned whimps run the fucking city, whole fucking world, you hear me."

Ace looked at Wanda and backed off from me.

"You're crazy, Dad. You're out of your mind."

"Yeah," I said, "I'm crazy . . . crazy as shit!"

I threw my napkin down on the table, spilling Ace's glass of juice.

"Now look what you've done," Wanda said. "Goddamn it, Red, get ahold of yourself."

She was right, I knew it. I had to stop it, but it was too late. The spring had snapped, and I was letting loose my parts all over the house. I could feel my arms pumping full of blood, my eyes exploding, and I wanted to waste it all, don't look back.

"Fuck Joe Lawrence," I said. "And the horse he rode in on."

"Screw you, Dad," Ace said. "He's my friend . . . Yeah, but you're a big shot. Why don't you go get drunk, and you and Dog can beat him up. You asshole!"

He turned and walked out of the kitchen, and I wanted to go for him then, turn him around and slap his face, and then suddenly I felt like I had to rip down the shelves we'd so carefully built into the kitchen wall. Rip them down, throw them away. Throw it all away . . . Burn it, axe it, kill all that's left.

"Red," Wanda said. "Did you take one of those goddamned pills?"

I turned and looked at her, wild-eyed. She knew about the pills. Of course, of course she did.

"No," I said. "What you been doing, spying on me or what?"

"Red, I'm telling you, don't go into work like this. Go back to bed . . . Red, listen to me."

"Don't worry about me, Wanda," I said. "I can handle it. I can handle all the shit they got to give."

"Red, you're sweating. God, Red, look at you."

I turned toward her and looked at her, and the pill lifted me out of myself, and I saw her there in front of me like a stranger. A ghost boarder in my home of strangers.

"Good-bye," I said, laughing. "See you after I get back from the office."

"Red, wait."

But I was headed for the door. There was something turning inside me, something old and savage, a hand gripping a throat. It didn't much matter whose.

I had to walk three blocks through the slush and could feel myself losing control, all of the pressures beating against me from the inside as though there were a cage of screaming monkeys trapped inside my body, trying to punch their way through the bars.

I was only a block away from the lot when I saw Dog. He was standing on the corner with Jackie Gardner, Jackie with his long, thin hair combed straight back like greasy pasta. Wearing his short leather jacket and old high-top tennis shoes, and Dog there in his ancient N-1 jacket, his arms wrapped around the lamppost. Just for a second, with the pill working inside of me, making everything shuttery and blazing bright, just for a second it was like we were all kids again, standing on the corner, laughing and getting ready to go off to a dance up at Patterson Park, just three young neighborhood guys hitting the streets . . .

Then I saw the bandage on the other side of Dog's head, his two-day stubble, and the gone look in his smile. Jackie Gardner stumbled against him and gave his little sad laugh. Jackie Gardner, who I hadn't seen since he told me about Billy Bramdowski.

Dog brought out the bottle of Maryland Rye to his lips. Some of the liquor dribbled down his chin.

"Hey, Red," he said. "Hey, babe, what's happening?"

"Dogger," I said, trying to cool myself down. But my voice sounded like an old, scratched 78.

"Hey, look who it isn't," Jackie Gardner said. "You come along the right time, Red. Just the right time."

He took the bottle and thrust it in front of him, smiling with one side of his thin mouth. One of his teeth was missing, and he gave that tired little laugh again.

"None for me, boys," I said, trying to sound casual but suddenly wanting that liquor more than breath.

"What's the matter, Red, you too fucking good to drink with us?" Dog said, putting his big hand on Jackie Gardner's shoulder.

"Too fucking good," Jackie Gardner said. "The guy is too fucking good."

"Hey, I'm on my way to work, okay?"

"Yeah," Dog said, "don't want to get caught drinking and driving."

Jackie Gardner hesitated a second while that seeped into his brain, then he opened his thin mouth and let out a little belch of a laugh.

"Drinking and fucking driving on the fucking parking lot. Fucking funny, man, that is fucking funny."

"Yeah, you guys are a riot," I said. "Too bad Ted Mack ain't on the tube anymore."

Jackie hesitated again and slapped his knee.

"Ted Mack . . . Ted Fucking Mack."

He opened his mouth and squeezed up his slitty eyes as though he were in convulsions, but no sound came out.

"Look, I gotta go. Glad to see you up, Doggie."

Dog looked at me dead-faced, and for a moment I got ready to take a shot in the back of the neck as I went by. But he let me pass. When I was ten feet away, though, I heard him say, "See you later, Jackie. I gotta talk to Red a minute." Then he was calling my name and walking toward me fast.

"Hey," Jackie Gardner said, "we going pussy hunting downa block or what?"

But Dog didn't answer him, and I saw Jackie open both his arms and then slowly slide down the lamppost, holding his bottle with both hands.

"Jackie's looking good," I said to Dog, which wasn't what I wanted to say at all.

"Hey, since when do you put down Jackie Gardner? He's a pal."

Dog stood there next to me, looking down on me as though he wanted to hug me or break my face.

"He's a good guy, 'at's the truth," Dog said. Then he grabbed my collar and shook me hard.

"Dog, Dog, hold on."

"Red," he said. "You think I'm a piece of shit out here, right?"

"No, Dog, just take it easy . . . Let go of me."

He turned me around and stared down at the freezing sidewalk.

"You want to know why I'm out here drinking like a goddamned bum?"

"Yeah, if you want to tell me."

"It's Carol, man. She's definitely fucking Dickie Nellis. But little Dickie's going to lose his dick, you hear me?"

He looked at me wide-eyed, his teeth clenched together, steam snorting from his nostrils like a bull.

"That's not true, Dog, I'm telling you, I know Carol."

He shut his eyes and put his right arm on my shoulder. But this time he sagged against me and gave out a low moan.

"I had this dream this morning, Red. I had my daddy's old shotgun, and I walked into my house, and it was all cold and blue in there, and there was Carol and the girls with Dickie Nellis. He was sitting there at the head of the table, and there was all this food, Red. Turkey and stuffing and shit, and it was Christmas, and there were presents everywhere, and I aimed the gun at them, Red . . . and blew them away. Oh shit!"

He looked down at me, and the tears came rolling down his cheeks, and I grabbed him and held on to his arms.

"Listen," I said, hearing a screaming voice in my own head, "it's not true, Dog. You know Carol. It's not true."

He shook his head slowly, and his breath came hard.

"But it is. You know why I'm out here? Because I'm afraid if I go back to the house, I might get out the gun and really do it."

"No, no, Doggie," I said. "You got to calm down. It's only a dream."

"You think so?"

"Yeah, I'm sure of it."

Dog's jaw hung open like somebody had busted the hinges. He nodded slowly.

"A man can't help what he dreams, isn't that so, Red?"

"Yeah, that's right. That's it."

"But maybe it's a sin to dream something like that. Maybe I oughta go to the church and see the father."

"That's right," I said, squeezing his arm. "That's a good idea."

"Go see the father uppa church," he said. "Hey, Red, how come you don't call the Dog up anymore?"

"The last time I was over you bounced me out," I said, trying for a smile.

"That was bullshit. You know that, Red. I just been feeling crazy. Nothing to do. You're lucky you got a job."

"Yeah," I said.

"You wouldn't have thought things were going to get like this," Dog said. "You would have never been able to predict it."

"Dog, I gotta get to the garage."

"I know, man. Listen, I'm going to go up and see the father and tell him that dream, that's the right thing to do, isn't it, Red?"

I smiled at him and gave his neck a squeeze.

"Yeah," I said. "That'll make you feel better."

"We're still friends," Dog said.

"We always will be."

"Shit . . . I know that. You're my buddy. I'm going down the kennel later. See Sadie. Maybe take the kids."

He squeezed my arm then and smiled at me through his great-gapped teeth.

"We gotta stick together, Red. You know? I just gotta find something I can do. You hear anything, let me know."

"I will, Doggie," I said.

"Yeah, okay . . . Hey, I feel better. It's just that I don't know what the fuck to do. You know what I mean? I mean, what the fuck do you do against this?"

I had thought he was calmed down, but I could see it rising in him again, the panic, the fear, and suddenly I had to get away from him. I was afraid it would spread to me, and with the pill pumping through me and the garage facing me, I couldn't handle it.

"Dog," I said. "Go up to the church. I'll call you later, okay?"

"Yeah, sure. Listen, Red, I got to tell you something, all right?"

"Sure," I said.

"I love you, you son of a bitch. You know that?"

"Yeah," I said, his words cutting through me so I could hardly breathe. "I know, Dog."

He turned away from me and walked down the street. Jackie Gardner slumped up against the filthy pile of blackened snow. The bottle lay at his feet.

When I hit the garage I was covered with sweat, and I saw Leroy mopping up the water that had dribbled down the entrance from the night before.

"Hey, Leroy," I said, "what's happening?"

"Nothing. You the latest."

I went into the office, turned up the heat, and sat down behind the gray metal desk. I told myself to do my paperwork, let the pill ride me over the rough spots, but the image of Dog out there in the snow, rheumy-eyed and half dead, kept flipping through my mind. That and Jackie Gardner in the street, and Ace thinking I was such an asshole, and Crystal leaving, and the way Wanda had made love to me. Like she was already gone and making it with a stranger, hard and hot, and who gives a shit?

Why was it like this? Was it the world or my own swollen pride?

I shut my eyes and rubbed my forehead, told myself to stop thinking about anything but my job. Get the pissant paperwork done before the mob of guys started coming in to get their cars.

But the pill kept flashing the pictures on-off on-off in my head. I wanted to slow it down, cut it out, but those photos were like a deck of cards which kept being dealt faceup over and over again. No way to stop them.

Sweat poured down my face, soaked my underarms through, and my heart beat wildly, jumping, starting, like an engine in some old wrecker. My throat was dry and stayed that way, even though I drank five Cokes.

I could feel that little man behind my eyes again, with his pinchers, pulling my skin tighter and tighter until the bones would break through and all I'd be was a naked, rotten skull.

It was then that our customers came in, and I saw them like a ghost looks at the living, standing there in front of me in their new winter coats, their polished shoes, and their sharp haircuts, and suddenly I wanted to grab one of them and scream "I'm still alive. I'm still fucking alive, you asshole, you hear me?" and this impulse became so strong that I said nothing for fear of not being able to control my tongue.

I knew they could see and, worse, smell my speed sweat. I knew they were laughing at the way my hair was matted to my head. Some guys I knew from Patterson, who had hated me for being the BMOC, guys like Steve Standowski, who had never been shit at basketball but had become a local lawyer. Though he didn't say a word (because he knew I could still take his head off), I could feel the happiness my misery gave him.

I got his midnight-blue Chrysler for him, and he handed me a fifty-cent tip.

When he got in I wanted to slam the door on his left leg, and it took all the rest of my willpower not to.

Which was too bad, because that was when Martin came in. Jake Martin was a financial guy from Washington. He had bought out a friend of mine down the plant, Terry O'Connell, who had moved his whole family down to El Paso to try and get work in the computer business. Martin wasn't a bad guy, just ordinary, pushy, trying hard to act and talk like big money. He was fixing up Terry's house so he could rent it to the new lawyers in the neighborhood for three times the old rates. And damn if he wouldn't get it too.

Only this morning was his unlucky day. The sight of him made me think of a time he'd come up the summer league and was playing on my team against Ace. Now Ace could eat him up around the basket, but two years ago he was still just finding his natural abilities, and Martin had elbowed him and pushed him and hooked him all afternoon until Ace complained. Martin had told him something like "Hey, kid, this is basketball, not the senior prom," which had caused me to say that if he didn't want the ball stuffed up his ass he might not talk like that to my kid.

It was all playground bullshit, and I'd thought nothing more of it. Until now. Now, with that dealer laying out those pictures in my head, and with the sound of the dripping water magnified a hundred times, and with Dog's dead face staring in my own, I could feel an anger like a flash flood sweeping through me.

Martin should have known, should have sensed it. But he was on a tear himself that morning. He started right in about his car.

"Baker," he says. "I came out of here last night, and when I got home my battery was worn down. Had to get it jump started this morning. You know why it was worn down?"

I was so close to exploding that I didn't even answer, I just shook my head.

"It was worn down because you or Leroy, I don't know which, was listening to the radio on it. You know why I know that, because I had it on an easy-listening station, WBAL, and when I got back last night it was moved over to the rock and roll station, so I know you guys were playing it. That hot shot at the gas station cost me twenty dollars today, and I don't like throwing money down the toilet. If that ever happens again, I'm going to report you to Mr. Morris, and you'll be out of work, you understand?"

"I don't think I heard you right, Martin," I said.

He moved toward me. Though he was a big guy, he moved pretty well. Even draped in his camel's hair coat.

"I said you pull that shit with my radio again and I'm going to talk to Morris. He and I are pretty good friends, in case you don't know."

I could see Leroy behind me, starting to move forward fast, and I told myself not to say a word or to just apologize. That was all he wanted.

But it didn't come out that way.

"You know, Martin," I said, "I been meaning to tell you this for a while, so this seems as good a time as any. You really are an original."

He looked a little shocked by that and tensed up his square jaw.

"I mean, you're the original vacuum around which the first asshole was created."

"You piece of shit," he said.

Then he swung at me. It might have been a pretty good punch if he hadn't had on that heavy coat. As it was, I was able to dodge it easily and move into him. I had raised my fist when I felt Leroy grabbing me from behind and pulling me back toward the office.

"Cool it, Red. Cool it, baby."

Martin was gasping for breath, and he looked at me with his little tense eyes. I tossed him his keys, and he was so surprised that he caught them.

"Okay, Baker," he said. "That's it. You're through."

"Get the fuck out of here before I decide to use your head for a mop," I said.

"You . . . you . . . nothing," he said. "You're a nothing. Mr. Hotshot. Well, we'll see. We'll see all right."

He jumped into his Mercedes and squealed out of the parking garage, laying a three-foot-long patch of rubber.

I turned to Leroy and shook my throbbing head.

"Thanks," I said. "You probably saved me a jail sentence and a nice lawsuit."

Leroy shook his head and smiled softly.

"Been nice working with you, Red," he said. "Maybe we be seeing each other up the summer league. 'Cause soon as that shit get back to Morris, you gone."

"How long do you figure it will be before Morris gets here?"

"I give you till lunch maybe. If he tied up with business and the lame can't get him on the phone."

"Yeah," I said, suddenly filled with relief, the picture slowing down in my mind, knowing that I was sinking but almost glad of it now. Let it come down over me like some black tent, but let it happen in the sunlight and not down in this white concrete tomb.

I got down to the Paradise about five. The two hours between the time I was fired and the time I pulled into the parking lot I spent at Horton's, drinking myself into a state of what they used to call (somewhere) "wild abandon."

The minute I walked into the Paradise and saw Dixie Lee dancing on stage and old Henry down at the end of the bar, eating his sub, and Crystal sitting next to him, smoke coming from her nostrils, I felt another chunk of burden break away from me, fly off into the stale air.

I walked right up to Crystal, who had on her spangled, tight-cut, two-piece work outfit, and I gave her a big drunken kiss.

"Red," she said. "What the hell are you doing here?"

"Waiting to talk to my broker," I said.

"No, really? Come on now. Tell me."

"Really? Really, I got fired. Canned. Turned loose. I'm now an ex-parking lot attendant."

"Oh God, you must be really down. Let me buy you a drink."

"Sure," I said. "But I got to tell you I feel fine. Hey, you look great."

"Red, are you all right?"

"Yeah," I said, motioning her over to our usual booth. She slid in next to me, and I put my arm around her and kissed her sweet-smelling ear.

"Red, you look drunk. Don't do anything crazy. God, I'm so sorry."

"No, no," I said, feeling my lungs rushed with air. "You don't understand. It's all right. It really is . . . You see, while I was driving down here, I was trying to figure out why I don't feel crazy or sad or desperate or anything, and I figured it all out, babe."

"Oh, Red, you're just drunk, baby. Come over and sit with me."

"No wait," I said, feeling the pill and the booze and my stone-cold fear make me babble on with no more idea of what I was going to say than a lunatic.

"You see, I figured it out. When shit gets to a certain point, when it's all coming down on you, I mean, then you either go mad or bust things up, like Doggie, or you just get happy. Because you're pushed up against the wall, Crys, and you think it's real, but suddenly you see that it was just something you made up. You don't have to take this shit, you don't have to live this way, you just thought you did . . . and it was thinking it, thinking you had to be some kind of guy . . . that was what was getting you down."

"Oh, Red, you don't know what you're saying," Crystal said. "Don't go on like this, don't."

"You want to go to Florida, Crys, I'm with you," I said. " 'Cause I tried it their way, you see, I tried it and it don't work, and there's nothing I can fucking do about it, you see. Want to get in a nice, big, white car and drive down there where the sun never quits. Get the hell out of this town. It's dead here, Crys . . . You know what I was thinking on the way over here? Baltimore ain't even a town at all. The whole town, it's really a hospital. People from other planets are the doctors, staring at us with one big eye through these giant microscopes . . . You know what I'm saying?"

I hoped she did, because I didn't have a clue. I was feeling all common sense drift away, gently, like a puff of smoke from my old train garden set. All my plans and brains floating away, and inside I felt either a scream or a new happiness which was impossible to explain. As though I were an inflatable doll, a Red Baker doll, all pumped up with air, and was taking off, flying over the tar-paper row-house roofs.

"Red, Red, calm down," Crystal said. "I'm worried about you, honey."

She held my hand, but it wasn't attached to my body anymore. I was flying, flying, no job, no hope and crazy in love with her eyes, her lips, her breasts. I needed all of her every single second.

"We're gonna live on the beach, Crys. We're gonna live like gypsies. I wasn't ever meant to be no family man anyway. You know that, you've always known everything about me."

And suddenly, right then, hovering over the bar, weightless and senseless, I believed whatever came from my mouth. I knew, knew that she really did understand me in ways that Wanda and Ace never could. In ways that I never could. Crystal, Crystal, Crystal . . . she was always there reading my mind, waiting for me to break out of my dead skin and fly with her to the golden beach . . .

"Red, Red, you're on those pills again."

But I was kissing her then and holding on to her, and the music was blasting out "Satisfaction," and this time I really did like old Mick Jagger, but he was wrong. There was satisfaction in everything in the world, there was a true happiness born of fear and terror, and it was flooding through me, filling me up, and I meant every word I said and forgot them as they roared out of my mouth.

"I love you, Crystal, I really do. We can make it all right. We can. I've missed you so much, baby."

"I've missed you too, but I want you to calm down now, hon. We'll spend the night together, and I'll take care of you, and you'll calm down. It's going to be all right."

"But that's exactly the point. It's *already* all right. I know what I want now, Crystal. I want to be with you . . . and maybe Dog . . . We get Dog to go with us . . . Just gimme another little shot of that Wild Turk, thank you, honey . . . Heading on down to Florida . . . Everything is fine."

I touched her electric skin, and she looked clean through my eyes. I had to have her now . . .

"Red, God, I love you. I'll take care of you, honey."

"I know you will. Come with me now, Crystal. Okay?"

"Red, I have to dance in twenty minutes."

"Okay, okay, just come with me, please. Outside for a minute."

And then we were walking across the cold parking lot, and I opened the door to my Chevy, and we climbed into the backseat, and I reached for her legs, and she was crying and saying, "Red, Red, I'll take care of you. Not like this, Red," but I had to have her, and I was pulling her leotard down and put my mouth on her nipples, and she was crying out and grabbing my cock in my pants and then unzipping them, and I peeled off her spangles, and she put her legs over my back, and I wasn't gentle, just put it inside her, ramming it in, and she was screaming, "Oh God, Red, Red . . . Red, wait, wait," and arching her tight little hips up, and then the world began to spin around wildly, and I came inside her and she came, both of us crying out and clinging to one another, crazy as hell. And in love some too.

Then I felt my head begin to ache, and this black bile started coming up in my throat, and I was covered with sweat, and I buried my head in her breasts and held on to her for a long time.

"Red," she said, "I've got to get back in there. Will you wait for me?"

"Sure," I said. "You know it, honey. Yeah."

We pulled back on our clothes and walked back inside, and she kissed me and ducked under the bar door just as Vinnie Toriano was starting to scream out her name.

"Hey, Baker, you keeping my girls from working?"

"No way, Vinnie," I said. "No way, babe. Here, let me buy you a drink. My buddy. Big Vin."

Henry looked up from his submarine sandwich and let out a piggy squeal.

"Hey, I don't believe this, Red Baker buying Vinnie a drink?"

"Yeah," Vinnie said, staring at me like a leper. "What's this, cartoons?"

"No way," I said, soaring again. "No way . . . Why shouldn't I buy my old pal a drink?"

And just then, just that second I meant it, because it seemed to me that it was right here in the body of Vinnie Toriano that I had at last found the truth. The truth that the eyes behind the knotholes down in my knotty pine basement had been trying to make me understand. That there was no law but what you made, there was no fortune but what you took, there was no love, no truth, no honor, no loyalty that could stand up to the terror of dying poor and alone.

It seemed to me then, drunk and staggering, that Vinnie was some kind of devil's priest, because he knew these simple facts long ago in his own reptile way. He had the wisdom of the sewer, the long rat-filled tunnel that was his church. And far from hating him, it now became clear to me that he had everything to teach me.

For I had bought a whole boatload of lies, and even as I raised hell and drank and saw Dr. Raines and ran around on Wanda, I really still believed in all that Boy Scout bullshit of my youth.

Now, standing there next to fat, greasy Vinnie, it occurred to me that I had been what my daddy used to call a "pure fool," and the thought about doubled me over with laughter.

I had believed that if you worked hard and kept yourself and your family together, it was going to pay off.

And worse, I had believed that it was not only going to pay off in this world but in the next one too. That was the greatest laugh of all.

Because standing there, looking at Vinnie, I was certain that he was God, him and all the men like him, bigger, stronger men who just went out and took what they wanted.

It was a fat, gold-chained greaseball who ran Baltimore, which was the only world I was likely to see.

I laughed wildly, and Vinnie stood there staring at me, half curious and half fearful that I was going to turn and pop him.

"Hey, Vin," I said, "take it easy . . . take it easy, babe. It's all right. It's all right. I gotcha now, Vin. I hear you."

"You been hanging around with Donahue too long, Baker. You're as crazy as he is."

"*You* liking Vinnie," Henry said in his high falsetto and pounding the bar. "Well, now this is a day I'll never forget."

"Shut the fuck up, Henry," Vinnie said. "You don't know anything."

Henry's mouth formed a small O, and then he sucked in his lips and looked down the bar.

"That's it," I said, suddenly feeling a great rush of liquor and food coming up in my throat. "You're the boss, big Vin."

Then I turned and walked through the wet canvas curtains and out the front door into the cold Baltimore night. The snow was coming down harder now, driving on the wind, and I staggered around behind the Paradise, into the weeds, and hung on to the freezing red drainpipe. My stomach heaved once, and I puked out my guts as the soft snow fell gently on my neck.

When I was done I slid into the parking lot and looked at my old Chevy as though it were at the far end of a telescope. I weaved crazily over the hard gravel, hearing the rocks crunch under my heavy boots.

I put the car in reverse and thought of Crystal waiting in there for me, remembered dimly some big promise I'd made about hanging around after the show, but it was no use, because I had to move.

I was filled with some strange new happiness that shot through me like a live hot coil of steel. It made me jerk and strut like a painted puppet.

I couldn't wait. Not for Crystal. Not for anyone. I couldn't wait ever again for anything.

I had to move, go places, make new friends.

God help those who got in my way.

I staggered everywhere that night. Up and down Broadway, in and out of Bertha's, and Ruby's, and Ledbetter's, and the Acropolis, where I fell in love with Athena the Belly Dancer, knew that we were right for each other, knew it as sure as I knew my own face, and forgot it by the third drink.

There were friends everywhere, new friends, great and fast friends, hands clasped, and people pounding my back, and songs sung, and promises made, and a little black man named Shorty who was my sidekick and told me as we weaved down the snow-filled, booze-lit street that he "loved me like a brother, and if you fall down I won't roll you, Red, roll most white mutherfuckers, but not you, Red." And I thanked him and told him I wanted to introduce him to Vinnie, he had to meet Vinnie, the man with all the answers. "Vinnie who, Red?" he said as we fell into Johnny Jack's Circus and watched a businessman try and climb the neon-pink stage to get at a fifty-five-year-old hooker named Lana Parr. "Vinnie who, Red? Where does the man live?"

"Everywhere," I said. "He lives everyfuckingwhere, but I didn't know it until tonight. You see that?"

"What's his gig, Red?"

"He don't work. He gives you and me the answers," I said, and then I fell down in the bar, but the bar floor turned icy and cold, and when I opened my dead, burned-down eyes, I was in the gutter out in the blowing, burning ice storm. Shorty was still there, holding my head in his hands and saying, "Red, man, you shouldn't get this way."

He helped me to my feet; then it was fading on me, all the new-found happiness, all the bright thoughts, and all that was left was shame and fear and anger rising from my stomach to my chest, like some belching blast of heat.

And then I was hanging over the Chevy's steering wheel like my old man with his cataracts, sideswiping parked cars in the pink-gray dawn and finally finding a parking space a block away from home.

A walk down Aliceanna Street, past the row houses, past the Formstone fronts, and the marble steps, and the screen doors with Olde English initials on them, and the *Sun* papers in their frozen plastic sacks, lying there like ticking bombs.

And then into my own house, so fucked and frozen, fumbling with the locks. Trying to move quietly, get upstairs to my bed, all the great thoughts of the night just one long revolting blur of colors.

Maybe Vinnie was right. Maybe I had become Dog. But he had never understood what happened to him.

Not that I understood this shit.

Instead of going right upstairs, I fell back for a second on the old black-and-white couch, and I could feel the shapes of things. The way the shag rug was like a dead animal beneath my feet, the way the television reflected a weird, distorted image of me, my big hands hanging between my long, wobbly legs. The way the house smelled, tight and closed and dusty, the way a plant hanging in the dining room looked like a crawling, unknown thing.

And then Wanda's voice coming not from upstairs at all but from the kitchen, where of course she had been sitting for hours.

"Red, is that you?"

"Yeah."

"Are you drunk?"

"Yeah, oh yeah."

"Can you make it into the kitchen?"

"Sure."

I rolled off the couch, half kneeling, then stood straight up and walked by the plant to meet her gaze. She sat at the kitchen table in her pink robe, her hair down, combed and clean. Her eyes were soft, forgiving in a final way.

"Red, I don't want to argue with you. I don't need a big scene. I know you got fired today. I knew you'd come back like this. I just want you to understand that this is it. It's over. Ace and I are leaving tomorrow. We'll be living with Ruth for a while."

I leaned on the door, shocked by the whiteness of the refrigerator. It looked like a great shining block of ice.

"No way. No way that's happening."

"It is, Red. I can't live like this. Don't throw a scene. You'll only hurt Ace."

I stood still and said nothing but felt the coil of live wire start up in my fingers, shoot through my arms, legs, chest. Felt its beat in my expanding heart.

"No way," I said. "No way. We're hanging in there, Wanda."

"Red," she said. "We're through."

"You got it wrong. I love you, Wanda. I love Ace."

I had started to sob, and the first tears sent a fury through me.

"I know you do, Red. But it's not enough. Please, don't scream and get crazy. I don't think I can stand it just now."

"You just walk?"

"No, I been here nineteen years. I don't just walk. I remember when it meant something."

"But Ace," I said. "Ace can't make it without me."

She nodded her head, just as calmly as an actress. I knew she had rehearsed this scene for years. She didn't even need me there to say the lines.

"He loves you, Red, but it's only because he's still young and doesn't know what a liar you are. How little you really care for him."

"That's bullshit," I said. "You've said just about enough."

I moved toward her and saw her eyes get big, and she put her hand to her lovely lips, and then I pushed her back against the stove, saying, "You don't leave. You don't pull this shit," and somehow she fell. Fell and cracked the back of her head, and I saw her slump forward, and I held my breath and called her name softly, and then she was up off the floor like a wild, wounded child, driving right into me, her long nails clawing at my eyes.

"You bastard. You bastard. You threw us away. You bastard."

She was hitting me then, and I could feel the scratch marks down my cheeks, and I slapped her hard in the face, and then I felt somebody jumping on my back, smashing me in the neck. I turned and threw my elbow back wildly and caught Ace right in the face and knocked him up against the dining room table, and he got up and started to come at me again but then stopped and started crying, and I said, "Son, I'm sorry, I didn't know . . ." but it was too late. He looked at me as though he were staring at a corpse. Then he shook his head and walked in the kitchen and helped his mother to a chair.

"We move tomorrow, Red," Wanda said.

"I didn't mean it," I said. "Look, I've been trying . . . You know that."

"You ever hit me or my mother again, Dad," Ace said, "I'll kill you."

He sounded like me when he said that. They held on to each other, and though I wanted to go to them, I turned and walked into the living room and sat down heavily in the old recliner and didn't say a word.

By midmorning they had both moved out. I even offered to help them and kept talking about how I'd come around and check up on them later, but neither of them would hardly talk to me.

Wanda kept moving fast, kept her eyes down to the floor, wouldn't say a thing. I knew I'd better leave her alone.

But I caught Ace looking at me a couple of times, and when I finally got ahold of him packing in his room, he was shaking and about ready to fall apart.

I leaned in the doorway, looked at him, and felt my hands tremble.

"Damn it, son, you know I love you. You can't just leave."

He said nothing but threw his underwear and colored T-shirts into his bag.

"Ace," I said, my voice cracking. "Listen to what I'm saying, son."

He stopped then and stared at me, so clear-eyed and in such pain that it was hard to meet his gaze.

"I do listen to you, Dad. I've always listened to you. The first thing you taught me was that it's not what a man says so much as what he does."

He began putting his T-shirts in the bag again, and I felt as though I was burning up from the inside.

"That's true, son," I said.

"I had a game last night, Dad. But you were too busy running around with that whore, Crystal."

There was an opening in his tone, so I went and sat down on the bed, watched him slowly drop his rolled socks into his grip.

"Look, son. I mean what I said. It *is* what a man does. But sometimes a man doesn't do the right thing, and if you can see his point of view some . . ."

He turned away from me, looking out over the backyard at the frozen mulberry tree. Icicles hung from its bowed branches.

"You mean because you got fired? Is that your excuse for everything?"

I didn't say anything but sat still, trying to calm my breath.

"No," I said. "It's not my excuse. I don't have an excuse for missing your game. And I can't explain to you about Crystal either. Things happen sometimes to a man, things he didn't count on, like getting older, like being broke, and if they hadn't happened all together, or at a certain time, he would have handled them better . . . but just now . . ."

My voice trailed off, and I dropped my head. I didn't want to cry in front of him, didn't want to beg.

When I finally got myself collected enough to look up, Ace was crying and shaking his head.

"I know it's hard for you, Dad. But it's hard on Mom too, and she hangs in there."

I wanted so badly to reach out to him, to take him in my arms like I did when he was a kid, pat his head and tell him it was going to be all right.

"Dad," he said, the tears streaming down his face. "You used to be *somebody* in this neighborhood. Look at you now."

"Ace," I said, but I didn't know what else to say. Was I supposed to tell him I had become nothing because of the parking lot. Because of the gray hairs in my head, because of the fears that set a man straight up in bed at five in the morning?

"And last night. You hit me and Mom. I never thought you could . . ."

He cried quietly, and I reached out for his arm, but he snapped it back and grabbed his suitcase off the bed. He started on an end run around me, and when I got up quickly he jerked as though I were going to hit him again. The fear in his eyes tore through me, and I backed away.

Slowly, I reached out to him and squeezed his shoulder.

"I know you got to go now, son," I said. "But I'm going to get all this taken care of. I mean it. We're going to all be a family again, Ace. I swear that to you."

He shut his eyes and nodded his head, and I pulled him to me and felt his whole body shudder.

"Ace," I said. "God, I'll make it up to you, son."

He clung to me then, like a little boy, saying, "Dad, Dad," over and over again, and then he stopped and pushed me away.

"Dad, I got to go. Mom can't make it alone. She needs me."

"I know," I said.

He walked past me then and quickly down the steps. I heard Wanda say something about getting a trunk, then I went to the window and saw them piling their luggage into Ruth's car. The snow was falling on them both, covering them up. Ace walked around the side of the car and opened the door for his mother. Then he turned and looked up at me. His eyes were blank, hollow now, as though he were beyond tears.

Then he walked around the driver's side, got in, and slowly they drove away.

I don't know a fancy way to put it. Just that it killed me.

Except that I wasn't dead. In fact I felt too alive, like a screaming note held on the guitar. For a week I walked through the house, staring at the dying hanging plant, opening and shutting the refrigerator to get my beer, tossing down my whiskey by 10 A.M. I would sit in a chair and try to think which way to go, where to look next for a job, but the electric fear and strangeness of all things familiar kept me prisoner in the house. Nothing looked or felt the same without them there. The smallest memory—Ace spinning his ball or Wanda smiling at me from the backyard while she hung out the wash—was like a surgeon's scalpel digging into my brain and heart.

I avoided listening to the radio at all or any of my old records for fear they would start the memory machine rolling out of control. I grew wary of Ace's room, shut it off, and avoided even looking at the door itself as I walked down the stairs.

The cellar of my house was a haunted place. All those eyes down there, watching me, judging me, and when I tried to get out of my own head, by calling Dog, his alcoholic babble would frighten me into hanging up.

I tried calling Ruth two or three times, but Wanda wouldn't talk to me. And Ace was always out. I wanted badly to go up to basketball, take him aside, and win him over, but I didn't dare it for fear of what I might do if he resisted.

So for the first week I stayed home, watching television, getting loaded until I was senseless. Afraid to go out to look for a job and not knowing where to go in any case.

At last I started up on unemployment again, but by the middle of the week most of the check was gone for booze.

By the eighth day I no longer moved from the bedroom. I woke up, reached for what was left of last night's bottle, and lay there in the stinking dirty sheets, watching "The Honeymooners," "Let's Make a Deal," "Leave It to Beaver," "General Hospital," anything that came on.

I say "watched them," but that doesn't really get it because they were really nothing more than part of my dreams. Staying there in bed for twelve and sixteen hours at a time, I never really woke up at all but lost myself in dreams of my youth, games I scored baskets in against Southern, and days walking Ace in the park, and Wanda and I making love out in the country by Pretty Boy Dam. Then when the memories would start to fade and I would realize the house was empty, that down there on the table there was nothing but a bowl of waxed fruit, I would fade into the TV shows, look at those old, comfortable characters, and pretend to myself that it wasn't any different now. Ralph Kramden and Ward Cleaver and Monty Hall and me, all the same guys, in the same room, with the wrinkled bedclothes, the twisted sheets, the quilt thrown on the floor.

I don't know which day it was I dropped the bottle of booze as I fell back into my sleep. But when I awoke I had to take a piss so badly I leaped out of the bed and stepped onto two pieces of glass. The pain shot through me so deeply that it startled me back to life. I looked down at the old hook rug and saw the blood seeping into the floor. I saw the widening red stain and thought of Billy Bramdowski, and then I reached down and picked up the glass and pressed it against my wrist hard, until blood began to squirt out and run down my fingers.

Then I remembered Billy Bramdowski's kid, with Billy's brains all over the garden trowel.

I stared at my room, at the six or seven glasses I'd brought up from the kitchen and the balled Kleenex which hadn't made it to the trash can. At my face in the mirror, heavy, jowled, with a four-day gray-and-black beard. My eyes hollowed out, blackened beneath like some zombie from a horror movie.

The blood kept pouring from my feet, making sticky, thick pools between my toes. I sat down on the bed, ripped a piece of sheet off, and began pulling out the glass.

An hour later I was bandaged up, in my Chevy, and on my way down to the Paradise. It was wrong, but Crystal was the only one left. And if I didn't move from the bedroom, it might have been Ace who found me lying across the bed.

She wasn't there when I arrived, only Henry sitting at the bar, staring into one of his subs.

"Hi ya, Red," he said. "What's happening?"

"Doing real good, Henry. How about yourself?"

"Well, I don't know. Still working down Mona Lisa Pizza. About killing myself. Vinnie's putting more stuff in there . . . all kinds of sculptures and stuff from Rome . . . got him a beer garden, getting ready for this summer. It's hard, but I ain't complaining. They gimme all the free pizza I can eat. Got this one called a Roman Pizza . . . There's mozzarella and anchovies and . . ."

She came in then, through the back door, but she wasn't alone. There was a young guy with her, with curly black hair and a face like an Italian movie star. He had a tattoo of an anchor on his arm, and a good, strong build. She didn't see me but slipped into "our" booth with him.

Behind me Henry droned on about the pizza, but I just sat there, stunned.

Crystal hugged and kissed the dark-skinned guy, and he ran his long fingers through her hair and kissed her on the ear.

Then she reached down and rubbed her hand on his leg, and I felt myself getting down from the bar.

Henry saw me and suddenly grabbed my wrist.

"Don't, Red, you don't need any more trouble."

I looked at Henry's sad, lopsided face and saw something decent and bright behind his clown's jowls.

I nodded to him and just stood there while the dark-skinned guy kissed Crystal again, walked around past me and out the door. As she waved good-bye to him she saw me, and her hand froze in the air.

"Red, you want to drink one with me?" Henry said. "I got some money."

"No, thanks," I said. "I'm going to talk to Crystal."

"You sure?"

I smiled at him and boxed his ear.

"You're a good ole boy, Hen. Thanks. I'm okay."

He smiled faintly and looked down at his sub.

I walked around the bar, not knowing quite how to hold my body.

"Hi," I said, trying to keep my voice down.

"Hello, Red," she said in a small, hoarse voice. She was pulling off being cool and calm pretty well except for her fingers, which she drummed on the table.

"Mind if I sit down?"

"Sure."

I slid in across from her and stared at her green cat's eyes, at her sweet smooth skin and her lovely open mouth.

"Who was he?" I said.

"Tony. A friend of mine."

"Looks like a real good friend."

She smiled sadly then and ran her right hand back through her short hair. It was a gesture I loved, and it cut me down, blunted my anger.

"Red, I have something to tell you."

"Yeah?"

"Tony and I are going to Miami together. He runs a charter boat down there, and he has some friends in the hotel business. He's going to get me a singing job at the Hilton."

"When are you leaving?"

"Two days. I was going to call you tonight."

"Oh. Thanks."

She looked straight at me, her mouth tightly drawn now, and her green eyes were flat, half closed.

"I couldn't wait forever, Red. I loved you, but that was finished the night you took me out in the car and left me here."

"Crys," I said, my voice breaking. "I'm alone now. My family's gone."

She picked up her drink and sipped it slowly. Then gently she put it down and held my hand.

"Red," she said. "Don't."

"Don't what?"

"Don't lie to me now. I want to remember you as a guy who maybe promised more than he could deliver . . . but who was a lot of fun. That's not the worst way to remember somebody. You lie to me again here, and I'll start thinking of you as just another bum."

"You think I lied all those nights we were together? You think I don't care about you?"

I reached over and grabbed her arm, but like Ace she jerked away from me.

"Red, don't try and get by on your charm. You know what my

daddy used to say—'Walk out while the music's still playing.' Let's leave it at that, hon."

"I love you, Crystal. You know that."

She shut her eyes, and a tear came down her face.

"I got to go on now, Red. Just like old times, huh? I go up and dance, and you slip out. Maybe that's how I'll remember you best, Red. The guy who was always sliding out the door."

"Crystal, things have changed. I need you, baby."

She shook her head and patted the back of my hand.

"You'll get them back, Red. You can't make it without your wife and Ace. Now get out of here before I cry and fuck up my makeup."

She got up and walked away, and looking at her straight, strong back and great legs, and thinking of all the fun we used to have and all our good nights together and how they were finished, made me almost get up and go after her.

But then I remembered Wanda and Ace out there in the snow, packing things into the car, and the way I felt every time either of them walked into the room, and I knew finally that she was right. Without them, though I'd fought against believing it all my life, I was nothing.

I could live without Crystal, although there, just now, watching her go, thinking of her with Tony, it almost seemed unbearable.

But she was right, just as Ace and Wanda were.

I had become nothing, a liar, a nobody.

I had hurt them all, and I'd hurt Crystal too with all my lies and bullshit about us going off to Florida together.

I looked up at her dancing to "Satisfaction" and then, corny gesture though it was, I raised my glass to her and smiled.

She smiled back at me, the tears rolling down her face, and then she strutted toward the other end of the platform. A drunken college kid yelled, "Oh, Crystal, do what you do, baby!" I took one last look at her and headed for the door.

It wasn't until I got to my car that I began to shake, and then I couldn't stop until I'd taken three good hits of rye and held on to the steering wheel like it was a life vest.

Wanda and Ace gone. Crystal gone. Dog, damned near crazy.

Was it all me? Was it my fault? Couldn't any of them see that I had to have money again? There was no chance at doing good, straightening out, no shot at anything unless I had the money to try it.

I started the engine, backed out, and then stopped at a snow-covered phone booth in front of Bud's Bait and Tackle Shop with its boarded-up windows and the old crayoned sign LIVE BAIT half eaten away in the window.

When I got the unemployment office, I had to wait fifteen minutes and keep popping coins into the slot, but finally Miss Motown came on. The booze was pumping through me, and I stammered and slurred my words.

"This is Red Baker. Just called to see if you had anything?"

"Mr. Baker, well as you know, I'm not supposed to discuss this kind of thing over the phone, but I do have something. I think Mr. Hardy discussed it with you. The maintenance job at Harborplace?"

"You mean the trash collector's job?" I said, suddenly wanting to smash the phone against the window.

"Maintenance, Mr. Baker. It includes grass cutting and painting too. It's a pleasant job when the winter breaks, and after all, it's not permanent."

"Okay," I said. "What's it pay?"

"Well, I can't discuss that now, but it's considerably more than unemployment. Are you interested?"

"When do I start?"

"The first of the year. That's about two weeks."

"Okay," I said.

"Does that mean you'll take it?"

"That's what it means."

"Excellent. I think you'll enjoy it."

"Yeah," I said. "Smart career move. Forty-year-old trashman."

"It would help if you could take the job with a positive attitude, Mr. Baker."

"I'm working on it," I said.

I hung up the phone and leaned against the glass for two minutes. Then I found another dime in my pocket and dialed again.

"Hello, fifth precinct."

"Choo Choo," I said.

"Red, that you?"

"Yeah, what you doing for dinner tonight?"

"Well, let me look at my busy calendar. Says here I'm having it with you, maybe eight o'clock at Hausner's. How's that sound?"

"Sounds fine," I said.

"That's good, Red. I always say we don't see enough of each other."

"Tonight," I said and hung up the phone.

My stomach was burning and my knees were weak. I sucked in my breath. It was just a dinner, after all. I was just going to hear what work he had in mind.

I got to Hausner's ten till eight and took a seat at a corner table the waitress said was reserved for Choo Choo. I had been coming to this place all my life and never saw a table reserved before. I ordered a shot of whiskey and a Boh back and told myself for the hundredth time that it was only a meeting . . . I could walk anytime.

All around me people were eating crab cakes, drinking beer, and admiring the paintings. The walls of Hausner's are covered with great art. Stuff like *The Blue Boy,* which is one of Wanda's favorites, and pictures of girls carrying milk cans through green fields someplace in Europe. And one Wanda and Ace and I all liked of a boy, a dog, and a waterfall. I stared at that painting now as the peroxided blond waitress, Daisy, brought me my shot. I tried to put myself in there with the kid, feeling the mud coming up between my toes, the hot sun on my head, knowing I could just drop my rod and reel and jump in the bright pond. It would be fine to be there.

Better than shaking hands with Choo Choo, who was suddenly at my table, wearing his black raincoat, with the collar turned up, his black hair combed straight back on his head, making him look like Sylvester Stallone or somebody who thinks he can box.

"Red," he said, hanging the coat on a hook behind our table. "How you doing, babe?"

"How do you think?"

"Yeah, well in every cloud, as they say. Believe me, I know about how tough it can be. You never know who to trust anymore."

"Listen," I said, leaning over the table. "I appreciate you laying out for dinner, but aren't we being a little obvious?"

Choo Choo smiled at that, then turned and waved Daisy to our table.

"I'll have a shot of Jack Daniel's. You okay, Red?"

"Yeah. Never felt better."

"That's good, hon," the waitress said. "Sooo many people sick

from 'es weather. My own mother has a sick headache all day long.
I'm getting the nuns to say a prayer for her."

Choo Choo winked at me and smiled up at big, wide-faced Daisy.

"You do that," Choo Choo said. "Stick with the faith, hon."

Daisy smiled as if he'd performed magic, and I suddenly thought,
"This is how it works. The war is fought between the Vinnie's and
the Choo Choo's. I'm just a soldier." The thought made me feel
clear-headed, stopped my hands from shaking.

"What were you saying, Red?"

"About this place. Isn't it a little obvious, you and me being seen
together?"

"That's just the point, Red," Choo Choo smiled. "I'm your alibi.
Everybody knows that you and me are pals. So we're establishing
ourselves right here tonight, a couple of pals having dinner. The
night of the job, you and me and Blazek and another guy, Bill Donaldson, are playing poker at my place. You see how we have it figured? I got three citations for bravery in action, and Blazek has
himself a couple. Nobody in the precinct is going to doubt a word we
say."

"I don't know if that makes me feel better or worse," I said,
staring at Choo Choo's blue tie with the Baltimore Colts horseshoes
on it. "I mean, are you figuring we're going to *need* alibis?"

"Red, Red, relax. I'm just making sure every inch of this thing is
covered. There's not a snowball's chance in hell that anything is
going to go wrong. It's like I told you before, it's a walk."

"Okay, but the problem is I don't trust Blazek to know this shit."

"Hey, I'm not saying he's a wild fan of yours. But this is professional. He does what I tell him to, for more reasons than one. I'm not
going into details, but you don't have a thing in the world to worry
about when it comes to him. I own the boy."

Choo Choo smiled and took his drink from Daisy.

"You figure on owning me too?"

Choo Choo laughed out loud at that.

"Red, your whole problem is you don't trust your friends. I would
never put you in a position like that. I want to work with you because you're a class guy, and I know you won't fuck up. Come on,
take it easy, and let's have some dinner."

I nodded my head and ordered imperial crab, coleslaw, and stewed
tomatoes, the best meal I'd had in six months, but when it came I

could barely touch the stuff. I was that spooked. Still, I made an effort to eat. I didn't want Choo Choo getting the idea I couldn't pull this off.

"There's one more question that occurs to me before you lay this out. If Blazek and Donaldson are covering for me, how much do we have to pay them?"

"Let me worry about that too," Choo Cho said, smiling and eating his fried oysters. "Damn, this *is* good food. Come on, Red, dig in."

I worked on my smile and dug in, but my stomach was tied in knots.

"I can tell you this, Red, not one cent of your share is going to them. Let me put it this way. They all owe me favors, and on this job I collect. Does that put your mind to rest?"

"Maybe."

"Look, Red, here's how it works. I came up with this plan. I cased it, and for that I get a third. You and the other guy get a third each. Like I told you before, you should take maybe fifteen thousand dollars out of this. That's five for each of us. And it's a lock. Nothing to it at all. The whole job is going to take maybe an hour."

"Where are you while it's going down?"

"Playing poker with you and the others," Choo Choo said. "God-damn these stewed tomatoes are the best. You know I actually got the recipe out of old man Hausner, went home and cooked them up, but they just didn't taste the same. They've got a touch here, Red. Real class. Have another drink."

"Sure."

We ordered a couple more whiskeys, but I sipped mine slowly. I didn't want to fog over what was left of my judgment.

"Now before I tell you about it, I want to ask you, as my partner, about a couple guys who are candidates to go into this with you. You know them all, and I want you to choose the one you'd feel best with."

"No," I said. "Don't name anybody. I already know who the other guy is going to be."

This set him back a little. He raised his thick eyebrows and cleared his throat and then took a long drag on his smoke.

"Okay, Red. I usually hire all the men, but tell me who you had in mind."

"Dog," I said.

He didn't say anything but ran his tongue around the inside of his mouth and tapped his fingers on the table.

"I don't know, Red. If you would have mentioned his name this time last year, I'd been behind you, one hundred percent, but he's been slipping, slipping bad in the past six months. Every time I see him he's drunk, falling down."

"Dog and me go way back, Choo Choo," I said. "It's him or nobody."

"Don't push me, Red, okay? I just want you to think this over a little. I know he's your best buddy. I know he *used* to be good. Hell, remember the shit we used to pull as kids? Great times. The best. But people change, Red. Dog might not have the nerve for this stuff anymore. You sure you don't want him just for old time's sake?"

"I want him because I know if anything goes wrong, he's there. I'm the one taking the risk here, Choo Choo, and there's nobody you could name who is half the man Dog is."

He nodded and sighed deeply.

"Red, have you approached Dog about this yet?"

"No."

"Then how do you know he'll want in?"

"I know Dog. He'll want in."

"I hope so, Red. All right. I'm going to give you your way on this. I'll tell you why. Because it's so fucking easy. I'm still not sold on Dog, but the way I figure it, all he has to do is keep lookout and drive. And the one thing I know for certain is that he can drive like a son of a bitch."

"Good," I said. "Now what's the job?"

"Mona Lisa Pizza," Choo Choo said, giving me a great big grin, and when I heard that, I couldn't help but smile back.

"I thought you'd like that. I know you and Vinnie aren't exactly asshole buddies."

"You got that right. But that brings up another question. I know Vinnie is selling a lot of pizza dough at that joint, but fifteen thousand dollars seems about seven thousand off. You wouldn't be bullshitting me on the take?"

Choo Choo laughed out loud and held up his drink to salute me.

"I knew I was getting the right man when I asked you. The other guys I had in mind wouldn't even have thought of that. Okay, here's the deal. Vinnie's average take from selling beer and pizza on a good

Sunday is about five to seven thousand dollars. The rest of it is
bookie money. You see, he's got a lock on the football pool. That's
his take, and that's where we make our bread. In fact, that's the
beauty of it. He can't come running down to the police complaining
about a dime of that shit. He's got nowhere to go."

"Nowhere except to his private army of goons," I said. "You know
he'll be breaking down doors."

"Yeah, maybe. But I kind of doubt it. Vinnie's hands are into a lot
of pies, and if he starts screaming and bringing down pressure on
innocent citizens, he could end up in a lot of trouble. A couple of
phone calls and we shut him up fast."

"You son of a bitch, you got it all figured," I said. I knew it was
wrong, but I could feel the fear leaking out of me and the excitement
and expectation pouring in.

"There's one more problem," I said. "I been laid off for quite a
while now, and I'm not sure what the hell to do with that much
money. I sure as hell can't stuff it into my bank account."

"No problem," Choo Choo said. "I got a lawyer friend down at
Charles Center. Used to be very close with the governor. He's very
good at hiding money. Knows how to put it to work for you too. You
want, I'll set up a meeting, and in no time at all you're a member of
the investment class."

"Hey, next I'll be in the fucking country club."

Choo Choo grinned and blew smoke from his nose.

"Yeah, and why not, Red. Look, I know you're a good guy, but
what you don't understand is that when you get right down to it,
everybody in this country is into crime. It's the American way, you
know?"

"Don't bullshit me," I said, pissed off suddenly. "I'm doing this on
my own. And I know it ain't right."

"Okay," Choo Choo smiled. "Here's how it goes down. On Sunday night at exactly twelve o'clock Frankie Delvecchio comes walking out of the Mona Lisa with the receipts. What he does is walk out
the door, turn right, and go into the parking lot. He gets into his car
and drives directly to the First National Bank, where he puts the
dough in the night deposit slot. Only this weekend he doesn't get
past the parking lot. You and Dog park just around the other side of
it. You know that little woods there?"

"Yeah, sure."

"Okay. I'm giving you both ski masks, but only one of you walks up. You come right at him with your gun out, take the money, and blink your flashlight to Dog, who comes around and picks you up. Then you ride away."

"What about Frankie?"

"You got a choice there. You can wait until he's unlocking his car door and bash him on the head, or you can shoot him in the leg. I can get a silencer for you for that. Personally, it's all the same to me, but as a matter of sentiment, I'd like to see the bastard on crutches."

"No shooting," I said. "No way. I can get up behind him."

"Yeah, that's the way I figure it myself. There's trash cans there, big green dumpsters. You come out from behind, whack him, grab the dough, and split. The whole thing should take twenty seconds."

"What if Joey or one of the other boys are there backing him up?"

"They won't be. Vinnie's such a cheap fuck he doesn't like to pay more than one guy for working late Sunday night."

We both had a laugh at that one.

"But what if they are?" I asked.

"Look, nothing is a hundred percent certain," Choo Choo said. "But I've been casing this place for five months, and they've done it this way every single time. One guy, that's it. Look, Frankie's a macho fuck and probably tells Vinnie he can handle it all by himself. Plus Vinnie thinks he's such a king shit that nobody would dare fuck with him. He's never been hit either there or at the Paradise or any of his card games. Never. He's gotten soft and careless.

"He always was soft," I said.

"Yeah, and we're going to hit him right in his nuts. Now, after you and Dog get the money, you drop the car off over on the Edison Highway at Lane's Used Car Lot. Just leave it there. I'll be there to pick it up. We go back to the apartment, split up the dough, and that's it."

"You're there alone, right?"

"Yeah, forget Blazek and the others. I already got rid of them."

"Sounds good," I said.

"Hey, it *is* good. It's going to work like a Swiss watch. You want some dessert?"

"Nah, I don't think so."

"Aww, come on. Let's have an amaretto and some peach pie.

Goddamn, I love this place, Red. They keep up the standards, you know?"

The night after I talked to Vinnie I went home and sat alone in the living room for a long time. I wanted to think it through, be straight about it all, come to some kind of logical decision. I even got out a piece of paper and a pen and wrote "Pros" on one side and "Cons" on the other, the way Wanda does when she's trying to make up her mind on something important.

But I didn't write one word pro or con.

I just sat there, feeling the loss. Ace and Wanda and Crystal, and Dog too almost as gone as Billy Bramdowski.

I kept thinking of going up for a jump shot over some defender's head, the ball arching out of my fingers and me knowing, knowing it was going to go in.

I thought of picking up trash down at Harborplace—trash thrown away by people with money, who could afford to splurge on the fast food they served down there or who bought those "New Baltimore" souvenirs, like the red pillows that said "Maryland is for Crabs!" on them.

And I remembered the parking garage, swirling down deeper and deeper, the breath being sucked out of me.

I knew there was more to it all than this. It wasn't enough to just let these pictures flash through me. I had to think about what I was doing, but after a few more whiskeys it was just all one long blur.

The bottom line was I had to have money, or we could never start again.

Choo Choo was a sleaze, but he wasn't any dummy. He had it figured, he'd done his homework.

I started talking out loud to myself, the way I used to do before tip-offs in basketball games. "You got it. It's going to work. It's like Choo Choo said. A walk."

Pretty soon I had myself pumped up. Maybe there'd even be more than fifteen in there. And Vinnie. Taking off Vinnie.

That was nice. Very nice.

I sipped my drink. I felt a calm come over me. I wasn't shaking at all when I picked up the phone and dialed Dog.

Through the snow-covered trees we could see the lights of Mona Lisa Pizza glowing under the black sky.

I sucked in my breath and looked over at Dog, who sat behind the steering wheel, his .38 lying in his lap and both hands holding his blue ski mask. He had on his black leather jacket, levis, and black rubber boots.

I looked down at my watch.

"Five minutes," I said. "I got to get behind those trash cans. You all right?"

"The Dog is in an excellent mood," he said. "Your flashlight battery working?"

"Yeah, and as soon as you see it, get your ass around there, all right? I don't want to freeze to death with all that cash in my hand."

"Hey, don't worry, compadre. You know I'll be there."

I reached over and gripped his arm, and he smiled and nodded to me.

"Red, I owe you for this."

"Cut the shit. I wouldn't be here with anybody else."

"You got nothing to worry about. This here car runs like a top."

"It's going to be a walk," I said, slipping the mask over my head.

Dog did the same, and we looked at each other and almost lost it.

"Got to get those eyeholes straight," I said. "Been practicing all week."

"You look like one of them skiers on 'Wide World of Sports,' "
Dog laughed.

"Three minutes, man. Just be there."

"Move it, Red. See you soon."

I held the gun in my right hand and got out of the car and made it
through the ten feet of trees that cut us off from the parking lot. I
took my time getting through there, remembering that three minutes
is a long time. We'd done a practice run only one night ago, and it
took less than a minute to set up behind the garbage cans.

Dog and I had discussed all that for four days, and both of us had
decided that the longer we had to wait, the more chance for bad
nerves to set in.

Do it, and do it fast. Don't wait, and don't think too much. Like
popping in a twenty footer. Nothing to it.

I had my black wool sweater and dark pants on and black high-
top basketball shoes, my old Celtics models. I knew the path and
stayed away from the slushy spots and the low-hanging branches,
which could cut up my face. In forty seconds I was out there,
crouching low behind the dumpster, which gave off the rotten odor
of sausage, rank pepperonis, and day-old anchovies. That was another reason for cutting it close. I didn't want to blow lunch as
Frankie came out the door.

Two minutes left, and I looked at the Mona Lisa, with its big
electric imitation sign of that strange smiling lady. Vinnie Toriano,
art lover.

I looked back through the woods and couldn't see Dog's car, and
yet I felt cool as could be expected because I knew he was there. The
same night I told him about the job, he'd looked physically better,
like old times. I know it was partially my imagination, but just having this, knowing he was trusted with it, had brought the color and
the life back into him like nothing since the day we'd been laid off.

He'd be all right. He'd be there. That was good to know.

But I still had to pull it off, and I looked at Frankie's car, not four
feet away from me. That was the tough part. Coming up behind him,
on the fucking ice, and not slipping and falling on my ass.

And not crunching it up either, which was why I'd worn the
sneakers.

I crouched, looking at the watch. Forty seconds to go, and Christ
let him be on time. The wind whipped across the parking lot, and I

adjusted the ski mask again and looked at my gun, the .38 special that Choo Choo had copped for me.

"Let it go smooth, Lord," I said. "Let it go smooth."

Then I saw the light go out in front. And heard the big oak door open, and I knew he was coming out; I sucked in the cold air and took a step forward, just a small one, so I could see around the trash can.

There was the sound of his footsteps coming across the gravel, and I ran my tongue around my freezing lips, forgetting that I had on the ski mask and getting a mouthful of lint for my effort.

He was walking toward the car now, I could see him plainly, and I prayed to God he didn't look straight ahead because I was in his line of sight.

But it was all right. He didn't look worried or cautious at all. He came around to the driver's side and reached in his overcoat pocket for his keys, and as he stuck them in the door I made my move.

The footing was better than I had any reason to hope for, and in a second I was on him. He heard me though, started to turn around, and said, "Hey, what the fuck?" But what with his keys and the money sack in his hand, he was in no position to fight back.

I smashed him on the back of his head with the gun, and he sagged to his knees. I hit him again, and he grunted and went over on his side.

I reached down and grabbed the canvas money bag from his left hand and his keys from his right and threw the keys into the woods. There wasn't much chance he was going to get up for any movie chase heroics, but I wanted to be sure.

Then I reached into my pocket for the flash, aimed it at the trees, and gave two quick blinks.

I heard Dog start the engine, and then from behind me there was a voice I knew as well as my own.

"All right," Henry said in his high-pitched squeal. "Drop the gun and don't move."

I turned and looked at him standing there, dressed in his court jester outfit, royal purple cotton bloomers that billowed like two sails in the wind.

"Well, well," he said. "Old Vinnie is going to give me quite a raise for this."

He moved toward me, holding his shotgun right at my stomach.

"Let's just see who's under that mask, pal."

He didn't get a chance to say much else. Dog came screaming around the woods and pulled into the parking lot.

Henry's fat face went white with panic, and he turned the shotgun on the car.

I could have shot him dead right then. I should have. I know it. I should have put a bullet right in his head.

But it was fucking Henry, whom I'd known almost as long as Dog.

Dog saw the situation clearly, and he didn't hesitate for more than a second. He got out of the car and kept his gun out of sight.

"Both of you don't move," Henry said. "Vinnie warned me about you boys. The Carruchi brothers, huh? We seen you casing this place. But you boys can't outsmart Vinnie. Now we're going right back inside the Mona Lisa, and I'm calling the boss. Move!"

I looked over at Dog, who shrugged as if this was okay with him.

"Henry," I said. "It's not the Carruchi brothers. It's me, Red."

"Red?" Henry's voice went up about two octaves.

"Yeah. Look, Henry, you can't turn us over to Vinnie. He'll crucify us. You let us walk out of here, we split with you."

Dog took a step closer. I could see the gun in his right hand, held just down behind his leg. He was still a good fifteen yards away.

"Red Baker?" Henry said.

"Yeah, you asshole. Red Baker. Look, we got to get out of here. You turn around, and I'll call you tomorrow."

"I can't do that, Red," Henry said. "I'm working for Vinnie. I told you the other night. I'm his new security guard."

I thought of what Choo Choo said. Vinnie was probably paying him half of what Joey would have gotten. The cheap fuck.

Dog took another step closer, and Henry aimed his gun at him.

"Who's that under there? Who is it, Red?"

"Don't matter," I said. "You just got to turn around and walk back in there. I'll give you a little tap on the head, and you can say we ambushed you, just like we did Frankie. Vinnie can't hold that against you."

Henry kept swinging the gun back from Dog to me. His legs were trembling, and his pants looked like they might float him away.

"I can't do that, Red. I'd lose my job. What the fuck else am I going to do?"

"You won't lose your job, Henry," I said.

I looked down at the ground. Frankie wasn't moving, but he'd come around soon.

"We're leaving, Henry," I said. I took a step toward Henry, still holding my gun at my side. "There are some heavy people behind this, Henry. You say anything and you're in deep shit, you hear me?"

"I got to take you in, Red. Wait, I know who's under there. That's Dog? That you, Doggie?"

"Yeah," Dog said. "Let us give you a little tap on your head, Henry. It won't hurt much. You won't need the job when we split with you."

"I can't do it," Henry said. "Vinnie trusted me."

"Vinnie wouldn't trust his fucking mother," I said, taking another step toward him. "Come on, now. Before Frankie wakes up."

"No way, Red. You got to come inside. I got to call Vinnie."

"Henry," I said. "Listen—"

But it was too late. Dog had lifted his gun from his hip and aimed it at Henry. Just as Henry swung the shotgun back toward him.

"No," I screamed. "Wait—"

The sound was strange. Dog's revolver, like a pop, with the silencer on it, and Henry's shotgun blasting away, a huge red spark blowing from its barrels. I saw them both fall, Henry staggering and then falling down on his face while Dog was blown back onto the hood of the Chevy.

"Jesus God."

I ran to Dog, who lay in front of the Chevrolet. Quickly I opened his coat, and there inside was leather and strips of plaid wool and this huge fucking hole where his stomach should have been. He was moaning and clung to me tight.

"Help me, Red."

"Don't worry, Dog," I said. "Don't worry."

I grabbed him and started dragging him to the car, but the blood and his stomach were trailing out behind him, and I reached down and tried to stuff it all back in.

"Dog, Dog," I said.

"Fucked up, man. Oh, Red . . . It shoulda been Vinnie."

"It's going to be all right, Doggie," I said, opening the door.

"No, Red," he said, grabbing me. His eyes were huge, and blood poured from his mouth. "Never lie to the Dog, babe. Get the fuck out of here, man."

"No way. Help me. You got to help me get you in the car."

But then he started to jerk and spasm, and he grabbed onto my neck and hugged me tight, and I said his name over and over again, I don't know why, until he was still.

"Dog," I said. "No, no . . ."

I held him close to me, cuddling his great, battered head in my arms, and I wanted to take his gun and put it in my own mouth, I swear it.

Instead, I ran over and took my gun butt and bashed Frankie on the head again and picked up the money bag as lights came on down the street. I ran from Frankie to Henry, who lay on his back, his purple jester's pants blowing around his waist.

Dog's aim had been true.

The bullet had gone straight into his head, just above the right eye.

Then I picked up the money bag and ran to the Chevy. I wanted to take Dog with me, but there was no time now, and I only looked down on him lying there with his arms spread open on the asphalt.

"Good-bye, Dog," I said. Then I jumped behind the wheel, peeled out of the parking lot, turned the car down Fort Avenue, and headed out toward the Edison Highway to meet Choo Choo at the lot.

W e got the biggest tree we could find down at St. Luke's that Christmas, a Scotch pine, full all the way round, with a good stem at the top for the old glowing star which Wanda and I had bought about ten years ago and which every year we debated about throwing out or hanging on to for one more year. Wanda always talked me into keeping it, and this time I didn't put up much of a fight. I was just so damned glad to have them back, I didn't want anything to screw it up.

What happened was that at the Mass for Dog I'd almost lost it. I got through the Latin part just fine, but when the Father started in with his speech about how Dog was a "loving and good provider, a beloved neighbor and friend," I felt like someone had put wires in my arms and legs. I wanted to leap out of the pew and scream, "It was me! I was his best friend and I got him killed." But just then Wanda grabbed my hand, and I held on to her tight, sagging in my seat.

She, Ace, and I went to the funeral together, too, along with her mother Ruth. We stood together and saw Carol and her girls, and all the guys from down the plant, standing there stiff like prisoners of war. And off on the side, leaning on his car was Choo Choo, just watching, not saying a word.

On the way home, riding down the snow-covered streets, I began to think it was like Easter a long time ago, Wanda and me and Dog and Carol heading to Hausner's. Dog would give Carol a box of marzipan candies, which she loved, but which always made me sick even to smell. I remembered biting into them, and I thought that guilt was something like that, some oversweet candy that you could never spit out, and I wanted to stop the car and wash my mouth out with snow.

When we arrived at Ruth's, I expected them all to get out and go inside, but instead Wanda walked Ruth to the door, and after whispering something to her, she came back down the steps and got inside the car.

"Let's go home, Red," was what she said, and so I drove the three of us back to Aliceanna Street.

The night before Christmas all three of us decorated the tree, and there was a lot of too polite discussion about which balls would look best hanging from which branches and how far away to space the lights. Wanda even found time to bake some peanut butter cookies, something she hadn't done in maybe three years, and I made a good stiff eggnog, using more whiskey than I ever had in the past, and then immediately worried: would Wanda think I was drunk and that this was just a way of camouflaging the beginning of a gigantic holiday bender? But she didn't say a word and drank as much as me, and we even let Ace have more than he should have. By the time midnight came, the tree looked better than the big one they had down Harborplace. Everything had come together just right, and we were damned proud of it and just stood there together, touching each other, sipping the eggnog, and commenting on what a fine job we'd pulled off.

In other words, things were as tense as hell. I finally tossed down two quick whiskeys in the kitchen to slow down my heartbeat, which was out of control.

In past years, when we were finished decorating the tree, we'd meet with Doggie and Carol and the kids, and go up the church to sing carols. But that was out of the question now. Just thinking about Dog's smiling face and his offkey bass sent chills down my back. I was afraid Wanda and Ace would suspect something, but they were real understanding about it.

"Why don't you go upstairs and take a little nap, and then we'll open the presents, hon," she said.

"Yeah," I said, "that sounds like a good idea."

I forced a wink at Ace and went up to bed, but there was no chance I was going to sleep. My body was as tense as a piece of steel, and every time a car went by, I would go to the window and stare out the smudged glass, expecting Vinnie and Joey and Frankie. And I thought a lot about Choo Choo, too. He'd been real slick, just like he promised, and the "investigation" of the crime was something like a joke. The cops had come around once. I told them I didn't know anything, that I hadn't seen Dog for a while, and they jotted down a couple of notes and were gone. I could see it in their faces—a couple of whackos killed each other at a pizza joint, and somebody else got the dough. Vinnie had always been a cheap fuck with his payoffs, and so nobody was going to break their chops to help him get his money back. I guess I should have felt grateful for Choo Choo holding up his end, but I didn't. I had a daydream that I'd go into his office and stick my gun up his nose and say, "You fucked it up. We walked right into a setup, and now you're gonna pay." Jimmy Cagney kind of stuff. And I might have done it too, except I had a wife and kid, and I could see him turning Blazek loose on them.

Besides, when I was in what was left of my "right mind," I knew it wasn't Choo Choo's fault. I had accepted his offer, knowing something could go wrong, knowing that once guns were involved anything could happen. It wasn't like I was an eighteen-year-old holding up the Little Tavern.

I had taken the risk, and I had talked Dog into it, like I could always talk him into everything, and the crazy bastard had done what he always did, tried to protect me.

And now he was dead. Hell, I had even used his funeral to get back together with Wanda and Ace. And I still had his share of his money, too. But it was going to be a while before I could get it to Carol and the kids.

So I lay there on Christmas Eve, tossing and turning until Wanda came up the steps into the room.

"Red," she said, "are you all right?"

"Yeah," I said, "sure. Look, I'm sorry about the carols. I know how much you and Ace like them, but it just reminds me of Doggie too much."

She sat on the edge of the bed and stroked my temples softly with her long fingers, pressing lightly, and I felt some of the tension disappear. God, I wanted to tell her the truth then, knowing that if it were someone else's story, she'd have her insights on the poor guy's problems and maybe even know what to do.

But I didn't dare tell her anything; instead I had to fake the reason I was grieving, saying things like "He was my friend and I feel responsible for him," and she held my head in her lap and said, "I know, Red. I know." And finally I held on to her and ran my hands through her hair, saying her name over and over again.

I don't think I would have made it through that night without her, but after a while, I was calm enough to sit up and pretend I was okay.

"Hey," I said, "let's go down and open the presents."

"Do you feel like it, Red?" she said.

"Yeah, sure. Then we can sleep later tomorrow." Which was another lie because I didn't sleep at all anymore. But I managed a friendly hug and we went downstairs, where Ace was already sniffing around the tree.

"Hey, Dad," he said, "is it time?"

"Sure kiddo. Let's go to it."

With all the dough I had, I at least wanted to buy them some hot presents—you know, maybe Wanda a car coat and something special like a small diamond ring, and Ace a great new guitar—but I had to go real light on all that. The case wasn't that dead. Not yet.

So I got Ace a new set of sweat togs, the kind he wanted, and a couple of those rock-jazz fusion records I can hardly stand to hear. And Wanda I got a new sweater from the bargain basement down at K-Mart and some fake pearls she could wear while she was hostessing at Weaver's. They gave me a rod-and-tackle set and a tool box, and, all in all, everybody faked it real well about how delighted they were with this stuff.

We'd had one more glass of eggnog and eaten a couple more of the cookies, and were about to unplug the tree and call it a night, when the doorbell rang.

My heart just about burst through my shirt. Vinnie, I knew it. This was the time to lay on the pressure. Oh yeah . . .

I wanted to sneak up to the door, peek out, and duck from the gunfire, but I couldn't do anything of the kind or Wanda and Ace would know. So I walked over cool as could be and opened it up, shutting my eyes as I did.

"Hello, Red."

It was Carol and the kids, standing out there in the slush. Her blond beehive was covered with snow, and her thick blue eye shadow had run down her cheeks.

"I know we said we couldn't make it tonight, but, well, the house was so lonely, and I thought . . ."

"Hey," I said. "Damn, it's good to see you, Carol. Come on in, hon. Get out of the cold."

I let her in with a big fake-hearty "Look who's here!" and damned if my family didn't come through like troopers, smiling and hugging the girls, and Wanda getting out the eggnog and cookies, and Ace taking the girls upstairs to his room so he could play them his new records (and probably play along with them on his Fender Telecaster, bought back in the good old days).

I stayed downstairs with Carol and Wanda and sipped another eggnog, and Carol talked about how pretty the Scotch pine was.

"It's so full. You know Dog always gets the kind that has a big hole in the back or half the branches are missing right in the middle of the tree."

I shot Wanda a look and felt my bones chill, and then Carol started to cry.

"Oh, Carol," Wanda said, coming over to the couch and putting her arm around her. "It's all right, honey. You just cry if you want to, hon."

I about lost it myself then but kept smiling and told a story about how Dog and I used to go sledding in Patterson Park, and he'd do all these crazy stunts just to impress Carol, and she cried again and looked up at us and said, "Red, I have to ask you something. I have to . . ." and I thought: here it comes, she's going to ask about the robbery and whether or not I was there. I sat as still as I could get, and then she said, "Did Dog tell you I was having an affair with Dick Nellis?"

This question threw me. I didn't know what to say.

"You're not answering me, Red."

"No," I said, "he never said anything to me about it."

She looked at me and shook her head.

"You're lying, Red. To spare my feelings. I've known you too long.

Oh God, I tried to tell him over and over it wasn't true. But he kept at me. He said that the only reason I was screwing Dickie was that he had money. Then, a few days before . . . before he tried that damned fool thing, he told me he was going to have a job soon. He had a new job all lined up, but he wouldn't tell me what it was, kept saying he was going to have plenty of money."

She began to cry more then, scraping at her face with her hands, and it was all I could do not to tell her it wasn't her fault, that it was my idea. I had gotten Dog killed.

But then Wanda would have known, and I would have lost her and Ace for good. Was it right to tell the truth? How could it be true that it was best to lie?

I looked over at the two of them sitting so still on the couch.

"It's not your fault," I said. "It's the way things went. He just wanted to feel like a man again. You know it's not your fault."

"But I wasn't sleeping with him," Carol said. "I almost did once . . . He took me home and I was feeling so low, but I didn't. I couldn't do that to Dog. I loved him too much. But he wouldn't believe me. God, Red, it's all my fault. I used to yell at him, complain about everything. Oh God, if I had him back again, I'd never do that. Never . . ."

She began to sob deeply, and Wanda put her arms around her, and I felt as though I'd suddenly got a nest of chiggers under my skin. I scratched at my hands and arms, felt hot flashes go up my spine.

It was wrong, but I felt I'd do about anything to get her away from us.

I sat there looking at them, then turned my attention to the tree and said softly, "Look at the light there. It's always the red ones that burn out. Now you tell me why that is." I touched the bulb and felt it scald my flesh but held on to it anyway, the pain numbing the pain within.

Then the phone rang in the dining room.

"I'll get it," I said, like a starving man handed bread.

I tried to walk casually from the room and thought how even my walk had become nothing more than an act. I wondered if that was it . . . something that happened to you after you committed a black enough sin. You got liar's walk, liar's smile, the old you was just a dummy leaking sawdust in some forgotten attic room.

I picked up the phone, but there was no voice at the other end. Only steady, deep breathing.

"Hello," I said, but I knew right away that no one was going to answer.

There was more breathing, heavy cigarette-smoker breath.

I waited, felt my pulse race, wanting to fake it, pretending it was one of the guys from the plant, but then he'd know that I was scared.

I was about to put it down when Vinnie came on the line. His voice was unnaturally low, his ultimate Godfather imitation. Only tonight it didn't seem funny.

"I know you got the money, Baker. Dog couldn't have pulled that job alone. I just wanted to call and wish you a Merry Christmas and a Happy New Year and to tell you that unless I get my dough back by January 15 you're going to be working down the Good Will in a wheelchair."

I felt the sweat pour down my face. My own breath was short.

"Hey," I said, "Merry Christmas, guy. It's really nice hearing from you. I'm real sorry about that accident you had down the plant. Broke your neck, huh? Well, hang in there, Phil. You're going to make it. And thanks for calling."

"Baker, don't you hang up on me. You come see me this week. You hear me? You come see me, you dickhead. I mean it."

"I'll try to stop in, Phil," I said. "You bet. Real sorry about your neck. Don't move a whole lot, and it won't get any worse—you hear me? Guy I knew once told me you make sudden moves, you could get paralyzed. Take it easy. Slow and easy."

After that Vinnie's voice went up a few decibels.

"Who else was in this with you, Baker? I bet I know . . . Gerard . . . or maybe the Carruchi brothers . . . Well, they can't protect you and your family forever, you hear me? We'll find you open one of these days. Sleep well, pal."

He hung up the phone, and I felt my mouth turn to cotton.

Would he come after my family? I couldn't believe it. Until I thought about him down there at the Paradise, of Joey and Frankie and how they got their kicks.

I went back into the living room, trying to look normal, smiling like a fool.

Both of them looked up at me. Carol's eyes were red, and her mascara ran down her cheeks.

"Guy I know. Slipped off the goddamned loading dock down the Boh plant and broke his neck."

"Calling here so late at night?" Wanda asked.

"Yeah, the poor guy couldn't sleep. He said he'd called every friend he had. Guess I'm at the end of the list. Sounded a little loaded. You know the old 'drink and dial' deal."

"Dog used to do that," Carol said.

"Dog," I said. "Old Doggie."

"Red," Carol said. "There's something else I have to know. I was going to ask you without Wanda around, but I don't think that's fair. We've all been close for so long, and I don't want to do anything that would change that. I know Dog would want it that way."

"Damn straight," I said, feeling numbed.

"Were you with Dog the night he tried that fool robbery?"

I looked her straight in the eye and then I kind of dramatically switched my gaze to Wanda.

"No," I said. "He didn't tell me a damned thing about it. He must have planned it with one of the other boys, Carol. You know I tried to get Doggie to go down to Meyer Clinic, and he threw me out of the house. He was real mad at me. Hell, we were like brothers. In a month or two it would have all blown over and he'd have been telling me what he was up to again, but for now he was hanging out with a lot of guys. It could have been any one of them, I don't know who. Maybe the cops'll find out."

I said all this real even, in a soft supervisor's voice.

Carol looked at me for quite a while and then nodded her head.

"I believe you, Red. Like Dog always said, you wouldn't bullshit about the important things."

"That's true," I said.

I looked at Wanda, who had avoided this question like the plague and whose whole face seemed to relax with my answer.

"A lot of people in the neighborhood think it *was* you," Carol said.

"A lot of people are wrong," I said. "They're the same jerks that think the Colts are staying in Baltimore. Believe what I tell you, Carol, it's the truth."

"Okay, Red," she said. "You were his best friend. And I'm glad you got a job."

"Yeah," I said. "Trashman. Wanda's going to disown me."

"You know that's not true," Wanda said. "And besides, it's only temporary."

"Sure," I said.

Then I heard it. A loud popping sound from upstairs. I could feel my whole body grow tense. The gun was hid up there in the attic. I'd kept it just in case Vinnie didn't know he was boxed in.

"Ace," I called, my voice breaking, "what's going on up there?"

There was no answer, but a second later I heard one of the girls shriek.

"What the hell?" I said. "Hey, Ace, what are you doing?"

"It's all right, Red, they're just playing," Wanda said.

"Yeah, sure," I said. "But I'm getting tired, you know? I could use a little less noise."

I got up, tried to be cool, but both girls were shrieking now.

"Ace!" they yelled. "Ace!"

I wanted to take the steps five at a time, but I kept it under control and walked up there, sweat breaking out on my forehead.

"Oh God," I said silently, "not Ace. Not Ace. I know it was wrong, but not Ace."

I walked straight to the attic stairs.

"Ace," I called. "You all right, son?"

There was no answer. Just the sound of the rock-jazz group blasting away.

"Ace," I said. "Ace?"

The door opened to his bedroom, and Lisa looked out.

She looked white-faced and scared.

"Mr. Baker," she said.

"What, honey?" I asked. "What is it?"

"Ace," she said.

"God, what?"

She smiled a little, and the color came back into her face.

"He made this balloon appear in my ear, and then he blew it up," she said. "It scared the hell out of me. Ace is a magician—you know that, Mr. Baker. He can do all sorts of tricks. We might go to Hollywood together. Be like Ginger Rogers and Fred Astaire."

I sagged against the rose-colored wallpaper as Ace popped his head out of the bedroom door.

"Hey," he said, "you want to see a trick? I got about fifteen new ones I worked on while we were visiting Grandma's."

"No, I think I've had about enough tricks for one night," I said.

"Aw come on, Dad," Ace said, smiling in that way I could never resist. "Just a couple. I need an assistant. To amaze and entertain our guests."

I could see he was doing it for them. That's how he is, my kid.

"Come on, Dad," he said, bowing like old Mandrake himself. "Step right this way to Ace Baker's Magic Parlor and be prepared for the fantastic, the mystical, and the marvelous. If you dare!"

"I could use a little of that," I said. Then I scraped myself off the wall and walked toward Ace and Dog's squealing, laughing girls, who waited for me in that small, crowded room.

It snowed for the next few days, big wet flakes that covered over all the potholes on the block, snowed over the dead mills, and the Paradise, where I didn't go anymore. Snowed over the white marble steps on our street so fast that even though I got them clean in the morning and laid down salt, they were covered over again in the afternoon.

I got up with Wanda now, and as I looked out the window on Aliceanna Street, I would think about the way Dog and I used to take our sleds to Patterson Park and slide down the hills in between the low-hanging, snow-bent trees, our whole life caught up in that one moment of pure speed, nothing else mattering but shifting the weight, seeing through the great mass of snowflakes, and at the last possible second making the cut that kept us from going out into the car-filled street. Then falling off our sleds on our backs and throwing snow up in the air, Dog giving out yells of pure pleasure and me feeling, even in all that cold, warm and contented, a pure happiness which would make me smile for reasons I could never name.

But now, as Wanda got up and looked at me with sleep in her eyes, I found myself turning away from her, looking quickly out the windows into the street.

"What are you looking at?" I said as she put on her robe.

"I was just thinking how tired you must be, Red. You were up and down all night. Is something wrong?"

"No," I snapped. "Why does something have to be wrong?"

She put her left hand on her hip and stared at me, then slowly shook her head.

I was about to say something about the snow, how I had to get down there and work on the steps, when I saw them. There across the street were five tombstones staring at me. White tombstones standing in front of five icy doors. I let out a cry, gripped the dresser's edge.

"Red, what is it?" Wanda said.

I blinked and looked again. Not tombstones at all, just the way the snow had piled on the stoops across the street, all white and shiny, like marble slabs.

I slumped back down on the bed and dropped my head to my chest. There was a pain in my neck, and I gasped for air.

"Red, honey," she said and reached down to hold me, but I pushed her away in anger, flailing my arms out wildly, striking her shoulder with the back of my hand.

"Get away from me," I yelled in a voice I didn't know.

"Red, what is it?"

But I shook my head. "Nothing," I said. "Nothing." Then I went downstairs, found my boots, hunting jacket, and snow shovel, and started working on the steps.

It was getting late, and I had to make it to my new job.

My job at Harborplace was only half a cut above the parking lot. Sometimes I painted over graffiti and other times I used a hammer and nails, but mostly I went around the docks carrying a stick with a nail on the end of it, picking up greasy waxed paper that the tourists and big shots left on the ground after lunch. People walked by me as though I was invisible, as dead as Dog.

Wanda never complained, and we even managed to eat lunch together, but I couldn't stand the shame of it. Once a couple of guys I knew who were still working down Bethlehem Steel came down for an afternoon with their families. One guy named Becker was real nice to me, talked to me as I stood there with my bag and my stick, but I noticed that he only looked at my eyes, and I thought that was exactly how I'd looked at the man with no nose. I'd tried only looking at his eyes and forehead, pretending he wasn't deformed.

The thought did something to me, opened up some place in my brain that had never been touched before.

I was like a cripple now, a war vet, or one of the "unfortunates" they always used to talk about in church. "And don't forget to help the unfortunates." It made me a little crazy, but for some reason I didn't flip out. Instead I just got quiet and began to look around.

I think it was the third or fourth day there when this happened. I had to work late, so Wanda took the car. I got on the bus, half dead from washing the hallways, smelling all that fastfood grease on my skin (and remembered how it sickened me when Wanda came home smelling of crabs).

Three black men sat in the back of the half-lit yellow bus, passing a bottle of cheap wine back and forth, and I wanted to go back there and drink with them all the way to the end of the line.

Half asleep, I thought of Crystal—gone down the highway, her new life with Tony already started. Maybe she was finally singing in some classy Miami club. Or maybe Tony was already gone and she was dancing for some other Vinnie in some new dive.

I stared half dead out the window at the bright new city, with its huge office buildings all lit up and empty, and suddenly I felt that it was a strange place—not Baltimore at all. What's more, I suddenly realized that it had been a strange place for a long time now, but because I lived in Highlandtown, because I had my job, my family, and my friends, I hadn't noticed how much it had all changed. Of course I knew it was different, more built-up, but none of that really affected me or my family. But now for the first time I saw things as they really were. I saw that the city had been pushing me and my friends all along, and we had been so caught up in just staying alive, that we had never once pushed back.

The bus turned down Broadway and took a left on Eastern Avenue, and then the row houses were on my right and Patterson Park on my left. I thought for a minute that being back in the neighborhood would make me feel better. But it didn't. Because I knew that it wasn't just the mill that was shut down. It was everything I had known and loved about Highlandtown since I was a kid, even the streets and houses themselves. Our whole way of life was going to go.

I knew it the same way I used to know my jump shot was going in. I was that sure.

I guess I was dazed by these thoughts because after the bus pulled away, I didn't see them for maybe three seconds.

But there they were, just behind me in their black Caddy—Frankie with his bandaged-up head, Joey, and in the back seat Vinnie.

I started to walk fast toward the end of the block, thinking if I could make it to the corner, I could cross and run like hell for the park, but I hadn't gotten more than a couple of feet, when they squealed up in front of me. Frankie and Joey jumped out of the car, and when I turned to look the other way, I saw Vinnie standing there with a gun.

I turned back toward Vinnie's two goons, thinking that if I could get one good punch in, I could bolt through them, and Vinnie wouldn't have a clear shot.

But I was dead-tired, and I never even saw it when Frankie bashed me on the side of the head with his gun. I started to go down, but Joey held me up, and then Vinnie kicked me in the balls. I groaned and fell onto the pavement, and somebody else kicked me in the ribs.

"That's enough," Vinnie said.

He reached down and grabbed me by the hair, and I could smell his tomato-and-sausage breath.

"This is as good as it's gonna get, Baker," he said. "You got three days to gimme back the money. Three days, asshole."

"Let me have him," Frankie said.

"No," Vinnie said, "that's all."

"Good night, Red," he said. He stepped on my left hand as he got into the car.

In the morning I told Wanda I'd pulled my back out the day before at work. When she left, I called Choo Choo.

He wasn't in. "Out in the field," the woman cop told me.

I went down the cellar and avoided looking at the walls. I went to the liquor cabinet, got out the bottle of Wild Turkey, and took three quick shots.

I hadn't had much to drink since Christmas Eve, and the liquor hit me fast, giving me a sense of confidence. To be honest, I should say "false sense of confidence," but for what I was going to do, I'd need all the help I could get.

I took the bottle upstairs, paced the floor, then called Choo Choo again.

"Detective Gerard is out on a case. He picked up your message. I'm sure he'll get back to you."

I was sure he wouldn't.

I wanted to work up a hatred for him, but it wasn't in me. He'd held up his end as well as he could, but when Dog died on the Mona Lisa Parking Lot, there was never any doubt Vinnie would come looking for me.

Who else would pull a job like that with Dog? Little Jackie Gardner?

The thought made me laugh out loud. Laugh in a way that was crazy, not my voice at all, but Dog's, laughing through me.

I had another drink, then went up to the attic. I turned over the packing crate and watched all the Styrofoam packing balls roll across the floor. Then I reached into the bottom and pulled out my gun.

I sat down in an old broken rocker and held the gun in my hand. My ribs ached, and I thought two fingers in my left hand might be broken.

But my right hand was fine. I took another drink, then went quickly down the steps, grabbed my coat, and left the house.

I wiped the snow off Weaver's window and looked inside the crab house. A couple of businessmen were surprised when I knocked on the glass. They glanced up but didn't like what they saw and quickly looked back down at their plates.

Finally I caught Wanda's eye, but she looked so startled by my appearance that she almost dropped her tray of food.

She nodded to me slowly, and I walked away from the window fast, putting my hands into my pockets and curling my right one around the gun.

The snow came swirling around me and around the ships tied up at the dock. It covered over everything with a clean whiteness so that it was impossible to tell where the land ended and the water began.

Across the way it swirled around the window of the new World Trade Center, and I could see people looking out the windows at it, office workers trapped inside, wondering if they were going to make it home.

I wiped the snow off the bench by the dock and sat down. The concrete was cold on my ass, and I began to shiver, but I sat there anyway, staring at the old tourist boat, the *Port Welcome*. Dog and I had gone out on that boat during Senior Prom Week with Carol and Wanda, twenty-two years ago. I remembered the blue and green party lights on deck, the sound of the Van Dykes, this black rhythm-and-blues band playing "Annie Had A Baby," and all of us dancing under the Chesapeake moon.

I shut my eyes and shook my head, and then I felt Wanda's hand on my shoulder.

"Red, what are you doing here? Are you all right?"

I looked up at her kind face through the swirling snow and reached up and cupped her cheek in my hand.

She sat down next to me and I pulled her close.

"Wanda," I said, "I want you and Ace to leave town."

She jerked away from me as if I'd hit her in the face.

"Why, Red?" she said.

"It's Vinnie," I said, looking out at the harbor. "He thinks I stole his money. He's not going to let it go."

"Oh yeah?" she said.

I reached into my pocket and pulled out the gun.

"What's that for?"

I'd expected her to gasp, to slap my face or in some way lose control, but she was cool.

"There's no other way," I said.

She stared at me for a long time.

"Red, you have to say it."

"Say what?"

She said nothing but wiped the flakes of snow from my eyes.

"Tell me."

"It was supposed to be a walk," I said. "I thought it would get us through."

"Oh Red," she said.

"I keep seeing Dog's face, Wanda. I keep hearing him scream."

Then I told her all of it, how Choo Choo set it up, how he gave me his word that Vinnie couldn't get back.

I was surprised how little time it took to tell. Only a few sentences really. In the first one Dog was alive, and in the last one he was dead.

Wanda stared at me and then back at the restaurant, where a waitress in a brown dress was standing at the door.

"Wanda, are you all right?"

Wanda turned and waved at her. The woman lingered a second and went back inside.

"So now you go after Vinnie?" she said.

"I don't see any other way."

"Red," she said, "you do that and you're just like him. There's no difference. But I know you, hon. You're a good man. You can't hide from that."

The words stunned me, made me feel as though I had altogether lost my way.

"You've got to leave, Wanda. Take Ace and go. I've got to settle this. You see that?"

"No," she said, "I don't see it. I don't see Ace and I going any-where without you. Do you think I came back here in order to leave?"

"You knew?"

"Vinnie won't hurt Ace or me. He always liked me in school."

"What?" I was shocked by the vanity in her voice.

Then I understood.

"You came back to protect me? Wanda, you don't understand."

"But I do, Red," she said. "I know you're what Ace and I got. When I left you, it about killed me. I won't throw you away, you hear me. And you won't talk like this again."

She reached down and took the gun out of my hand. She looked at it for a long time as the snow covered her face and hair, making her look like a graveyard angel. Then she stood up and walked away from me.

Stunned, I followed her. When she reached the end of the pier, she dropped the gun into the water. It sank right away.

She turned to me.

"Red, can you get the money?"

"Yeah."

"Then do it. We're leaving Baltimore."

She stared at me, so serious and strong that I could only nod my head. Then she walked past me by the bare trees, through the snow, and back to work.

As I write this, the sun is coming up over the desert. Wanda is working as a secretary for the university in El Paso, and Ace is going to the local high school, where he's starring on the Thunderbirds basketball team. Me, I got a job through my friend Terry O'Connell making metal detectors for stores and airports. Helping the world be safe from the bad guys who take what they need.

All my life I've lived by the water. Worked with Dog on the harbor, spent every vacation down the ocean, or crabbing in the Chesapeake Bay.

I never thought I could survive without the sound of lapping water nearby, without being able to smell the salt air.

Here on the desert outside El Paso, it's dry, burning dry, the sun boring into you like it's got some kind of score to settle. The cactus, the tumbleweeds, the cows and chickens in the Mexican backyards— all of them are parched, walking in circles as if they're trying to quench an unending thirst.

At first I didn't think I could stand it.

But I'm making it. For myself and my family.

It won't ever be easy. I hate my job checking the parts as they roll off the assembly line. It's work for a robot, and by next year they'll probably have one.

Which is why I'm going to computer school. Classes begin in two weeks, and just thinking about it makes me want to take a drink. But

I haven't yet, and I don't think I'll start. If Ace can handle it, so can I. He misses his friends back in the neighborhood, misses Patterson Park worse than I do. But he doesn't bitch about it, and he's playing ball, showing these southwestern boys how we do it in Baltimore. Averaging fourteen a game and nine rebounds.

Wanda misses home too, but she loves working over at the university.

So we're going to make it.

But sometimes I find myself feeling strange. On a good night I walk out on the desert, look up at the millions of stars, and think I can see Dog's face. Or see his shadow just beyond the next dark cactus.

Or hear his voice laughing at me, feel him punching me on the arm.

When that happens out here, in the terrible dry heat, I take off my shirt and walk for miles at a time. Walk under the round, yellow moon and brilliant white stars, and then I hear Doggie's voice, his great laugh, and I begin to run fast, faster, and the sweat pours off my face and chest, and something explodes within me, some love and terror too, for my family, for Wanda's strangeness, for old Dog, my dear, dead friend.

And when I stop, with my chest pounding, the dust blowing up behind me, it's almost like I know something.

Something about friends and what sets one man apart from another. Not brains or money but what he will risk for love.

In his dim way, Dog loved me well. He lived to protect me, so I might live better for both of us.

But what gets me sometimes is what Wanda said to me that last day at Weaver's.

Am I the same kind of guy as Vinnie or Choo Choo? Or am I the good man my wife and son know and love?

Maybe that's what I'm doing out here. Like old Job after all. Living through the heat to find out.

Is there something out there, watching, judging, the stars mere knotholes from which some haunted face peers through?

Is Dog out there now too, watching with his fierce, tender eyes?

I still can't say.

But I know this:

When I stop running and stand there among the cactus and tumbleweeds, I sometimes climb up on the great rock a mile or so behind our house. I light a cigarette and watch the smoke trail upward through the desert moonlight, and I think of Baltimore and Dog. I feel his spirit, the spirit of our whole dying neighborhood, deep inside me, and sometimes I laugh out loud.

Then I stare down the flat desert path and see the blue lights from our kitchen shining through the night. I flick the cigarette out into the dirt, jump to the dry ground. And begin my long, tough run toward home.

"Feverish and funny...could only have come from the very talented, slightly twisted mind of Robert Ward."

—George Pelecanos, bestselling author of *The Night Gardener*

"Noir for the lost, heartbreaking, hilarious, and so beautifully written."
—Ken Bruen, author of *The Dramatist*

"Ward lays bare the dark, weird soul of the American Dream."
—Jerry Stahl, author of *Permanent Midnight*

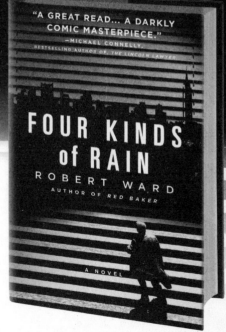

"A GREAT READ... A DARKLY COMIC MASTERPIECE."
—MICHAEL CONNELLY,
BESTSELLING AUTHOR OF *THE LINCOLN LAWYER*

FOUR KINDS of RAIN

ROBERT WARD
AUTHOR OF *RED BAKER*

A NOVEL

Down on his luck, psychiatrist Bob Wells finds himself caught in a dangerous scheme involving one of his delusional patients, a legendary mask worth millions, and a woman he'd do anything to keep.

AVAILABLE WHEREVER BOOKS ARE SOLD

ST. MARTIN'S MINOTAUR   www.minotaurbooks.com

SWAMPSCOTT PUBLIC LIBRARY

3 1996 00230 9708